3

The Forgotten One, is the highly anticipated conclusion to this gripping trilogy. A fast paced, thrilling ride that will leave you wanting more.

Don't forget to get Beyond the Red Carpet and Heart of Stone Today.

Get your copy today and join my mailing list to keep up to date on all upcoming releases.

www.debbralynn.com

Debbra Lynn

The Forgotten One

ISBN – 978-0-994-9873-2-7

The Forgotten One

Copyright @ 2018 by Debbra Lynn

Cover art by Riley Grant of Hoplite Solutions

Editing by Sandi Jewett

Website photos by Jaclyn Miller Photography

Author photo and website photos by Karla Muzyka of Lipstick and Lace

Acknowledgments

From the moment I decided to start writing I knew it was going to be quite the journey, and I was right. I wrote and released the first two books of this series in one year. Beyond the Red Carpet and Heart of Stone came so easily to me, however I discovered the true meaning of "Writers Block" trying to complete this third book. There were several times, and I mean several where I thought I was just going to call it quits, be done with it, after-all who would really even notice. I am so glad I did not let that defeating thought get to me in the end. I was invited to a book club event in my home town, and it was there that I saw I actually had fans. I had people eagerly waiting for me to release the next book and that was enough to push me to continue. I was terrified to release my first book, I am not a writer, I have no experience so how was I supposed to create a story people would fall in love with? Those were my thoughts but I took the leap and I just took a dream of mine to be an author and I went with it. Now 3 years later I have the proof in the form of 3 novels to prove that hard work and dedication are all it takes to begin the journey of making your dreams come true.

My husband Robin, was my sounding board, he heard every chapter as I went, and I am thankful to him that I had someone to bounce my ideas off of. He has supported my journey right from the start and insisted I did not quit at those dark times.

I am so thankful to Matt Harris for his amazing work on all three of my covers, and I will continue to work with him on all my future work. This time around I had to find a new editor and I am so happy I found a great one in my area named Sandi Jewett. I had such a great experience working with her and again, I will continue to work with her for my future work. And my two amazing Beta Readers, Cheryl Pangrass and Amber Lafitte, you ladies are so detailed and help us catch all the little things. Thank you both for taking the time to be the first readers of this book.

Prologue

She could feel her heartbeat heavy in her throat as she cautiously allowed her feet to lead her down the dark hallway. Tiny beads of sweat formed on her forehead and then slowly rolled downward until they dropped from her brow to join the tears that she so desperately tried to keep at bay. Step by step she continued, her legs trembling beneath her. The darkness surrounding her was terrifying, she wanted nothing more than to turn around and run back towards the light. But, her body betrayed her and the only choice she had was to try her best to summon the courage to go on. Her stomach was in knots. Confusion and disorientation surrounded her, and although the blackness enveloped her, she knew she must keep going. She could make out every crack and crevice along the wall, as her fingers slid along it. The wall was the only thing at this moment that gave her any solace, guiding her through the darkness. After what felt like an eternity, a faint glow flickered in the darkness. She knew now only a few feet in front of her was a door. A small sense of relief filled her at knowing she could escape the suffocation of the darkness if she could just make it beyond that door. She reached slowly, grasping for the door knob, fumbling to latch onto anything that would allow her access. Panic began to rise in her chest as she thought perhaps it was just all in her imagination. Perhaps someone was just trying to play a trick on her, someone who was wanting to give her a false sense of hope, when there was none. And as the panic rushed through her body, she felt it, her hand felt the door knob and she gripped it with all of her might. Holding it tightly to make sure it could not slip through her shaking fingers. Alone in the shadows of the unknown she stood holding onto the knob now with both hands, willing herself to take a deep breath, to open the door, to find out what was powerful enough to draw her here, wherever here was. She found her strength and allowed her trembling hands to turn the knob, slowly, and carefully, until she felt the door open, just enough to allow her to peak through the crack with one eye. An illumination of soft glowing light filled the small room, and she allowed herself to push the door open further. At first, she stood in place, not wanting to cross the threshold, just studying the surroundings before her. It was nothing more than an empty room, a metal chair in the far-left corner, and an old plastic table sat in the centre with an array of candles that lit up the barren space. The heaviness on her shoulders lifted as the feeling of impending danger subsided as she walked into the room. She looked from one end of the empty room to the other and walked up to the table, gliding her finger over the freshly fallen wax of the candles. She was certain she was going to find something here, she could feel it in her gut, something had led her to this room. Then she heard the footsteps behind her, she knew someone was standing at the door and slowly turned around to see who was there.

"Caleb!" she sighed heavily with relief.

"Oh, my God, Caleb? Are you okay? Please tell me you are okay?" The worry was evident in her quivering voice as she rushed towards the one man she thought she would never see again.

But, she was stopped instantly in her tracks. The blood drained from her face as the man she once shared her career with, the man she shared all of her secrets with and the man she desperately fell in love with, stood before her with tears glistening in his eyes. He quickly pulled out his gun from his holster and placed it tightly against his temple.

"No Jill, I'm not okay,"

And with those words the blaring bang of the gun rang piercingly in the air, deafening any sounds around her, and again, the darkness came.

ONE -September 28, 2015

Jill Keller sat upright, bringing herself out of a dead sleep, grasping at the sweat soaked sheets as if trying to grab hold of something before falling to her death. Her heart was pounding, her breath was rapid and shallow as she fought to bring herself back into her own bedroom. She swung her head, squinting her sleep blurred eyes so she could see the time. The numbers glowed 4:28 AM. Slowly her pulse began to slow down as she realized the horrific images that she had witnessed only moments ago were only an insanely vivid nightmare. Regardless of the relief in knowing it was only a dream, tears began to threaten her, she did her best to hold them back. It was only a dream after all, she just needed to shake it off. She fell back onto her bed and her feather filled pillow, hoping now that she was awake the image of Caleb with the gun to his head would start to diminish. But as she lay there and stared into the darkness with only the faintest of light from the streets coming in, she knew that the image would be stuck with her forever.

"God Jill, it was just a stupid dream," she muttered quietly under her breath.

She restlessly rolled onto her side, bunched her pillow under her head and closed her eyes. She hoped she would be able to fall back asleep at least for a little while. Her shift did not start until seven, and the last thing she needed was to be sleep deprived after the day she had had yesterday. She tossed and turned for a few more minutes before conceding that more sleep wasn't going to happen. She reached for the lamp on her bedside table and turned it on. Throwing her legs over the edge of the bed she dragged herself up and headed towards her ensuite bathroom. The lights glared brightly when she turned them on, forcing her to squint at the very unwelcome light. Jill glanced at her reflection in the mirror and shook her head in dismay.

"Jesus, you look like shit," she insulted herself, as if expecting a response. Turning away from the mirror she stripped off the white tank top that clung to her sweat dampened skin, tossing it on the floor. Turning on the shower, the water came beating fast and hard from the shower head. Jill ran her hand under the water until it began to slightly scald her skin.

"Nothing better than a scorching hot shower to wash away the memories", she thought to herself as she climbed into the hot stream, shrinking away from it at first. She slowly moved under the shower as her skin began to adjust to the heat and relaxed as she began to enjoy the warmth run over her entire body. The dream played itself over and over in her mind. She was hoping the shower would help wash it all away, but her mind was stuck in that room with Caleb.

She was bothered by it even though it was only a dream. She knew it must have had something to do with the conversation she had with Olivia Donovan the day prior. As she stood with her shoulders slumped and her head hung as the water washed over her, she brought her mind to yesterdays conversation.

"I'm sorry Olivia, you need my help with what? Jill repeated the question, as Olivia Donovan sat stoned face serious directly across from her.

"Detective Keller, I need you to help me prove that Sophia Donovan killed my brother, Marcus. You're the only one who can help me," Olivia answered.

Jill processed her words for a few seconds before continuing.

"Ms. Donovan, as you are well aware this case has been closed, it's finished so I am not exactly sure what you think I can do for you?"

Olivia sat back heavily in her seat and sighed deeply with apparent frustration. Jill could understand what she must be going through, what her family must be going through, but she could not understand why Olivia was here asking her for this kind of help.

"Listen, Detective Keller, something isn't right with this whole thing. I know she killed Marcus, I just know it, and I need you to help me prove that," Olivia's desperation was clearly written on the lines of her face.

"I understand this is hard for you Ms. Donovan, but…"

"Please don't call me that," Olivia abruptly cut off Jill. "That makes me think of her and I am nothing like her. Sorry, but please just call me Olivia."

Jill tilted her head in acknowledgement of the request and continued. "No problem Olivia. As I was saying, I know this has to be hard for you and your family, but the case is closed. There is nothing left to pursue. Sophia was cleared in all matters of this investigation. It is time that we all move on from this, despite whatever hard feelings you may be holding for your sister-in-law," as soon as the words were out, Jill wished she could take them back.

"She is not my sister-in-law, that evil bitch is not part of my family any longer. She destroyed my family, she took it all away. She took Marcus away. I know that, and I think you know that too, don't you Detective Keller? You're not convinced that Sophia is innocent in all of this, are you?" Olivia stared intensely at Jill awaiting her response.

Olivia was right, Jill had been suspect of Sophia Donovan from the beginning. The whole case went so seemingly smooth and she was not shy about bringing that up to Caleb during the investigation. But every corner they turned and every break in the case, it all only validated Sophia's innocence, it never did sit well with Jill. However, regardless of her own personal feelings regarding Sophia Donovan, Jill did what Caleb asked, and had accepted how it played out, despite her uneasiness.

"Olivia, I don't know what you are expecting me to say here? This case is closed, it's over, despite how you, your family, or I may feel about it"

Olivia gave a laugh of evident sarcasm, "My family…my parents are fooled, just like everybody else. They are so blinded by her act, her holier than thou façade, her fake tears of losing the man she loved, God, it's such crap. They certainly don't want any part of this, but you, you can help me, right?

"I'm sorry Olivia, but it's time to move on," Jill answered sympathetically.

Not appeased at all by her response, Olivia briskly stood up and stormed towards the door of Jill's office. She spun around before leaving the room, with frustration and anger lacing her voice.

"If you won't help fine, I will do this myself Detective Keller, but don't you sit there and try and convince yourself that any of this is okay, that you don't know the truth. You told us when you met us that you were going to help us find out who killed Marcus, that you would stop at nothing. Well, if this how you do your job on all of your cases and you're the one who is supposed to be protecting this city, then I feel deeply sorry for the people of Los Angeles," With those last stinging words she slammed the door behind her, leaving Jill alone, her ears still ringing from Olivia's harsh insult.

The hot water flowing from the shower was slowly going tepid when Jill pulled herself out of yesterdays conversation with Olivia Donovan. Her words still stinging. She knew she should not be taking it so personal, but she could not help it. Her career was something Jill prided herself on, she knew she was a great detective. Jill tried her very best to just ignore what Olivia said to her. It was obviously out of sheer anger and desperation, but after last nights dream, it might not be so easy to ignore. She believed Olivia was right, but she knew it was over. Jill knew full well she had better take her own advice and move on. That's what Caleb wanted.

Turning off the faucet of the now cool water Jill just stood dripping wet, her hand still resting on the faucet. *That is what Caleb wanted* she thought to herself. Maybe that wasn't enough anymore.

TWO - September 30, 2015

"Can I get a Miller, please?" Olivia Donovan asked the busty red head behind the bar as she took a seat at one of the stools lining the bar.

"Here you go sweetheart," the waitress set the cold beer down in front of her with a quick wink and a snap of her gum.

Olivia gave the waitress a somewhat uncomfortable grin and brought the beer to her mouth. The cold beer hit her lips, the taste of the bubbly drink was a welcoming comfort to her, especially after the last couple days. Beer, well alcohol period had quickly become Olivia's best friend. In fact, right now it was her only friend. Since Marcus was taken away from her she felt like she had nobody in her life, not even her parents seemed to care anymore. Taking another swig of her drink, she glanced casually over her shoulder, observing the other people who also had nothing better to do on a sunny afternoon. There were not very many people in the bar this time of day. A young couple sat side by side in a booth, she was giggling wildly, as he inappropriately slithered his fingers up her bare legs. Olivia turned her attention away from the couple in the booth and turned the other way spotting an elderly man, probably nearing his 80s, gripping his mug of beer as if it could possibly be his last. Maybe sensing her staring, the old man turned and caught Olivia's gaze. She swore she could see years and years of hurt and pain in his eyes, and with nothing more than a sullen grimace, the man turned his focus back to his drink.

God, is that what my life is going to come to? Olivia thought to herself. Spending my days alone in a dark and nearly empty bar, with no family or friends. Wallowing in self pity while trying desperately to drown all my feelings with cheap beer. There was a small flat screen TV above the bar running sports highlights, something she was pretty sure nobody cared about, including herself. She took another long swig of her beer, her thoughts going back to the conversation she had had with Detective Keller yesterday... Every time she thought about the conversation with Detective Keller, she got irritated and angry. How could the detective dismiss her so easily? That woman just totally rejected anything she had to say about Sophia. She had thought the detective would have been the one person she could go to, for some reason. Maybe it was the fact that during the investigation Detective Keller was clear in saying she would do anything to find out who killed her brother. Well obviously, she won't do anything because her brother is still dead, and his murderer walked free.

Feeling the intense frustration building again, Olivia downed the rest of her beer and slammed the empty bottle on the wooden bar. The waitress walked over to Olivia.

"I take it you want another one?" Red asked.

"Actually, this time make it a whiskey, whatever you got, I don't care."

"Rough day?" Red inquired as she set a shot glass in front of Olivia, filling it to the brim with the smoky smelling liquor.

Olivia glanced up at the waitress with a suspicious glare, surprised that anyone was showing interest in her pitiful life, then replied dejectedly.

"Ya, I guess you could say that."

The waitress smiled at Olivia. "Well, you're in the perfect place then. You here alone?"

Olivia grabbed the shot glass, and in one quick motion knocked back the stiff drink, the burning sensation immediately hitting her throat. The taste was not pleasant, but right now she didn't care.

"Ya, well no, I'm actually waiting for someone."

"Oh, that's too bad," the waitress replied flirtatiously as she refilled her shot glass. "Let me know if you need anything else to help with that bad day. My name is Zoe," and with a wink she turned her attention to the lonely old guy at the end of the bar.

Olivia sat stunned for a moment. Was she being hit on right now by a woman? She was not sure if she should be offended or flattered. She was certainly not here to be picking up people to take home. She had way too much going on to be worrying about where her next lay was going to come from. She especially wasn't interested in a desperate bartender, who probably makes it a habit out of fucking her constantly revolving door of patrons.

Olivia sighed heavily and put her head in her hands. Maybe she was reacting to harshly due to her current mood. She glanced over in Zoe's direction and gave her a faint smile, hoping it would make herself feel better for being so instantly judgmental. Zoe smiled back, Olivia was surprised how striking she found the red head, after all women were not typically her thing. Olivia's musings were disrupted at the sound of the bar door swinging open. The afternoon sunlight pouring in, exposing an ample amount of dust floating lazily in the air.

"Oh, I am so glad you came," Olivia stood up.

"Hey Olivia, it's good to see you."

"It's good to see you too, thank you so much for coming on such short notice," Olivia awkwardly stepped forward for a hug.

"What's going on? You didn't sound very good on the phone," Alex Preston responded as he pulled out of the uncomfortable embrace.

"I need to talk to you Alex. It's about Sophia. I need you to tell me everything you know about her and my brother's relationship, and I mean everything."

Alex took a seat next to his best friend's sister and did his best to prepare himself to what was going to be a very long conversation.

THREE- September 30, 2015

Caleb Stone was alone as he sat on his balcony overlooking the beautiful blue waters of the Caribbean. His body slumped heavily in the wicker chair as his empty gaze watched the small waves flow easily onto the fine powder sand. It was as if he was hypnotized by the waters dance, but he was not. In fact, his mind was on Sophia. His attention broke from the ocean as he reached down beside him for the cold bottle of beer and took a long drink. It should have been refreshing, especially under the heat of the Antiguan sun, but the sensation was lost on him. He could do nothing to numb the pain he was feeling inside. The last time he recalled feeling this much pain was when Kirsten was murdered… and that was a long time ago. A time in his life he still hated to think about.

As he sat alone in this magnificent place, his heart ached with the same fierceness as it had so many years ago. He sat his beer down on the small table beside him and stared at the joint he had set there earlier that morning. Caleb picked it up and rolled it gently between his fingers, bringing it to his nose to inhale its pungent scent. A faint smile came to his lips as the memory of the last time he had smoked a joint came into his mind. He had snuck behind the garage of his foster parents, Tom and Elise's house and Tom had caught him. He recalled how terrified he was, he was certain that they were going to send him away for it, but they hadn't. In fact, after a lengthy lecture on drugs and alcohol from his foster father, Caleb swore he would never touch the stuff again. Tom promised that nobody but them needed to know about it, including Elise. He could feel his heart stiffen with the memory of the parents who raised him, knowing that they too were gone from his life.

"Screw it!" Caleb mumbled under his breath, grabbing the lighter off the table. He held the flame to the end of the joint and inhaled deeply, bringing it to life. He inhaled deeply allowing a billow of smoke to enter his lungs. His lungs had not experienced smoke in a very long time. He began to cough uncontrollably, trying to clear the sensation in his throat. He took another long swig of his beer to clear the uncomfortable irritation. When he brought the joint back to his lips this time, he inhaled a little more softly, being sure not to choke himself again. His head filled with a familiar fog, but that pain, that unspeakable pain, was still there lying heavy in his chest. He glanced toward the small love seat across from him, the last place he sat with her, the last place he held her in his arms. His heart broke into pieces as he remembered their very last conversation that haunted his memory.

"What is it, babe? What is going on in that pretty little head of yours?"

Sophia had decided to just go ahead and bring it up. She was sure it wasn't going to be a big deal for him to share it all with her now, knowing that there had been many things he hadn't wanted her knowing to keep her safe.

"Oh, nothing, I'm fine. I've just been thinking so much about everything, and how perfectly it all went. Caleb, I'm so thankful you were with me every step of the way. I'm just curious about something though, who was the person that Marcus hired to kill me?"

Her question caught him off guard. He had been tormented with guilt about the situation, but he truly never believed that she would bring this up. As her words hung heavy in the air, he desperately tried to figure out just how and what he should say. He was terrified of telling her the whole truth. He feared she wouldn't understand, and that he would lose her because of his role in the entire operation. He loved her more than anything in this world, and if he wanted a solid future with her, honesty was going to be the best policy. It was time to tell her the whole truth. He turned his gaze back to the sunset as it slowly dipped below the horizon, he was just praying he was about to do the right thing.

"Caleb? Are you okay? Listen, baby, I didn't mean to upset you. You don't have to tell me anything. I know I was probably kept out of the loop on a lot of things to protect me. I just can't seem to figure out who he could have hired. I don't know how you managed to stop it from happening, either. That's all. If you don't want to tell me anything, I know it's for a good reason. I'm sorry for asking, but it's been really bothering me." Sophia felt horrible that she put him on the spot and reached for his hand. Caleb grabbed her hand and prepared himself for what he was about to say next.

"Sophia, there's a lot I have to tell you. Please know it's not going to be easy to hear but you deserve to know the truth. You know that I would never hurt you, nor will I ever hurt you intentionally. You deserve to know everything that happened. I will tell you absolutely everything you want to know, but I'm begging you to hear me out, and let me tell you everything before you make any judgments. Please, understand why I wanted to protect you from this. There is something about me that you don't know. I'm telling you because I know you love me and you know I love you. In order for you to truly love all of me you need to know all of me, all the good parts, and the not so good parts."

Sophia could feel his palm sweating in her hand, she felt a sudden panic rise in her throat. She trusted Caleb more than anything, but she knew he was hiding something serious to keep her safe. As she studied his expression carefully, it became abundantly clear that it was something she wasn't sure she wanted to hear.

"Caleb, you're scaring me. You know that you can always tell me anything. Whatever it is, please, I want to know. It's all over now, so you can tell me. Baby, does this have anything to do with who they hired to kill me? Oh, God, do you think I'm still in danger? Do you know who it was?" Sophia begged, as the panic began to deepen. "Caleb, who was it?" She now raised her voice. "Please, tell me. I need to know."

His throat felt restricted, and his mouth had lost all moisture. He hated to see her so scared and panicked. He knew she was no longer in danger, but the fear of losing her nearly paralyzed him. Still, he knew she needed to know everything about him, everything that would eventually lead him directly into her life. There was no turning back now, he turned to face the woman he so desperately loved and started the entire story that had been burdening him since the moment she was brought into his life.

"It was me, Sophia. I was the one he hired to kill you."

Silence hung in the warm air, a silence that made Caleb question if he made the worst decision of his life. He could not keep this from Sophia, not if they wanted a life together. He knew it was the best thing to tell her everything, but as he watched the colour drain from her beautifully tanned skin, guilt began to blur his judgment of telling everything to the woman he loved.

"What do you mean?" She asked him with no clear emotion to indicate her feelings.

"Marcus hired me to investigate you. He was certain that he was in danger, and he hired me."

"Caleb, I don't understand, did he hire you to investigate me or kill me?"

Caleb's heart began to beat wildly in his chest, but he knew he had to continue and tell her everything. "He hired me to investigate you, to find out if he was in danger. He needed to know if you were trying to take him down in any way, and..." Caleb's explanation was cut off without warning.

"Caleb! Why the hell would Marcus have hired you? I don't understand, I mean Christ I know he was a monster, that I get, but I don't understand how you are involved at all. You were a cop, a

detective, so how did he find you? How?" Now her face was beginning to express escalating worry.

"I'm sorry Sophia, I am, shit, I should have told you sooner."

"Told me what Caleb? Tell me! Why the hell would Marcus ever even come to you in the first place? Don't you lie to me now, tell me the truth."

"Because Sophia, I'm a contract killer, I'm a fucking hitman, I kill people for money!" The words came out before Caleb could formulate the softest way to say them. He instantly regretted the bluntness of his confession. He watched Sophia intently, she pulled away from him, but her eyes held his.

"A what?" was the only thing she could reply.

"Listen to me Sophia, you have to understand, I only wanted to help people."

"Help people? By killing them?" Sophia stood up, her eyes still locked on his. "How could you not tell me this? How could you lie to me for so long about this? I trusted you Caleb. I trusted you with everything inside of me. The whole time you were being hired to kill people, including me, for money. How could you do this to me?"

Caleb felt like someone had just kicked him forcefully in the stomach, the air nearly knocked out of him completely. He needed her to understand.

"Baby, please, just let me exp...." Again, he was cut off.

"No, I can't! I can't!" The tears now rushed to Sophia's eyes. She did her best to muster the strength to utter her last words before

turning and running out the door. Caleb stood up quickly and started after her but thought better of it and stopped abruptly.

"Sophia," he called out loudly after her, hoping she would change her mind and come back so he could explain. "Sophia, please, come back," he cried out again, only this time only loud enough for himself to hear.

The wafting smoke drew Caleb's attention back to the present. He took one more drag off of the joint before he snuffed it out on the bottom of his sandal, tossing the remnants over the railing. It had been three days since she had left, and Caleb had not heard from her. He was increasingly becoming more worried about her. He had no idea where she was, but he knew he had to go to her and try to explain everything. She needed to know that that part of his life was over, that she was what he needed in his life now. He dug into the pocket of his cargo shorts and retrieved his phone. A picture of them smiling lovingly into one another's eyes coming alive on his screen. He thought perhaps the more he checked his phone, the better chance there would be that she would call. Nothing. He hit the email icon and saw the unopened message from Jill. He had seen it the day Sophia ran off, but he had had no interest in anything other than her at the time. Pressing on it, the email filled his screen, and he read:

To: Caleb Stone

From: Jill Keller

Subject: Happy Birthday

Hey there, you old fart! I just realized as I am sitting here in my nice new office, that you so kindly left to me, that today is your birthday. I guess I will just have to take myself to Joe's tonight for our annual tequila shot and steak. Well, that is unless I take my new boneheaded partner with me. Ya, you heard me

"Boneheaded". Maybe it's just me being too hard on him because he isn't you. In fact, I am sure that is what it is. Anyhow, I'm not sure where you are, maybe sailing around, laying on a beach somewhere or maybe you're living up in a tree somewhere, I am not too sure. Hell, I don't even know if you are checking your emails. Regardless, I just wanted to say Happy Birthday, and that wherever you are, I miss you. It still isn't too late to come back home either. I would maybe, just maybe, even consider giving you back your office. Well, I should go but I would love to hear from you, to hear all about your crazy adventures.

Talk to you soon,

Jill

A feeling of guilt washed over him after reading her email. Aside from Sophia, Jill was one of the closest people to him, and he had lied to her too. But he had no choice, if she knew the truth about him it would have destroyed everything. Caleb knew that he had to protect Sophia, no matter what. The one sure thing Caleb knew in all of this chaos was that he would do anything to protect Sophia Donovan from ever being hurt again by anyone, and he meant anyone.

FOUR -October 1, 2015

The door to Zoe's small apartment was flung open, banging heavily against the wall. Olivia and Zoe were tightly entwined as they entered the apartment. Zoe's hands wrapped in Olivia's long dark hair, their lips hungrily locked together. The apartment was dark, neither one of them caring that they banged into every object that got in their way. Zoe managed to use her foot to kick the door shut, being sure not to release Olivia from her embrace. Olivia pinned Zoe against the first wall she could feel, their bodies writhing in hunger. She brought her lips away from hers for a moment. For a second, Olivia questioned if she really wanted to do this. It did not take long for her to have her answer, as she looked into Zoe's eyes, her breasts heaving with desire against Olivia's dewy skin. Olivia crushed her mouth back onto Zoe's, pulling at the bottom of her tight tank top as she did so. With one quick motion Olivia pulled the shirt over Zoe's head and tossed it on the floor beside them. Zoe pushed herself away from the wall and pulled Olivia with her down the hall into the bedroom. In the bedroom, Zoe reached for a small lamp on her bedside table and turned it on, before turning to face Olivia. They stood looking deep into each others' eyes. Olivia now feeling somewhat shy as Zoe studied her. Zoe reached and hooked her index finger into the waist of Olivia's pants, pulling her gently towards her. Reaching out, Zoe slowly took off her shirt.

"God, you're sexy," Zoe murmured, as Olivia stood in front of her. Her small breasts now covered with nothing but a simple black bra.

Zoe reached behind her to unclasp her red lacy bra. Letting it slide to the floor her lush full breasts were taut with wanting. Olivia's pulse started to race. She had never gone this far with a woman before, but as Zoe stood in front of her, Olivia knew this was exactly what she wanted and needed right now.

"No, you're fucking sexy," Olivia growled with desire as she pulled Zoe to her, exploring her mouth with her tongue. Gently she laid Zoe back onto the bed and straddled her. Olivia captured both of Zoe's arms above her head and slowly ran her tongue from her throat down to her breasts. Moaning, Zoe arched her back slightly, as Olivia gently held Zoe's nipple between her teeth, feeling it stiffen with a craving for more. Olivia heard a soft whimper escape Zoe, and it excited her even more knowing she was in control of their lovemaking. As she continued her exploration of Zoe's sweet and soft body, she flicked her tongue over Zoe's nipples and placed butterfly kisses over her breasts. Olivia continued downward from Zoe's breasts and gliding over her soft stomach, gently placing kisses along the way. Olivia stopped for a moment admiring how perfect Zoe's stomach was as she gently played with the pink butterfly that dangled from her belly button. Zoe was writhing beneath her in anticipation. Olivia started to feel like her nerves were beginning to overwhelm her. What if she were horrible at pleasing a woman she thought to herself. Olivia knew she could please a man, but she had never been with a woman before, what if she couldn't please her?

"Please baby, I want you so bad," Zoe pleaded with desire.

Olivia seductively looked up to meet Zoe's heated gaze. Reaching up she fondled Zoe's breasts one more time before her mouth continued downwards, stopping at Zoe's red lace panties. This was it, Olivia thought to herself, this is happening. She hooked her fingers in the waist and pulled them down Zoe's long legs, tossing them on the floor beside her. As her tongue traced a seductive line up the inside of Zoe's trembling thighs, Olivia became aroused in a way she had never experienced before. The moment her mouth tasted Zoe's sweetness, Olivia, without any further hesitancy, plunged wildly into an intense new sexual experience. "Wow, just wow," Zoe exclaimed in between panted breaths.

Both women were laying naked and sweaty, on their backs. Zoe's arm flung lifelessly over her head, as she tried to catch her breath. She rolled over on her side, propping her head up on her elbow. Her long red hair spilling onto the pillow around her. Olivia rolled over facing Zoe.

"That was incredible," Zoe continued.

Olivia responded with a shy smile, which was strange because she certainly was not acting shy five minutes ago. Now that it was over she was not sure how to act. If this had been a man she would probably be getting up, grabbing her clothes and heading out the door, but right now she did not want to be anywhere but here.

"It was," Olivia replied coyly.

Zoe watched Olivia's reaction for a moment, seeing a myriad of thoughts flicker through Olivia's eyes. She gently reached across and pushed a loose strand of Olivia's dark hair out of her eye.

"You okay? You seem a little lost in thought?"

"I'm great, honestly, that was amazing. Surprisingly amazing actually," Olivia answered honestly.

"Surprisingly?" Zoe laughed. "Did you think I was going to be a shitty lay?"

Olivia heard the hurt in Zoe's words and realized her response had seemed insulting, and that was not at all what she meant. She thought for a moment and decided she should tell Zoe that this was in fact something that was totally new to her. "Shit, no sorry, I did not mean it like that. I meant surprising because, well... I wasn't sure what to expect at all, I have never done this before."

A complete look of astonishment washed over Zoe's face.

"You're a virgin?"

Olivia almost laughed out loud, god she was far from it. "No, no of course I'm not a virgin. I just mean that was my first time with another woman."

The shocked expression remained on Zoe's face a few seconds longer. Olivia could tell she was trying to make sense of it all in her head.

"You're screwing with me, right?" Zoe replied.

"No, I'm serious, I mean I have kissed a couple chicks before, nothing serious, but this was my first time, you know... doing this..."

Zoe's eyebrows rose with surprise.

"Well, I would have never guessed that. You seemed to know exactly what you were doing, that was seriously intense, I felt like my body was literally going to explode."

Olivia smiled at the compliment.

"I have always wanted to try it, I have always found women beautiful."

"And..." Zoe asked, drawing out the word.

"And... you were here, you know exactly what you did to me, no man has every made me cum like that, seriously." Olivia pulled the sheets up to her waist, feeling suddenly introverted again.

Zoe slowly brought her mouth to Olivia's, softly kissing her on the lips. Not a kiss filled with desire, just more a kiss of understanding and appreciation. Olivia returned the kiss, enjoying the subtle connection. Zoe laid her head back on to her arm.

"Well, I must say, I am glad you chose me. Can I ask you why?"

"Why what?" Olivia repeated Zoe's question back to her.

"Why me? Why tonight? I mean I could tell you were having a rough day when you came in, but what made you want to be with me?"

Olivia wasn't completely sure how to answer that question. She thought for a moment before responding.

"I don't know, I just have been having a shit time lately and really needed a distraction. I obviously was not out looking to just hook up with someone. But look at you, obviously, you know you're hot, you would have to be blind not to notice that. Something about you got me. That smile, those eyes, those," Olivia teased sexily as she caressed Zoe's large breasts with her fingertip.

Zoe giggled, and grabbed Olivia's hand, entwining her fingers into hers.

"I'm glad I can be here to help. But you know I can help in other ways too. I am actually known to be a great listener, it's actually one of the requirements of being a bartender. I am basically just a way cheaper shrink," Zoe chuckled.

"Oh, I don't know if you want to enter my fucked-up world just yet. It's kind of crazy to say the least, or maybe it's just me who is crazy, honestly I don't know anymore."

"Ah, don't say that, we all have a little bit of crazy in us. I am sure whatever is going on isn't easy to deal with. But I mean it, I am a great listener, if you ever need someone to just listen, and I am also a problem solver, if you have any problems that need solving."

Olivia squeezed Zoe's hand firmly in hers, and replied with an intensity, she knew Zoe would not be expecting.

"I appreciate it, I'm just not sure how you would be able to help me take down the bitch who killed my brother, and destroyed my family's life, that's all."

The words hung awkwardly in the air as Olivia studied Zoe's reaction to her abrupt reply, she was sure that she probably blew it, and Zoe was going to think she was in fact crazy, but to her own surprise she was wrong.

"Your right, that is a pretty shitty day, but hey, I'm always looking for a challenge."

FIVE - October 3, 2015

The cup was warm against Jill's hand, as she slowly inhaled the fragrant aroma of the freshly brewed coffee. Her office was quiet at this hour, she had decided to come in early to check some emails before the craziness of her day began. With heavy apprehension, she turned on her computer and opened her emails, only to be disappointed yet again. Sitting in the silence of her office she tried her best to bury her displeasure of the fact that she had not heard back from Caleb. It wasn't like she was expecting him to reach out to her every day and keep her informed as to his every move, but she was expecting him to at least give a quick reply to the last email she sent. It had only been a few days since she sent him the birthday email, so maybe her impatience was getting the best of her. As much as she didn't like to admit it though, the idea of him out there, wherever he was, was getting the best of her. She missed him, a lot, and Jill knew full well it was not just the fact that her partner and friend was gone, she missed him. Seeing him every day, his face, his smile, hearing his laugh, she missed everything about him. As much as she tried to pretend she didn't miss him, she did, more than she thought possible.

Jill gripped her mug firmly in between both hands, she slowly leaned back in her leather chair, and rocked back and forth. She wished Caleb were here, not only because of her own personal feelings, but also because he would know what to do about the whole Olivia Donovan situation. He would know how to handle her. Jill could relate to Olivia in a sense. She could understand the constant nagging intuition that something about the whole Sophia and Marcus Donovan case was suspicious. She had felt that way through the whole investigation, but she also knew Olivia Donovan had seemed highly unpredictable. Jill knew one thing more than anything and that was the fact that she trusted Caleb. She trusted his abilities as a cop and she trusted that he was always doing what he was able to as to make sure cases got solved. She suspected that he possibly had some sort of soft spot for Sophia. Jill could hardly deny the fact that she was a beautiful woman so what man wouldn't, but to prematurely close an investigation due to that was something Jill knew Caleb would never do.

Jill rested her head back and closed her eyes, the tension was radiating throughout her neck. She was not quite sure why this was eating at her so much, but it was. She was not sure if this was something that deserved her to look further into or if she should just follow Caleb's advice and just shut the book on the whole thing. Olivia was clearly unstable, they discovered that during the investigation. She was highly uncooperative and seemed like she would be a nightmare to deal with. Did Jill really want to get into that with her when the chances of it leading no where was highly probable? Olivia was angry. She had lost her brother, that part was understandable. But was her anger misdirected and out for some sort of unsupported retribution? These are the questions that Jill was uncertain about, and these were the reasons why she didn't think Olivia Donovan deserved any of her attention. Struggling with her thoughts, the silence of her office was abruptly disrupted by a quick rap on her door.

"We've got to go," Detective Joshua Landon exclaimed urgently as he downed the last of his coffee.

"What do we got?" Keller replied as she quickly jumped out of her chair, grabbing her gun, and putting it securely in its holster.

"A body was found under the Santa Monica Pier, early this morning."

Jill followed her new partner out of her office.

"Just lovely," she uttered quietly under her breath, closing the door behind her as she raced to follow her partner.

The black Dodge Charger came to a grinding halt, Keller and Landon jumped out simultaneously, slamming the doors behind them. There was already a thick crowd of curious gawkers gathered behind the crime tape, which had been set up a couple hours earlier. Jill pushed her way through the sea of the curious mob.

"Out of the way people, make room."

Frustrated by the fact that some people were oblivious that they were trying to get through, and not moving an inch, Jill shouted in her most intimidating tone.

"Everybody back away and let us through, right now. There is nothing to see here, carry on with what you were doing and let us do our damn jobs."

That got mostly all of their attentions, and they separated allowing the two detectives to make their way down the path which led to an open sand bar under the pier. The two patrolmen that were called in were on the scene waiting for the two detectives. The youngest one walked up to them, he looked like he was fresh out of the academy, the paleness in his skin indicating this was one of his first homicide scenes.

"What do we have here?" Jill inquired as she was putting on a pair of latex gloves.

"A woman looks to be in her early twenties, no I.D. She was found early this morning by two guys on their way out to surf."

"Well, then those two must have just missed it, the tide's lowest in the morning, so if her body is still here..." Landon stated.

"That's the thing," the young, pale faced cop interjected. "She has been here for awhile."

"What do you mean?" Keller asked as the officer led them to the body.

"Oh, I see," Jill exclaimed with understanding. "Christ, whoever did this wanted to make sure she suffered."

The woman's mutilated and swollen body was tied awkwardly to one of the pier posts. Her back pinned to the wooden post, her arms bound tightly above her head. A rope was tied firmly around her chin, which Jill guessed was so she was forced to watch her impending death as the waves grew higher and higher. Her feet were also tied tightly together, strapped to the post. The worst part was she was stripped naked and multiple wounds covered her entire body. Seaweed matted in her hair. Her probably once beautiful face, distorted from the beating and drowning.

"Jesus Christ," Detective Landon muttered under his breath, though loud enough for Jill to hear. Joshua Landon had just recently become detective, so she knew he had seen his fair share of grizzly sights, but the first few scenes as a detective can be overwhelming. Landon continued.

"What kind of pyscho would do this to someone? I think drowning would be one of the worst ways to go, and to not be able to at least fight for your survival…my God."

"Forensics arrived shortly before you guys, and we are just waiting for the coroner," the rookie cop informed the two detectives.

"Thanks guys," Jill replied. "We got it from here."

Jill watched as the two patrol cops headed back to their patrol unit, then turned to face her partner.

"Looks like we got a sick son-of-a-bitch on our hands here."

"No shit, we've got to find whoever the hell did this, and soon, so the sick bastard doesn't do something like this to someone else."

Jill walked closer to the lifeless body, studying her face more intensely. She sighed deeply with disgust then turned away.

"We will figure it out, whatever sicko did this will get his, I assure you. Jesus, what I wouldn't give to be able to take justice in my own hands sometimes," Jill proclaimed angrily.

"I hear ya, Keller, it's shit like this that makes you wonder just how far a person could go to keep scumbags like this off the street."

Jill nodded in agreement with her partner, patting his arm gently.

"I certainly wouldn't blame them," Jill agreed, as she glanced over to see the coroner making his way to them. Then repeated her statement before walking to meet the balding man heading toward her.

"I wouldn't blame them one fucking bit."

SIX -October 5, 2015

"I got her."

"You got her? Caleb's heart nearly stopped cold in his chest. "Where is she?"

"Her mom's, she just went in. When you messaged me last night, that was the first place I decided to go and bingo." Trent Ford replied to Caleb's urgent question.

"Thank God." Caleb exclaimed with understandable relief.

"Listen, man I know how you feel about her, I do, but are you sure that she is not going to say anything? Are you honestly sure?" Trent's concern was highly evident in his tone.

Caleb sighed deeply, mostly out of pure reprieve in the fact that his friend found her so quickly. He could completely understand where Trent's apprehension was coming from. Trent did not know Sophia Donovan the way that he did, and he was convinced that she would never say anything, no matter how much Caleb had betrayed her trust.

"She won't" Caleb began to answer and was quickly interrupted.

"How do you know?"

Caleb continued. "I just know. Look, I know she is hurt, I know she is angry, but Sophia would never do that to me, I am not worried about that at all."

"Well, I'm not going to lie and say it doesn't worry me, but I guess if she does she is only incriminating herself, she was involved."

This time it was Caleb who suddenly interjected.

"No, listen to me, I don't care what goes down, I don't give a damn if I get caught or if for some insane reason she does say something. Under no circumstances, and I mean not one fucking circumstance, is she to be brought into this, do you understand me? No matter what happens, she is to be kept safe."

There was a bitter silence over the phone for what seemed like an eternity before Trent spoke again.

"You can't let her take us all down, Cal, I will not go down for this shit," frustration was deeply etched in his voice.

Caleb felt his own frustration building. He knew this whole situation had the potential of getting severely messy, but it was up to him now to make sure he kept everyone involved safe. If he had to take the hit alone for all of it, he would. But his main priority was Sophia, she needed to be kept out of it all together and he would figure out Luke and Trent as he went.

"You are not going to go down, I promise, just trust me. Look, now that I know she is there, I am going to get on the first flight out of here. I am going to be home in a day or so. So, just please do me a favour and don't panic, it's going to be fine. When I get home, I am finally going to get a chance to talk to her. She just needed some time to cool down and process what I told her. But I need you to stay calm, tell Luke to stay calm, and just try and watch her for a bit for me, okay?"

Again, the silence was deafening through the phone line. Caleb was feeling a sense of urgency to make sure Trent was on the same page as him. He was about to ask him again when Trent replied begrudgingly.

"Okay, I get it. I will talk to Luke. The kid is freaking out that she is going to say something. I will try and keep things calm over here until you get home. But, man you really need to make this shit right with her, I don't want to feel like there are any loose ends, I hate loose ends."

Caleb did his best not to take Trent's last comment as a threat, the last thing he wanted to do was create any more tension in the situation. He trusted Trent and he knew that he was just freaking out, Caleb knew that if he could rely on anyone to keep things calm and controlled, it was him. They have too much history and too much information on each other for them not to trust each other.

"I will get there as soon as I can, I promise. It's all going to be fine, no one is going down, no one is going to get caught, and no one has to freak out and panic. Just go have a beer and relax and tell the kid to do the same thing. I will let you know as soon as I can get my flight, and you can pick me up then."

"Fine, just hurry the fuck up and get home," Trent replied half heartily and half with serious intent.

Caleb chuckled into the phone to do his best to ease the tension.

"Relax man, because I'm coming fucking home."

SEVEN - October 5, 2015

Sophia Donovan gently shut the front door of her mother's house, and within seconds Isabelle Vaughn came dashing out of the kitchen to meet her daughter. A dish towel was slung over her shoulder, she wiped her damp hands quickly on her pants before reaching to pull her daughter in a tight hug.

"Mom," Sophia murmured as she clung to her mother. The tears she had been fighting came rushing to the surface with intensity. Sophia kept her face buried deep into her mother's shoulder as Isabelle rubbed her back, not saying anything in that moment. After several moments Isabelle whispered in her daughter's ear.

"It's okay honey, everything is going to be okay."

Sophia slowly brought her face out of Isabelle's now wet shoulder, her mascara smudged and running black down her cheeks. Her eyes were red and swollen, but more than that, they told her mother that she clearly had not slept in days.

"I don't think so Mom, I don't think anything is going to be okay."

"Honey, come, let's get you a cup of tea and you can tell me what happened," Isabelle responded as she led her daughter back to the kitchen.

Sophia put her arm around her mother's waist and walked with her into the kitchen, which smelled of fresh flowers. As she took a seat at the island in the centre of the room, she glanced over to the table and verified the smell, a beautiful bouquet arrangement of lilies sat perfectly arranged in the centre of the kitchen table. Isabelle walked over to her kettle, filled it with water, turned on her stove and let the water come to a boil. She took a seat next to her daughter and grabbed her hand in hers. Sophia could tell by the look on her mother's face that her heart was breaking seeing her like this.

"Sweetheart, what is going on? What happened?"

Sophia sat quietly, unable to look her mother in the eye. Fear formed a bubble in her throat. She could feel her palm begin to dampen in her mother's grasp, so she gently pulled her hand away and buried her face in her palms.

"Sophia, talk to me, you know you can tell me anything. I hate to see you like this, but I cannot do anything to help you if you don't talk to me."

Before Sophia could answer the piercing whistle of the tea kettle interrupted them. Isabelle jumped off her stool and took the pot off the burner. She grabbed two mugs and poured them each a steaming cup of the hot water, plopping an Earl Grey in each. Isabelle placed the hot mug in front of her daughter and returned to her seat.

Sophia's tormented gaze met her mothers.

"Mom..." those were the only words that managed to escape Sophia's trembling lips before she broke down in tears once again. Isabelle allowed her daughter the time she needed to gather and process the thoughts that were clearly tormenting her.

"I don't know what to do."

"About what?"

"Everything," Sophia replied bluntly.

"Whatever it is, we can get through it together. Tell me what happened, and we can fix it."

"This can't be fixed Mom," Sophia whipped herself around, so she was fully facing her mother.

"What I did, cannot be fixed. It's done, and I cannot take it back."

Although the actual words did not come, Sophia could see in her mom's expression that she knew exactly what she was talking about. There was an immediate unspoken understanding that hung between them, and they sat staring at each other, waiting to see who would speak first. Isabelle took a deep breath, just then her own tears surfaced, relief evident on her features.

"Baby, what did that man do to you?" her voice now quivering.

Sophia steadied her herself and prepared to be totally honest with her mother. She deserved that, Isabelle had been there for her for her entire life. Sophia knew she could always rely on her mom, no matter what life threw at her. She just never ever wanted to make her a part of this. She never wanted to speak the truth because once those words were out, there was no turning back. The thought that she could upset her mother the way this information would upset her was not something she ever wanted to confront, but right now was the time. Her mother knew, she knew the whole time, but now it was the time to share it all.

"Mom, I don't want you to have to hear what went on between Marcus and I, but things were not good, not at all..." Sophia began but her mother cut her off.

"Sophia, I need you to tell me what that man did to you. I have to understand fully why you did what you did."

Sophia was surprised at the bluntness of her mother's statement.

"How did you know Mom?" She asked

"Honey, you are my daughter, I know you better than you think. I know you were miserable and unhappy with him. I know you were not telling me the truth about what was truly going on. I wasn't entirely sure at first. Were you capable of doing something like that? But when I finally realized my instincts were right, I knew that you must have gone through some sort of vial hell to force you to do it. When you told me about Caleb, when you finally admitted to me that you were in love with him, and that you wanted to go be with him, is when I allowed myself to accept the truth. But, baby, I need you to tell me it all. What did that man do to you, that forced you to kill him? And why are you home so soon? What happened with Caleb? I need you to tell me, be honest with me, and we will get through it together, I promise you that. I need to know the truth, all of the truth."

Her mom was right, she had to tell her. She had to talk to someone about everything that was going on. She should have come to her right from the start, but she chose to keep her in the dark. However, now she needed her Mother more than she has ever needed her in her life. She braced herself as she was about to relive her most terrifying and disturbing memories. She reached for her cup of tea, blew gently and took an easy sip, she placed the hot mug back down on the counter and sighed heavily. She turned back to her Mother, this time she reached for Isabelle's hand and squeezed it firmly. Sophia knew she had to start from the beginning, it was time to tell her Mom everything, every dirty and dark lie that she had been keeping from her over the last 12 years.

"You're absolutely right Mom, things were not good at all, there was a lot of things I kept a secret. Things started to go bad very early, but I never ever expected things to go this bad."

EIGHT - October 6, 2015

Olivia lay entwined in Zoe's arms, their legs mingled beneath the rumpled sheets. Olivia's head was resting on Zoe's chest, slowly rising and falling with each breath. Zoe's fingers gently combed through Olivia's long dark hair. As it fell softly on her bare back, Olivia could feel her eye's getting heavy. It had only been about a week since they had met, but since that first night they had been spending every spare moment together. Olivia had never imagined herself in this type of relationship with another woman, but there was just something about this amazing red head. Zoe, unlike any man that Olivia had ever been with, could please her in ways that she just did not believe were possible. She was attentive, and gentle when she needed to be. She was fierce and passionate when Olivia needed and desired it. But it was not only just the sex, Zoe listened to her, she never felt judgment from her at all. There was an unbreakable level of trust that she felt when it came to Zoe. In just one short week, Olivia had been able to share some of her deepest secrets with Zoe, and she had been there to listen to every detail of her thoughts on her brother's murder.

"What's going on in that pretty little head of yours?" Zoe interrupted Olivia's musings.

Olivia sighed, placing her hand on Zoe's stomach. "Nothing much, I was just thinking how crazy it has been since I met you."

"Oh? Crazy good or crazy bad?" Zoe questioned.

Olivia chuckled softly. "Crazy good of course, you know that. You just get me in ways that nobody else has ever gotten me before."

"Well, it's really not that hard to figure someone out, when you just take the time to listen to them. I don't think anyone has really ever heard you before. Or they just have not taken the time to want to hear you. I don't know, maybe we just connect on a different level and that is why we mesh so well."

"You don't judge me, no matter what I say or do, you just don't judge me. I can be myself with you. I can express myself without feeling like you might think I am a nut job. Every time I try to be myself around anyone else they think I am being dramatic or overreacting to the situation. I love how you just let me be me." Olivia tilted her head up, allowing her gaze to meet Zoe's.

Zoe bent her head down, allowing her lips to softly touch Olivia's, they held them there briefly and then Zoe pulled away as she continued to look in Olivia's eyes.

"I want you to be you, I love who you are, I don't want you to pretend to be someone you are not. You give me excitement and it is unpredictable. And God it has only been a week, I honestly cannot wait to see what you have in store for me," Zoe smiled widely, a slightly crooked tooth exposed.

Olivia brought her head down again, and she traced tiny circles with her finger around Zoe's belly button, admiring her flat stomach and appreciating just how beautiful her body was.

"Olivia, you know you can always talk to me about anything, anytime you have anything on your mind, I am here to listen. Don't ever feel like you cannot talk to me."

Olivia nodded her head, before replying verbally.

"I know that."

"So, that being said, is there anything on your mind?"

"I just wish my family would listen to me like you do, I wish someone would listen to me about my brother. My family thinks I am being resentful and difficult. They think I am just trying to lash out for Marcus' death. That fucking bitch cop, Keller doesn't want to listen to me. I don't get it, why can't anyone else see this for what it is? Why can't everyone see it as clearly as me that Sophia had something to do with my brother's death." Olivia could feel her throat tighten, frustration building.

Zoe did not respond at first, and Olivia knew she was trying to formulate the best response. That is what Olivia appreciated so much, Zoe listened to her instead of jumping at her like everyone else. She thought about what to say back instead of just spewing insults.

"Baby, I believe you. You know that I believe you. I hate that your parents, and this cop chick do not want to hear it. There has got to be someone or something that we can do though."

"Zoe, I have tried. I talked to my brother's friend Alex the night I met you at the bar, and he really didn't say much that I didn't know. I guess he was under that bitch's spell too. What the hell is it about that woman that people just fall for her shit? She tries to be this innocent damsel, and I know that she is not. Christ, I lived with them, I heard them argue and fight. My brother was not always perfect, but neither is she, she is far from it. I just know that she had something to do with it all." Olivia now sat up, pulling the sheets up around her as she sat and faced Zoe.

Zoe reached over and tucked a long dark strand of hair out of Olivia's face.

"All you know is that she is out of town, right?" Zoe asked softly.

"Ya, I have no idea where she is, or where she would go. What the hell does she need to leave LA for? That is what I don't get. Her friends, her family, her life was here, so now that the investigation is over, she's just gonna run and hide, with her tail tucked between her legs?" The anger was becoming evident, as Olivia's cheeks began to feel flushed.

"I wish I knew what to do to help find her for you. I want to get these answers for you baby, I do, I just wish I knew what to do to get them."

Olivia grabbed Zoe's hand and held it firmly in hers. She leaned in, and Zoe kissed her again. This time Olivia could feel Zoe's tongue as it slowly crept between Olivia's lips. Her breath instantly deepened, and that familiar rush of desire flooded through her body, and all with just one kiss. As it deepened, Zoe's hand reached behind Olivia's neck and she pulled her firmly towards her, so their breasts were pressing together. A soft moan escaped Zoe. Olivia pulled away long enough to whisper.

"You have no idea how much you mean to me."

Zoe seductively licked her full lips, her hand still grasping Olivia's neck. Her breath already growing heavy with anticipation of what was about to come, and before Zoe pulled Olivia back to her awaiting mouth she responded.

"I love you Olivia, and there isn't anything I wouldn't do for you, anything."

NINE - October 6, 2015

The sun was just settling over the horizon, the LA smog laid a smoky haze against the dusk of the sunset. Sunsets were always beautiful, even in LA. In fact, the orange glow cast from the descending sun would always beautify even the evident issues of the LA air quality. Trent Ford sat inside his parked Toyota Tundra, with the heater running on low. The October air was brisk, especially with the sun slowly making its departure. The music was low, loud enough for him to still make out the song but low enough that he could still hear his own thoughts. He was parked on a side street, facing the front doors of a tiny little bar called "Last Call". His engine purring quietly and his headlights off. He had followed Sophia Donovan here, he barely had left her side since he found her yesterday. The feeling of exhaustion starting to creep up on him.

Sophia was alone. Trent was fairly certain that not many people knew she was back already, and why would they? He was sure she was not jumping to tell people what had been going on in her life, he found himself worrying if perhaps she had told her mother anything.

His phone was sitting on the seat beside him, and it beeped loudly with a text message. He flipped open the phone to retrieve the message. Every time he used the burner phone it reminded him of just how much he actually hated these phones, but burner phones were the only way of communication when it came to business.

"Be at the Airport to pick me up at 7:30 AM."

Trent read the words projected on the tiny cell phone screen. Caleb was going to be home in the morning and he was relieved. He still could not for the life of him understand why the hell Caleb chose to tell Sophia everything. She was already in too deep as it was, but exposing them like he did, Trent could not make sense of it. He got that Caleb was in love with this woman, but why could he not have just left well enough alone. Trent was highly exasperated with the situation they were now in, but all he could really do now was just do what Caleb asked him to do and keep an eye on her. The rest they would have to sort out later and hopefully now that Caleb was coming home, he could make things right with her.

He had watched Sophia get out of her car, about 10 minutes prior, and head into the bar. He thought perhaps he would go inside and keep an eye on her but then thought it was probably better if he just stayed out here and just waited for her to come back out, then follow her to wherever she was going to next. He at least wanted to find out where she would end up for the night, so he could leave to pick up Caleb in the morning and then he could take over. Trent was a little surprised that she went to the bar, he knew she was not much of a drinker. A part of him immediately went with the notion that maybe she was meeting someone there. No new cars had pulled into the parking lot, so he felt somewhat assured that perhaps after all this she really just did need a drink. Hell, he needed several of those shots he had taken last night while he sat outside of Isabelle Vaughn's house, waiting for Sophia to finally move on. He typically did not like to drink while he was on a job, but he needed something to keep him alert and awake while he kept his eye on her.

Sitting alone with nothing but his music and his thoughts, Trent thought back to all of the events over the last several months. The three of them, himself, Caleb and Luke had managed to keep very low key, they ran a very successful operation and then one woman comes into the picture and has the potential to blow it for everyone.

He was definitely more worried than he wanted to admit. He had kept that to himself when he spoke with Luke, but the idea that they could be exposed after all this time because of Sophia had him on edge. He did not regret his part in helping with it all, not at all.

Marcus Donovan was a waste of skin in his personal opinion and what he had done to Sophia was disgusting. But at the end of it all, he was still very concerned that she would break, and say something to someone. At the same time though, he was slightly reassured that by her exposing them, she also exposes herself and that was probably the last thing that she wanted or needed.

The whole reason he got into this was because of his daughter, losing her almost devastated his entire existence. It tore apart his marriage, it tore apart his life, and he did not want other people to have to experience that if they did not have to. That is why he got into this business with Caleb Stone in the first place. And that is why he had no problems helping in any way he could when it came time to take care of Marcus Donovan. It was unfortunate that Cat Walker had to get herself involved. She had become a threat in the end. She was just as much a danger to Sophia as Marcus was, in fact, she was probably more of a threat. By the end of it she was willing to do anything to eliminate Sophia out of their lives, so she could have Marcus to herself without any complications. It was just a shame that she allowed her life to get tangled in Marcus Donovan's malicious web.

Trent looked at his clock, the numbers told him it was now 7:45 PM, he was surprised that he had already been sitting here for an hour. A few cars had now parked in the parking lot of the bar, however observing the new patrons, he found himself not at all concerned that they were there to meet Sophia. After doing this for so many years, he had developed a strong knack at reading people, even from a distance, and knowing what their intentions are. He was fairly confident that two young girls, not even legal age of drinking, bouncing arm in arm into the bar, and a depressed looking old guy, with a newspaper folded under his arm, were not too much of a concern for him.

Trent let his head fall easily on the leather head rest, he was starting to feel a bit of impatience creeping up on him. It had been a lot of long hours, and he was hungry, and growing very tired. He wished he had more Jack Daniels in his flask, but he finished it all off last night, while he waited for her at her mom's. That probably was not really helping in the way he was feeling now. He reached for the volume dial on his trucks radio, and turned it up just a little bit more, hoping the music would help wake him up. Trent stared at the front doors of the bar, mentally willing her to come out of there, so he could at least get a change of scenery, but after several moments he realized that was just not working. He drew in a deep breath, and quietly hummed along to the Eagles singing "Take it Easy".

And after only a few more moments, Trent's eyes grew very heavy, and as they slowly began to close the last thing he remembered thinking to himself as his conscience mind drifted off to sleep was, "Man, do I ever love the Eagles."

TEN - October 6, 2015

The bar was so quiet at this time of the day, which was good because Zoe was feeling very drained from the afternoon she had spent with Olivia. She wished she did not have to come to work at all this evening, but bills were not going to pay themselves… and she had a lot of them. What Zoe wanted more than anything was to just go back home and crawl back into bed, and not move again until the sun rose the next day. Not that they would have gotten much sleep, but that was fine with Zoe.

"Miss, can I get another beer?"

Her thoughts were interrupted by Gus, a cranky old coot that came in everyday, sat at the end of the bar and drank nearly all afternoon. Even though Gus had been coming in for as long as Zoe had worked there, she still chuckled every time he called her miss. He knew her name, but he just kept to himself every day, it was just him and his Miller. He did not want to come there to chat with the other customers, or make small talk with the flirty bartender, he just wanted to come and sit at the end of the bar and drink his beers.

Zoe grabbed a Miller Lite from the beer fridge, popped the top and placed it in front of Gus.

"Here you go Gus," she said politely as she took his empty bottle away. He gave her nothing more than a nod and continued on to himself.

Besides Gus, there were only a handful of other customers in the bar. It was still fairly early, that is why she did not like starting earlier, because the tips and the customer conversation were highly lacking.

She pulled the towel off of her shoulder and began wiping the bar down… a pointless task she thought to herself, no amount of wiping was going to get this bar clean. She wished the owners of the place would just suck it up and put some money into it. There were so many things that needed updating in the place. New furniture, new art work, a new pool table. God, people were lucky if they actually got to play after they put their money in. It was kind of a luck of the draw, sometimes that damn table would take your money and let you play the game, or sometimes it would take your money and you were just out of luck, no pool game for you. But, most of the time it was the same faces that came in, with the same stories, and the same problems. So, when the bells on the front door chimed, Zoe was actually very relieved to see a new face.

She continued to wipe the bar down, as a noticeably beautiful woman walked towards a stool and took a seat at the bar. The first thing Zoe noticed was the woman looked very sad. More than sad, she had a look of heartbreak etched all over her face. One of the cool things about her job was it usually was not long before they were sharing their stories with her, so she had a reason as to why people were the way they were.

After giving the woman a moment to get comfortable, Zoe approached her.

"Good evening, what can I get for you?"

The woman looked up at Zoe, almost dazed, like she did not comprehend what was just asked of her. Zoe did not press though, it was clear this person was not having a good day.

"Um… I don't know, I guess I will have a glass of your house Merlot."

Zoe snickered under her breath, *house merlot,* this obviously was not the type of place this chick was used to coming, but nonetheless Zoe grabbed a wine glass, which of course required a quick rinse. The dust had settled quite thick over the barely used glasses. Zoe dried the glass and did a quick search for a bottle, any bottle of merlot that she could find. Most of their wine was served out of boxes. After a minute of searching she managed to find an unopened one under the bar with a few other abandoned bottles of red wine. It was very obvious that this really was not the place of wine drinkers. Zoe located a cork screw and uncorked the bottle. She poured a healthy glass and set it in front of the woman. Again, Zoe noticed how attractive she was. She, like Olivia, had long dark hair. But Olivia had a different kind of appeal to Zoe. Olivia to Zoe was incredibly hot. She was small framed, she had a paler skin tone and she had blue eyes which pierced through Zoe's sole every time Olivia looked at her. This woman was beautiful, she had a very calming presence about her but at the same time, her presence indicated some sort of heartache. Although Zoe, since meeting Olivia, had not even thought of being with another woman, she still noticed them when they sat down at her bar, it was hard not to.

Zoe left the woman alone. It was apparent she, like Gus, was not there to mingle. So, Zoe continued cleaning up.

"Excuse me."

Zoe glanced over to the direction of the voice. She walked over to the woman.

"What do you need?" Zoe asked.

"Do you have the time?"

Zoe glanced at her watch.

"It's ten to seven," Zoe answered her.

"Oh, okay, thanks," was all the woman said.

Zoe could tell whatever this woman had gone through, it was clear that it was not good. Zoe could read a pain in her eyes unlike she had seen in anyone's before. Olivia was quite upset the day she came into this bar, and it actually turned out great for Zoe, but this was different. This was pure heartache. There was evidence of crying and pain in her red, swollen eyes. Zoe did not want to pry, but she wanted to find out what could be causing someone this much agony. So, she thought maybe it best to strike up a casual conversation and see if she opened up.

"Are you meeting someone?"

"No."

Well that was nice and blunt, Zoe thought to herself. "Ah well a nice evening out by yourself is always good too," Zoe could not help but feel awkward, and that was rare.

The woman's gaze lifted up to meet Zoe's, and she did not say anything this time. She just took a sip of her wine.

Just then the front door opened and the bells jangled again. Two young girls walked casually into the bar and sat next to the woman. Zoe turned to them, knowing instantly that they were both too young to be drinking. The taller blonde summoned Zoe over.

"Yes?" Zoe asked.

The tall blonde replied. "Can we get two vodka cranberry please?"

"I'm gonna need to see some ID please?"

The girls looked at each other with astonishment. A look of who does this woman think she is asking us for ID. Obviously we are 21.

"Really?" The other girl replied.

"Really!" Zoe said seriously.

With a huff they both reached for their purses slung over their shoulders and retrieved two pieces of ID. Zoe grabbed the ID's and studied them closely for about 2 seconds before she handed them back.

"Nice try ladies," Zoe rolled her eyes.

The blonde sulked, "What do you mean nice try? Those are our IDs."

"Listen ladies, you can go back, and you can try and play some pool, you can grab yourselves some cokes, or you can leave. I am not gonna kick you out, but I am not going to serve you booze, do you understand?"

They both dropped their shoulders in defeat, actually shocked that their $20 fake IDs did not pass the test. Actually, most nights in here it probably would. Most of the other people who worked in here did not give a shit about how old you are, but Zoe tried her best to be on top of that.

"Fine," the blonde said and grabbed her friend by the arm. "Come on, Trin, let's go play some pool then."

Trin followed her friend as they headed back towards the pool table.

Zoe shook her head as she headed back over to the woman sitting at her bar. The woman actually had a small smile on her face.

"Can you believe that?" Zoe asked rhetorically.

The woman allowed herself to actually giggle. Zoe felt good knowing she helped the woman have at least a few minutes of laughter. The woman grabbed her purse, off the stool behind her and pulled out her wallet. Zoe hoped she was not leaving already, watching as she opened her wallet and pulled something out, handing it to Zoe.

"Here you go, just in case you think maybe I'm trying to pull a fast one on you too?"

Zoe laughed at the woman, and took the drivers licence out of her hand. And just to go along with her in the moment she studied the ID.

"There, now do you think maybe I can have another glass of wine?" the woman teased.

Zoe's stomach lurched into her throat, and her heart sped up, beating fast in her chest. Her legs got weak, and for a second she almost did not know what to do. She wasn't even sure if her reaction was pure excitement or disappointment. She knew that she had to remain calm and act normal, because the last thing she wanted to do was give her a reason to get up and leave, not now. Not when she was here sitting right the hell in front of her. She handed her ID back and mustered a fake and flirty smile.

"Absolutely, Sophia, let me grab you another glass of wine."

ELEVEN -October 6, 2015

Olivia was soaking her exhausted body in a mountain of fragrant bubbles with a glass of red wine in hand. Her long wavy hair was piled high on top of her head, wispy, damp strands falling around her face. It was not a large tub, Zoe's apartment was small and so was the tub, but it still felt good to let her body relax in the hot water, the suds dancing on her skin. Her eyes were closed as she was drifting back to earlier that afternoon. Her and Zoe spent hours making love, sometimes wild and untamed and other times were slow and passionate. Whatever it was they were doing, Olivia could not get enough of this woman and she thanked whoever was listening out in the universe every day that she stumbled into her life. She lifted her petite foot out of the mountain of bubbles and traced the outline of the faucet with her brightly painted toe. Taking a healthy sip of the Malbec, she savoured the vibrant taste, relaxing even further. She had a little bit of buzz after only about half of a glass, the heat of the water and the lack of food that day were starting to show. Olivia glanced at the clock on the wall and was disappointed that it was only quarter to eight. Zoe was not going to be home until at least three in the morning, but that was the life of being a bartender. At least she had a job, and that was more than Oliva could say for half the men she dated in her life. Her phone, which was sitting on the ledge of the tub, beeped loudly and Olivia glanced down to see the message glow up on the screen of her iPhone.

"Hi Honey, I just wanted to see how you are doing."

Olivia's eyes nearly rolled into the back of her head as she read the incoming text message from her mother. *Like she gave a shit how she was doing,* Olivia thought to herself. Since she met Zoe in the bar that night, she really did not want to speak to either one of her parents. Olivia did finally tell them both about Zoe, they tried to act supportive but she knew deep down they did not approve. After all, they have made it clear to her very often, they just want her to find a nice man and settle down and have children and move on with her life. They wanted her to stop obsessing about her brother's death and the fact that she thought Sophia might have had something to do with it. *No, not might...* Olivia corrected in her mind, she does have something to do with it. She knew that deep in her heart the only person who wanted to hear it was Zoe. Zoe did not think she was a lunatic for not dropping her nagging intuition. In fact, she wanted nothing more than to be able to help her prove herself right. She just did not know how to go about it. Zoe did not have the chance to meet Marcus, and she did not know anything about Sophia, other than the information Olivia had shared with her. Olivia decided she was just going to ignore the text from her mother. She really did not want to talk to her right now. Setting her wine glass down she reached for the wash cloth draped over the handle in the tub and plunged it under the water. Bringing it up and wringing it out before she placed it on her face, rubbing the remnants of old mascara from her eyes. The water was still hot, and still very relaxing and comforting on her tired body.

Olivia knew she was going to have to try and get some sleep this evening before Zoe came home, because once she was home they probably were not going to go to sleep well into the dawning of the sun. The only thing Olivia was feeling, was tired. Since meeting Zoe, the sleep deprivation was definitely more than she was used to. She was happy she did not have to work right now though. Marcus had left her a small inheritance in his Will which allowed her to just be free to investigate things a little bit further, and of course spend more time with Zoe. He had also left some money to his parents which was good. They were both retired and at least now they did not have to worry so much about living on a limited income. When Marcus was alive, he helped them or tried to, but they were both stubborn and they did not want to accept his money. He made a ton of it, but they always said, he worked hard for his money, and they did not want him to hand it out to them. Olivia, on the other hand was fine with taking whatever help he wanted to offer her. He even let her live with them for awhile, rent free of course. But, she could not stand to be there with Sophia. It was then, while she lived with them, that she really saw Sophia for what she was... a greedy, selfish bitch. Marcus worked so hard to give them the life that they had, and she worked at some stupid gossip magazine. Olivia was sure she probably had made decent money, but for a woman who wanted to write, she sure did not try too hard to achieve that goal.

Olivia would hear them arguing about her living with them. She had heard Sophia many times saying that she needed to leave and be on her own. There were many times that Olivia wanted to just walk into those arguments and tell Sophia to go screw herself, that it was Marcus's house, it was Marcus's decision as to whether or not she got to stay there. She always kept out of it though, she did not want to make things any more difficult than they already were for her brother. Anytime Sophia was in the room with Olivia, she could just feel the tension increase. Olivia did not like her, and she was pretty certain that Sophia was not too fond of her either, but Olivia honestly could give two shits what Sophia Donovan thought about her. After Marcus asked Olivia to move out she was hurt, of course, she felt like her brother was taking Sophia's side. He was in a way, but she also knew that he had to ask her to leave or Sophia would make his life miserable. God forbid anyone do anything other than what she wanted. Olivia did go though, she did not hold any ill will towards Marcus about it. They had still maintained their relationship, for the most part, but Olivia had no reason or want to talk to Sophia after that. That was until this happened.

Olivia sank deeper into the warmth surrounding her, her mouth almost submersed in the water. Sighing heavily, she tried to get her mind to think about something else. She really did not like it that other than Zoe, Sophia Donovan was all she could seem to think about. It annoyed and infuriated her because right now she had no idea what the hell she was going to do about it. Olivia had always played out the different scenes in her head of what she wanted to do and say to her if she had ever been given the chance again, but most of it was just wishful thinking. She honestly did not know what she would do if she saw Sophia again. She did not know to what lengths she would go to get her to tell her the truth about her brother. Olivia did know that she wanted retribution for her brothers' murder and part of that was to hear the entire truth about what happened that night. Her hate for Sophia was strong and she often wished her dead, but at the end of the day, she was just never sure exactly what she would do if given the chance. Olivia closed her eyes again and tried to force her mind to go to a more calming place. Again, her phone beeped beside her.

"God mom, I'm fucking fine," Olivia muttered to herself, sounding severely annoyed. She gave her hand a quick shake, to try and air dry some of the wetness off before grabbing her phone. Maybe if she just replied back her mother would leave her alone for the night.

Her breath caught in her throat, and she froze in a state of utter shock at the message that was displayed on the screen in front of her.

"Baby, I need you to stay calm. I'm not too sure what to do right now, but Sophia fucking Donovan is in my fucking bar, right now."

"Holy shit," Olivia said out loud to herself, before jumping out the tub, sloshing nearly half of its contents to the floor. She reached for the white fluffy towel hanging on the back of the door and wrapped it tightly around her wet body. She fully dried her hands and replied back.

"Don't let her fucking leave that bar, do you understand me? Do not let her leave!"

Olivia turned toward the foggy mirror and wiped it off with her hand. She was staring at her reflection, she looked pale, and she could feel her body trembling. She could not believe this was happening right now. She wondered how Zoe knew it was Sophia, she did not know what she looked like. She did not care about that detail right now, she just continued to stare at herself in the mirror, and after a moment she spoke to her own reflection,

"Well, I guess it's time to find out what that bitch did to my brother, once and for all."

TWELVE - October 6, 2015

"Don't let her fucking leave that bar, do you understand me? Do not let her leave!"

Zoe read the words that Olivia had typed back to her almost immediately. Zoe could not even imagine what must be going through Olivia's head the moment she read her text. If Zoe was in this much shock that Sophia Donovan was sitting at her bar, she could not even contemplate what must be going through Olivia's mind right now. All she knew was she had to keep Sophia here, she had to distract her long enough for Olivia to get here. Zoe had no idea what Olivia's plan was though, was she just going to show up here, take a seat at the bar next to Sophia and strike up a conversation? Did Olivia think that Sophia would just sit here and talk to her, explain what happened that night? Olivia was smarter than that, she would know that talking to Sophia would be a waste of time, but what exactly was her plan? Zoe could not answer that question, so the only thing she could do was keep Sophia here and then find out when she arrived. Zoe clicked her phone off and shoved it in the back pocket of her Levi's. She turned back to Sophia and offered her a timid smile, trying her best not to show her distraction.

"How's the wine?"

"Good, thank you," Sophia replied.

"Can I grab you another one?"

Sophia lifted her nearly finished glass and studied it for a second before she responded.

"I probably shouldn't, but oh well. Sure, I will have one more."

Zoe could tell the second glass of wine had helped let Sophia's tensions ease a bit, and although she was still in an apparent state of melancholy, her guard did seem to be lowering slightly. That was good for Zoe, because that meant she would hopefully be able to keep her talking until Olivia arrived. Zoe grabbed the bottle of open Merlot and she filled Sophia's glass about half full.

"Thank you," Sophia smiled softly.

"No problem," Zoe answered as she put the bottle, now only a quarter full, back on the shelf. Zoe glanced at the end of the bar, and Gus was sitting there watching them, seemingly just out of boredom not pryingly. Zoe figured she would go check on him now she had his attention.

"Another beer Gus?"

"Okay."

Zoe popped another Miller and placed it in front of him, again not much acknowledgement.

The two young girls were giggling over at the pool tables, the tall blonde teasing the one named Trin because she missed her shot. At least they managed to get a game in before the table decided to eat their money. She didn't mind if they were in there as long as they were not causing any ruckus and honestly right now, they were the last things on her mind. She walked back over to Sophia.

"So, are you from around here? I have never seen you in here before." Zoe asked casually.

"Yes, I'm from around the area."

"Cool," Zoe tried to sound only somewhat interested.

"I usually see the same faces in here, that's why I ask."

Sophia nodded her head slowly before responding.

"I'm not much for these types of bars," she glanced around the small bar.

At first, Zoe felt somewhat insulted. She was not sure what she meant when she said *these types of bars,* but then she remembered the way Olivia described Sophia. She did say she was pretty stuck up and thought she was better than anyone. It was hard to tell from the lack of conversation if that was her persona, she actually seemed like she was probably a very nice woman. However, she also trusted Olivia's judgment and that comment made her think that Olivia was probably right. Then Sophia continued.

"I don't mean anything against your bar, I just meant I don't usually go to bars alone and drink. You have a fine bar," Zoe could tell Sophia realized how insulting her remark was as she now tried to correct herself. Zoe felt her sincerity.

"I know what you mean, no offense taken, the place is kind of a dive. It's actually not my bar, I have worked here for long enough it feels like it might as well be, but no. The owners are rarely here and to be honest, as you can see, they have not put much thought into the place. I have tried to convince them to spruce up the place, they just don't want to put in the money I guess," Zoe explained and found herself being able to easily share with Sophia.

It was strange, being a pretty good judge of people, she did not entirely get the sense that Sophia was what Olivia described, but she was sure that is why so many people got blinded by her. She could put on a good front. Maybe that is what was eating her so much, maybe that is why she looked as devastated as she did, maybe she did have something to do with Olivia's brothers' death? Zoe thought to herself that must be it, that must be what was happening. As to why she was here, when Olivia said she left LA, well, Zoe knew she could not answer that.

"Hey, listen I know this is probably not my place at all to ask you this, it's just you seem like maybe you have had a bad day. Are you okay?" Zoe decided just to come out with the question she had been wanting to ask since Sophia sat at the bar.

Sophia's eyes locked onto Zoe's, and again, Zoe could read that pain behind them. For a brief moment she wanted to feel sorry for her, she wanted to honestly have her share with her what caused that pain. But she knew for right now she just needed to keep her entertained in a meaningless conversation, no matter how much she may have actually cared what the answer was.

"I'm fine."

"Are you sure?" Zoe pushed just a little further but felt regret as she could see the offended look on Sophia's face. "Sorry, I didn't mean to pry, it's just I'm used to people sharing their problems with me. It's kinda what I do besides serve them drinks to try and drown the issues away," Zoe tried her best to ease the tension she felt between them. She could see Sophia relax a little bit.

"Thanks for asking, but honestly I am fine. It's nothing a couple glasses of wine cannot fix," Sophia replied before taking another sip of her drink.

Zoe smiled at her, and decided it was best just to leave it at that. She would have to find something else to talk to her about.

"Where's your bathrooms?"

Relieved that she could take a break from trying to distract her, Zoe pointed towards the back of the bar and answered.

"Back there, towards the back of the bar, and I got to tell you, if you are this impressed with our bar, you are going to be blown away by the bathrooms."

Sophia let out a sincere laugh at Zoe's sarcasm, and she reached for her purse, threw it over her shoulder and headed towards the bathrooms. Zoe watched her walk away and put her hands on her hips and sighed deeply. She felt a buzz vibrating from the pocket of her jeans and she pulled out her phone.

"I'm here, is she still there? Please tell me she is still there?"

Zoe replied without hesitation.

"Yes, she is still here. She's in the bathroom so please hurry up."

Again, she placed her phone in her back pocket and felt herself relax. Now Olivia was here so she could finally talk to Sophia and hopefully get the answers she was looking for once and for all.

THIRTEEN - October 6, 2015

Sophia walked into the small bathroom. The lights were very dim and there were only two-bathroom stalls, one sink and a mirror, direct opposite of the stalls. Sophia noticed immediately how hot it was in there and the smell… well the smell was not putrid, but it was a far cry from being pleasant. What she had said to the bartender earlier was true, she was not used to being in places like this. She had frequented her fair share of bars and clubs, but those were in the days with Marcus and typically they were of a much higher standard than this. The last time she could recall being in a dingy bar like this was with Caleb. The day he showed her the emails between Cat and Marcus. The day she was faced with the realization that her marriage was over and that her thought-to-be best friend was betraying her, as well as her husband. She knew long before that, that her marriage was over, but she had been handed a double blow when she found out that it was in fact Cat that was involved with Marcus. That was the start of it all. That was the beginning of the end, and that was the day that Caleb Stone told her that he was in love with her. A day she would never forget.

Sophia walked to the sink and braced her hands on either side, raising her head she looked at herself in the mirror. She was shocked even under the dimness of the lights how crappy she looked. No wonder the bartender was asking her if she was okay, she looked and felt like hell. She could not believe how devastated she felt. Honestly, she would be lying if she said she did not miss Caleb. She missed him so much it was killing her on the inside. After he told her the truth while they were in Antigua she did not know what to do but run, she had felt horribly betrayed. But now, after a couple weeks of thinking, she wondered if maybe she acted too quickly with her decision to leave. What she shared with her had shocked her. The fact that he was hired to kill her right from the beginning, and that he had been following her, spying on her and watching her the entire time. How could he have not told her about that once they had gotten close? How could he help her with this entire thing, including helping her murder her own best friend and husband, and not say anything? When he had told her the truth she went into denial. She did not want to believe what he had told her, so she fled. She did not know what else to do at the time. And when Caleb had incessantly tried to reach her, she chose to ignore him instead of talking to him. Sophia did not know what to say to him, she was hurt and angry, but at the same time she questioned herself if she was allowed to feel that way. After all, she had drawn Caleb into her mess. He had already been involved, but she did not know how involved he was at the time. But still she asked him to help her, knowing full well that he was a cop and that his choice to do it could have ruined his entire life.

Sophia turned on the water faucets and ran her hands under the chilly water, bending over she splashed a small amount onto her face, hoping it would some how make her look somewhat human again. Grabbing a couple of paper towels, she blotted her face and her hands dry. Looking back in the mirror, she realized that the water had done absolutely nothing to make her look or feel any better.

Sophia reached into her purse and pulled out her phone, she had not heard any alerts, but a part of her was desperately hoping that maybe there would be another message from Caleb, because this time she was ready to talk to him. She knew she wanted to see him, she wanted to talk to him, she wanted to find out more and have him answer the questions she had. Now that she has had the time to process what he told her, she had a ton of questions. But more than that, more than anything she wanted him, she needed him. Needed him to hold her and tell her it was all going to be okay. She wondered if she had blown it with him. Maybe her reaction to everything he had told her was telling him that he could not trust her enough to be honest. It probably took so much courage for him to get to the point of being able to share that with her, and she had just runoff and ignored him. She regretted the way she had handled the whole situation. She had not heard from him for a couple of days and it was scaring the hell out of her. What if he had given up on her? It probably seemed to him she had given up on him when she walked away.

"God dammit!" she was staring at herself in the dirty mirror when tears began to surface again. She could not keep those tears at bay. The second she thought of him, she crumbled.

Sophia had not wanted to bring her mother into any of this. As it turned out, Isabelle had known all along. She worried that if her mother had figured it out, did anyone else suspect anything? This was partly why she needed Caleb right now. She was starting to freak out and lose control; besides her mother, Caleb was the only person that could help keep her calm and make her feel like everything was going to be alright. Enough is enough. Sophia knew she needed to reach out to him. She needed him to know she wasn't going to run from him again. She needed him to know that she loved him before it was too late. She slid her finger on the screen of her phone and found him in her contacts and hit send before she second guessed herself. It went straight to his voicemail; her heart instantly sank. After his very brief instruction to leave a message she did so.

"Caleb," she whispered. "Caleb, it's Sophia…," she took a second to compose herself and continued. "I'm sorry… I'm so sorry, I shouldn't have run away, I didn't…um… I didn't know what else to do. But I am so sorry, I need you to call me back. We need to talk, I need to see you… Caleb…I love you, I love you so much. Please call me back," Sophia went silent and waited. Somehow hoping that he would come on the line and tell her he loved her too, and not to worry everything was going to be okay. Only the silence came through, so she hit end. She put her phone back in her purse and wiped her eyes again. She did not want to give that bartender anymore of a reason to pry into what was wrong with her. She did have to admit, she felt a little bit better now that she had reached out to him. She felt like now they can move forward. Caleb loved her, she didn't question that, she just hoped that he would want to talk to her again after running off and ignoring him for so long. All she could do now is wait for him to call her back. She fiddled with her hair and took a deep breath and headed back into the bar. As she headed out of the bathroom she was startled by a familiar voice behind her.

"Hi Sophia, it's been awhile."

Sophia turned around and the last thing she remembered seeing was the evil look on Olivia Donovan's face. A look of hatred, vengeance, and then blackness, nothing but pure blackness.

FOURTEEN - October 6, 2015

"I can't believe I am letting you talk me into this!" Jill Keller exclaimed before she shoved a handful of popcorn into her mouth.

"It's about time you got yourself back out there Jill, it's been way too damn long," Rachell Bishop said, as she threw herself down onto her overstuffed beige couch. She dug her hand into Jill's full bowl of popcorn, retrieved a handful and leaned back against a fluffy cushion. She extended her long legs in front of her, using Jill's knees as a foot stool.

Rachell Bishop was Jill's best friend and had been for about the last 8 years. In fact, Rae as Jill and most people called her, was one of her only close female friends. Jill was not the type who had a ton of friends, let alone female friends. Jill had met Rae through her ex husband back when they had started dating. Rae had been dating Jill's exes' friend. Although that relationship had been very short lived, the two-woman had hit it off finding that they balanced each other out. Jill had always been reserved, and introverted, Rae was the exact opposite. She had high energy, she was outgoing, and she was fun to be around. She always seemed to be able to bring Jill out of her shell a little bit. For some reason Rae was the only person in her life that was able to do that. Rachell was strikingly attractive, but in a very simple way. She was not the type of woman who liked the flash and dazzle, she was plain and modest, but nonetheless a natural beauty. Her skin was the colour of milk chocolate, smooth and flawless. Her eyes were an intense shade of green, almost crystal and her hair was raven black, with wild curls. Her father was white and her mother was African American, and she inherited obvious stunning features from both of them.

"Well, it hasn't been that long," Jill interjected.

"Ha," Rae let out a sarcastic laugh. "Jill? Come on!" You have not been serious with anyone since you and John divorced… that was what? Six years ago, now?"

Jill popped another handful of popcorn into her mouth and grabbed her bottle of beer to wash it down with before she answered.

"I have seen people since then."

Rae cocked her head to one side and looked at her friend with the *are your serious stare.*

"Which people are we referring to here? Do you mean gas pump Gary? Or perhaps strap on Steve?"

Jill let out a loud howl of laugher. The fact that Rae had nicknames for every person she had ever dated highly entertained her.

"Hey, strap on Steve wasn't that bad!" Jill replied in between fits of laughter.

"Wasn't that bad?" Rae chided. "The guy liked to fuck you with a dildo, what kind of dude would rather screw a chick with a dildo than his own junk?"

Jill was laughing so hard, she had tears streaming down her face. She knew she shouldn't have shared that piece of info with her friend, poor Steve would never be able to live that down.

"Okay, well he was still nice, and Gary, what was so wrong with Gary?"

Rae nearly choked on her mouthful of beer when Jill asked her the question. She managed to swallow it down before she answered.

"Gas Pump Gary? Well, the fact he picked you up while you were pumping gas with the line, how about you let me fill your tank, isn't enough of a reason?"

Again, Jill laughed. This was probably the most she had laughed in months, but she knew she could always rely on Rae to help her with that.

"Hey, at least he actually liked to fuck me with his own dick!" Jill defended.

"Ya, you and half the city of LA."

"True," Jill agreed. She definitely had not had anything serious since her divorce. She had a string of random flings, that was about the extent of that. She knew there was a reason for it. Her mind was somewhere else and on someone else, but that was not information she was willing to share with anyone, not even her best friend.

"Look, just go out with Eric, he is a super nice guy, he is sweet, and I am sure he is not a fricken wierdo like you seem to love so much. Just a dinner that's it. If you don't like him fine, but at least give it a shot," Rae was adamant she was going to get Jill to go on this damn blind date.

"Jesus, fine! But just a dinner that is it. And if I am not feeling him, I swear to God I am leaving. I don't want to sit through another painful date with some boring, self-indulged, ego maniac. I'm doing this for you to get off my back!" Jill looked her friend dead in the eye, trying to maintain seriousness. "You know that right?"

Rae shrugged Jill's contemptuous look off with a wink.

"Ya, ya, just go on the bloody date, okay? Then maybe I will think about leaving you alone for a bit."

Jill squeezed Rae's big toe, and she flinched in over reactive pain, then slapped Jill's hand away with her foot before jokingly sticking her toe in her face.

"You're such a jerk," Jill bellowed with playful laughter.

"Ah, but you love the shit out of me anyways, don't you?" Rae teased as she brought her legs in and positioned herself cross legged on the couch.

Jill smiled at her long-time friend, she wasn't sure if Rae knew how important their friendship was to her. Now that Caleb was gone, she was the closest person to her in her life and she was extremely thankful to have her. She wished she could share with her the feelings she had been harboring for Caleb, but that was something she did not want to put out there, because as soon as she put it out there she had to deal with them. If she kept it to herself, maybe with him being gone, they would subside and she could try and move on with her life.

"Don't ya?" Rae humorously pestered.

"I do, I love the shit out of you Rae, but seriously this is the last date you are allowed to set me up on. Because if not, I might just have to kill ya," Jill gave her friend a playful wink then downed the last of her beer.

Rae scoffed sarcastically.

"Well now if you did that, who would be left to set you up on anymore blind dates?"

Jill tossed a throw pillow at Rae before she stood up with her empty beer bottle and headed towards the kitchen.

"Do you need another beer you little brat?"

"Why yes, I do, my little Jilly Bean," Rae answered as Jill reached the fridge.

Jill shook her head, smiling to herself, it was a nickname given to Jill by her father a long time ago. Only Rae could get away with calling her that now, only Rae.

FIFTEEN - October 6, 2015

"Oh my God, Olivia, what the fuck did you do?"

"She's fine, I just knocked her out," Olivia responded assuredly.

Zoe and Olivia were both standing in the back alley behind the bar, Olivia's white Lexus engine was purring quietly, her headlights off, and Sophia Donovan passed out cold in the back seat.

"What do you mean you knocked her out? You punched her?" Zoe exclaimed.

"No, I used this," Olivia answered retrieving an empty syringe out of her back pocket.

Zoe was clearly confused at what was going on at that moment and did not even think to ask what was in the syringe or where Olivia got it.

"Baby, listen, I will figure everything out okay, but I had to do something fast. I could not just walk into the bar and sit down beside her and ask her to tell me the truth. This is my chance to find out the truth, this is fate, fate brought her into your bar," Olivia held Zoe at arms length firmly by her shoulders, staring at her deep in the eyes.

Zoe held her stare, her heart beating out of her chest. After a few moments she broke her attention away from Olivia and shrugged away from her. She wrapped her arms around her bare arms and attempted to warm herself in the brisk air.

"So now what? What the hell are you going to do now? What if she wakes up?"

Olivia shook her head in quick response. "She won't wake up for a few hours."

"How do you know that?" Zoe replied desperately.

"Because, I used Etorphine, so trust me she is gonna be out for a bit."

Again, confusion passed across Zoe's face. It was apparent that she had no idea what Olivia was talking about. Olivia knew she had a million questions but now was not the time to talk, not standing here in the chilly night with an unconscious Sophia in her back seat. She had to figure out what she was going to do next.

"I have to know the truth Zoe, you understand that, right?" Olivia pleaded.

Zoe rubbed her hand across her face, trying to clear the shock of the moment away. She was silent for a moment, and Olivia feared that she had finally acted in a way that was going to convince Zoe she was crazy. Zoe walked over to the car and peered into the back window, Sophia was still out cold. She turned back to Olivia.

"Yes, I understand, of course I do. I just… what the… what the hell are we supposed to do with her?"

"Maybe, I will take her to my place, wait for her to wake…"

"No. You can't do that, don't take her to your place," Zoe interjected.

"Well, I have to go somewhere and soon."

Olivia was beginning to feel panicked at her knee jerk reaction to do this. Her body started to tremble, anxiety crept over her.

"Fuck," Olivia cursed, stomping her foot into the pavement. "Fuck, I had to do this. This was my only chance."

"Okay, okay, baby, just calm down. I know where we can take her," Zoe pulled Olivia into her hoping a tight hug would help calm her down.

Olivia wrapped her arms tightly around Zoe's waist, and breathed a slight sigh of relief into her chest and murmured.

"Where?"

"My cabin, out towards Lake Arrowhead."

"Cabin? Like your family's cabin?" Olivia asked.

"Yes."

"Are you sure? Is it safe there?" Olivia questioned her wearily.

"Yes, it's totally safe and private. Nobody has been out there for at least 2 years. I have been trying to get my family to sell it but for some reason they just don't want to let it go. It's secluded, no neighbors around for a couple miles. It's the only place right now, just you have to take her there.

Olivia pulled out of Zoe's hold and kissed her hard. As usual a rush of desire coursed immediately through both of them. It was Zoe who pulled away.

"Give me your phone," she demanded. Olivia pulled her phone out of her other back pocket and handed it to Zoe. She watched as Zoe clicked around and input some information, then handed it back to her.

"I put the directions in there. Just follow them exactly as it says, don't stop anywhere, just go straight there. There is a spare key to the cabin under the broken plank on the front deck. It's probably going to be fucking cold in there, so you're going to have to start a fire."

"What about you?" Olivia's big brown eyes were filled with worry.

"Her car is in the front of the bar, I'll take her car and follow you as soon I close up here. I will leave my car here until the morning. Tommy won't be here until about noon tomorrow to open up, so I will get my car before then. But you need to go, just take her there, get her out of here."

Olivia quickly followed what Zoe was saying, gave her another quick kiss and turned towards her car. Zoe turned back towards the bar and then stopped in her tracks and turned abruptly back to Olivia.

"Wait."

Olivia stopped before she got into the driver side.

"What?"

"I need her fucking keys, they are probably in her purse, did she have her purse?"

Olivia ducked into her car and fumbled around for a moment, then she popped her head back over the roof of the car.

"Here catch," Olivia said as she tossed the set of keys towards Zoe.

Zoe reached her hands out and caught the flying keys. Without saying anything further she rushed back into the bar.

Olivia stood staring after her, as if perhaps waiting to see if she would come back out again. After a couple seconds she hopped into the driver seat of her car, slammed the door and sped quickly out of the back alley, her taillights fading away in the darkness.

SIXTEEN - October 7, 2015

The LAX baggage claim was very busy for the early time of the morning. Caleb Stone stood waiting impatiently for his bags, the conveyor belt sitting motionless. Sometimes he wondered what the hell took so long for the damn bags to come. He was anxious to say the very least, at getting out of here and going to see Sophia. He wasn't sure if it was going to be as easy as that though, because he was still not sure if she was going to talk to him or not. Caleb pulled his cell phone from the inside of his jacket pocket and saw his battery indicator at one percent. He wouldn't have enough life left to check the voicemail that was sitting unheard. It was probably Trent he thought, telling him he was on his way to pick him up. He slipped his nearly dead phone back in his pocket and continued waiting for the belt to move. He glanced at the clock on the far wall of the baggage claim area, and it read 7:55am. He knew he should have felt more exhausted considering he barely slept a wink on the plane. He just had way too much on his mind, it would not stop the whole way home. The anticipation of seeing her again was overwhelming and there was no way he could sleep. The crowd grew slightly bigger as more people came to retrieve the bags, it was not only Caleb that seemed to be getting annoyed by the wait. A small child in a stroller was making it very clear that he was ready to go home, and that is exactly how Caleb was feeling.

Caleb knew one thing, after these last couple weeks being apart from Sophia, he knew that he did not want to live without her. He had hated every waking moment without her, hell every sleeping moment as well. She would haunt his dreams every night. One that stood out clearly came rushing back to him as he stood and waited.

It was dark and cold, all around him, and he was alone. The only light that relieved the blackness was the moon and a dimly lit street lamp. Caleb looked around, confused at first by his surroundings, and why exactly he was there. But upon closer inspection he stood alone in the middle of the street, in an isolated, seemingly abandoned town. There were no cars, there were no people it was just him standing motionless and confused. And then out of the darkness he heard it… her voice, calling his name softly, but he did not know where it was coming from. He yelled out for her.

"Sophia? Sophia is that you?"

Then silence, he turned around in circles, trying to see her, trying to see where her voice was hiding, but unable to find her. Then again.

"Caleb, help me."

Caleb felt his heart tighten and a sense of dread wash over him. She was in danger and she needed his help, but he could not seem to will himself to move from the spot in the centre of the road, standing under the dim streetlight. So, he tried to call again.

"Sophia, where are you? I love you, come to me and it will all be okay."

Again, there was nothing but an eerie hush, a silence that was beginning to drive him mad. He was desperate to find her, to find out where she was calling from, but he couldn't move to search for her. He could just turn in circles, there in the isolated street. And finally, he saw a figure emerge from the depths of the darkness slowly walking towards him and his heart leapt with relief. At first, he could not make her out, but as the glow of the streetlight impaled her face he knew it was her, his love, Sophia. He tried running to her, to grab her and hold her tight, but his legs felt as if they were being swallowed by quicksand. He could see his legs, he could even feel them, they were both there so he was maddened by the idea he could not seem to move. Sophia walked, almost floated slowly towards him. He noticed her face, still beautiful, but haunted and shallow. As she continued to get closer she reached her arms out to him.

"Caleb, my love, help me."

"Sophia," he tried moving again, but no matter how desperately he tried to get his legs to function he was stuck, powerless, waiting for her to come to him. So, all he could do was reach his arms out to her in return. But then she stopped, her arms coming back down to her sides and she just stared at him. Eyes dark and void of emotion. Just a stare that terrified Caleb.

"Sophia, please come to me," he begged her. She just stood there, about 15 feet from him. So close but still so painfully far away. "Sophia, please," tears of desperation now escaped him, as he tried his best to urge her to him.

Then he saw blood, it slid out of her eyes, and slid down her cheeks, and then followed next from her nose. Her skin was placid and pale, no colour left in her beautiful skin.

"Sophia!" this time he yelled as loud as his voice would allow him. "What's happening? Sophia, baby, tell me what's happening?" His arms were outstretched as far as he could get them, praying that it was enough to reach her, but even though she seemed so close, to touch her was an impossibility.

"I'm sorry Caleb." Her voice whispered hauntingly.

Those were her very last words, and she crumbled, she collapsed to the street beneath her. Her head bouncing fiercely off the concrete. This time when Caleb tried to move, his body listened. He bounded towards her with a speed he never knew he had, as he got to her body he fell to the ground to scoop her up into his arms. But when he got to her she was gone, she just vanished beneath his grasp. He lay sobbing, and wailing, again alone in the middle of the street.

"About damn time."

Caleb was jerked back to reality by the frustrated woman beside him. The baggage belt came to life and the suitcases came tumbling out of the opening. Caleb took a moment to catch his breath, even the memory of that dream haunted him. It was one that stuck with him, no matter how much time had passed. He knew he needed to get to Sophia, he needed to talk to her and to fix all of this.

Caleb tried his best to patiently wait for his bag to make its appearance, his foot tapping uneasily on the ground. Finally, he could see his red bag, coming slowly towards him. He did not wait for it to get to him, he gently pushed his way through the small crowd and grabbed it from the conveyor belt. He hurried towards the doors to go find Trent, who was to be waiting for him. As he suspected, Trent was there, waiting, but with a look on his face that Caleb had not seen before. Caleb approached him, and the two men quickly exchanged a welcoming hug.

"It's good to see you," Caleb exclaimed.

"You too," The look still spread across his face.

"Come on, let's go I'm double parked out there," Trent grabbed Caleb's suitcase and wheeled it out the front doors.

They got to the awaiting Tundra and Trent put Caleb's suitcase in the box, both men jumped into the truck. The moment they hopped in, Caleb reached for Trent's phone charger and plugged his dead phone in.

"I'm guessing you left me a message here?" Caleb asked not expecting Trent to deny his question.

"No, I didn't call you, I just came straight here," he replied, his voice was riddled with an unknown worry.

Caleb, waited a moment for his phone to come to life and hit his voicemail icon, quickly punching in his password.   He stilled when he heard Sophia's voice.

"Caleb," Caleb's heart jumped into his throat at the sound of Sophia's voice. He continued listening.   "Caleb, it's Sophia...," there was a brief moment of silence and then she continued. "I'm sorry... I'm so sorry, I shouldn't have run away, I didn't...um... I didn't know what else to do. But I am so sorry, and I need you to call me back. We need to talk, I need to see you... Caleb...I love you, I love you so much. Please call me back," Then he could hear her hang up. Caleb ended his voicemail and stared at his phone blankly for a second. Trent watched him and then inquired.

"What? Who was it?"

Caleb turned to him, with a clear look of relief and elation, then he replied.

"It was her, she wants to talk. She said she was sorry for running away, and that she wants to talk. Oh my God, thank God," Caleb pressed his phone to his forehead closing his eyes, enjoying the moment. Quickly he brought up Sophia's number and hit send, his heart beating fast in his chest, he could not wait to talk to her. But her phone went straight to voicemail. Caleb was surprised that when it was time to leave her a message, her mailbox was full, he thought that was strange, but hung up and turned back to Trent.

"Come on, let's go. Her voicemail is full, and I can't wait for her to call me back."

Trent's chest heaved slowly, and he continued looking at Caleb, he was evidently trying to formulate what to say.

"Let's go, man, where is she? I need to go see her right now," Caleb exclaimed again.

Trent turned his attention out his front window, both hands on the steering wheel.

"I don't know where she is."

"What do you mean you don't know where she is? You were on her last night you said, where did she go for the night?" Caleb's voice was filled with obvious concern.

Again, it was obvious Trent was finding the best way to answer Caleb.

"I did, I was with her, she was in that bar, she was in there for awhile."

"Well, so where did she go after?"

Trent inhaled a deep breath then answered.

"I don't know, I fell asleep. I was fuckin tired man. I had not slept at all since I found her. I'm sorry but I fell asleep. I woke up early this morning, and her car was gone. I drove by her moms on the way here but she wasn't there."

Caleb did his best to maintain his calmness.

"Christ."

"We'll find her, she will call you right back."

"Why didn't you put a fucking tracker on her car?"

"I didn't need to, I had her, and don't worry, she will call you back. Just hang tight, she will see that you called, and she will call back. I give it five minutes."

Trent put his truck into drive and pulled out of the pick-up area and headed towards the city. Caleb shook his head, frustrated that Trent fell asleep, but still relieved that she called him. Trent was right, Sophia would call him right away, as soon as she saw he called. He just had to wait for her, before he knew it, they would be together again, she would be with him, safe, exactly where she belonged.

SEVENTEEN - October 7, 2015

Sophia slowly tried to pry her eyes open, they were so dry, it felt like someone had sprinkled dust directly in them. It took her a few solid attempts and even when she finally managed to get them open it was as if they were still shut. She turned her head cautiously from side to side and all that she could see was darkness, not black, but dark. She was able to scarcely make outlines of some objects, but she had no idea what they were. Her mouth was stale and pasty, and she was thirsty. She could not, in all of her life, ever recall feeling so thirsty. Her mind was a massive cloud of fog and she willed herself, with everything she had, to remember what she did last night to have her waking up feeling like this. Her head pounded, like a thousand hammers were trying to break her skull. She must have gotten very drunk last night. The last thing she remembered was sitting at that bar, drinking wine, and talking to that red-headed bartender. She searched the corners of her memory for more information.

Yes, she remembered talking to her, she remembered two young girls coming in and trying to pass for 21. She remembered the old guy sitting alone at the end of the bar... and then what? Yes, she thought to herself further, she remembered going to the bathroom, and...Caleb, yes, she remembered she called Caleb. Then nothing. A curtain was pulled over her recollection of what happened after she phoned him. Was he here? Sophia tried to roll over, attempting to get up to see where she was. She was able to slowly bring her feet to the floor but as she managed to summon the strength to stand she realized something had abruptly stopped her. Confused, she reached down and felt something cold and hard around her ankle... was that shackle? She was only barley able to make out her own foot in front of her, she grasped at the object and followed its' trail, leading her back to the foot rail of the bed. She was able to determine that her ankle was shackled by a handcuff of some sort, and the chain was attached to the metal foot board. Then in a panic she grappled desperately with the metal cuff, but to absolutely no avail. She frantically looked around the room trying to see something, anything. She could see shards of daylight peaking in from a window in the back corner of the wall behind her. She followed her only instinct and began to scream for help.

"HELP ME! SOMEBODY HELP ME!"

There was only silence, she could not hear anything, so she tried again.

"PLEASE, SOMEBODY! WHERE AM I? HELP ME, HELP, PLEASE HELP ME!" she pounded her fists into the mattress with complete and utter desperation that nobody was hearing her call out for help. Then she heard it…a car door slam outside. For a brief moment she was overwhelmed with relief, that someone was here to save her from whoever put her here. She thought now was the time to start yelling again, she had to make sure they heard her.

"HEY, HELLO, IS SOMEBODY OUT THERE? CAN YOU HEAR ME?"

Again, nothing but silence, for what seemed like an eternity and then she heard someone in the other room walking around.

"HEY, PLEASE SOMEBODY I'M IN HERE, I'M IN THE BEDROOM, PLEASE HELP ME!"

Nobody came to help her, so it very quickly registered with her, as much as she wanted to deny it, that whoever she was hearing was the person responsible for her being cuffed to the bed. Frustrated and scared she forcefully began yanking on the chain, silently praying with every angry yank, it would somehow miraculously come undone. And nothing… what had she expected? Exhaustion from the drugs, and the extraordinary stress she was feeling, made her quick to weaken and quick to defeat. Tears were now the only thing she could summon the strength to produce. She leaned her back against the cold wall and began to sob.

"Why?" Sophia asked herself in between breathless cries. Again, she could hear someone outside of the room. She could hear cupboards banging, and footsteps walking over the creaky wooden floors. That was the only thing she knew for sure about her surroundings, the floors were wooden and cold to the touch.

"Why? She asked again, only this time to the empty room, barely audible.

"GOD DAMMIT, WHY?" This time she bellowed fiercely with a raspy, hoarse voice, and this time she was heard. The door swung open, hammering hard against the wall behind it. Sophia glanced weakly towards the door, the last remnants of colour drained from her face as she recognized her captor.

"Would you please shut the fuck up!" Olivia came into the room carrying a candle. She set it down on a little table next to the door.

It took Sophia a moment to comprehend what she was seeing, who she was seeing, and then a flash of memory assaulted her mind.

She had gotten up to go to the bathroom... yes, she remembered that. She recalled looking in the bathroom mirror thinking how horrid she looked. And she remembered calling Caleb... and...it was foggy but she forced herself to remember what happened next. And... then... she walked out of the bathroom...and... then...she dove deep into the last memory she had and then it finally came. Yes, she remembered someone saying something to her, she did not remember what, but she remembered turning around and seeing Olivia standing right in front of her. That was it, that was the last thing she remembered.

"You can yell and scream all you want Sophia, nobody around these parts are going to hear a goddamn thing. You might as well save your breath and your energy, because you're going to need it.

Sophia just stared at her, stared at her image, illuminated only by the light of day coming in behind her and the soft glow of the candle. She could not seem to muster any words, she could not even fully comprehend why this was happening.

"And there is no sense wasting your energy or ruining your pretty little manicure trying to get that thing off, because it is not coming undone, I will promise you that."

Sophia managed to gather enough saliva to moisten her dry mouth, she swallowed hard and finally managed to speak.

"What are you doing Olivia? Why I am here? What do you want from me?"

Olivia stood staring at her as a look of disgust spread across her face, and for several moments Sophia did not think she was going to answer her.

"Oh, Jesus Sophia, you know damn well why you're here. Don't sit there and try to act all fucking innocent with me, I'm not buying your bullshit. I'm not gonna stand for the lies, no more, it's over."

Confused Sophia replied,

"What? What's over? Olivia what the hell are you talking about?"

Sophia could immediately tell that Olivia was infuriated over her questions. She could see the anger spread across her whole body. Olivia lunged at Sophia. She stopped short of hitting Sophia and ended up standing over top of her, shaking with fury. Sophia had only ever seen from Marcus.

"It's fucking over Sophia! Do you hear me? And I swear to you, I swear on Marcus's dead rotting body, that you are going to tell me the fucking truth. You're going to tell me exactly what you did to him that night, or I am going to make you wish and pray that you had never come into the Donovan family, ever. Do you hear me, you crazy fucking whore?"

Sophia's empty stomach flipped inside of her, it felt like the room surrounding her was closing in on her. Her breathing became shallow, her chest tightened, her heart pumped wildly and that was it, that was all her body could take in that moment. Once again, the darkness over took her and Sophia slipped into unconsciousness.

EIGHTEEN - October 8, 2015

Caleb threw his phone onto the couch in complete and utter frustration, he paced back and forth, wearing a path in the carpet of Trent's living room carpet.

"God dammit, Sophia, where the hell are you?" he asked out loud.

He could not understand it. Why would she call him and leave him that message, and then not answer him? Her phone just kept going straight to voicemail. Her phone must be off, but why? She had called him while he was in the air coming back to LA. Her message said that she wanted to see him, that she loved him. Caleb, for the life of him could not understand why she was not calling him back. His instincts, which were typically highly credible, were nagging at him, badgering him that something was wrong, something was very wrong. He tried his best to ignore the intense bouts of anger he was feeling towards his friend and colleague, Trent. Caleb had trusted him to keep an eye on her and he fell asleep, then she had disappeared right out from under his nose. If Trent had just put a fucking tracker on her car, this would not be happening. As much resentment and anger he felt at Trent, he had to also understand he put him in an awkward situation, Trent was not comfortable with the whole situation. He was anxious about Sophia's unexpected return to LA to begin with and following her every move for over an entire day, was a lot on him. Yes, he had made a mistake, he fell asleep while on watch, but as angry as it made Caleb, he realized that no one could go days on end without rest. Just then the front door of Trent's apartment swung open and an exhausted looking Trent came in. Caleb turned to him, anticipating some sort of good news.

"Did you find her?"

Trent shook his head with a negative response.

"I went everywhere I could think, she is not at her mom's, she is not at her friend Samuel's. I drove to her old office building to see if she was there, I even went back to the bar."

"Shit!" Caleb replied, his voice overcome with defeat.

"Hey, we will find her, it's only been a day, she will show up at her mom's again. At least her mom lives here in LA now, and not down in San Diego. She is more likely to go stay with her. She will show up, and she will call you." Trent tried his best to reassure his panicked friend.

"She should have called me back by now. Why would she call me telling me those things and then turn her phone off? If she was wanting us to talk, and to see me so badly, why the hell has she not called me back yet?"

"Caleb, listen to me, she doesn't even know you are back in the City. For all she knows you are still in Antigua, just give her some time, calm down."

"Calm down? Trent, I can't calm down. Something isn't right, I just know it. No," Caleb shook his head, "Nope, something is definitely not right. I can feel it. I won't calm down, not until I talk to her."

"Okay, we will keep looking until she calls back and we know where she is. She can't be too far. I will keep searching for her."

"Why didn't you just put a tracker on her car?" Caleb asked Trent calmly.

There was no response for a moment. Caleb could see Trent was asking himself that very same question.

"I had her. I didn't want to use a tracker, I didn't want to rely on it. I wanted to stay on her until I had to come for you. I was positive she would have just ended back up at her Moms for the night. I'm sorry, it was a shit call on my part. I feel like crap about it, but there is nothing I can do about it now. She will show back up at her Mom's, I know she will."

Caleb walked into Trent's kitchen and grabbed himself a beer out of the fridge. He could care less that it was only mid-morning, he needed a damn drink. He cracked the top and tossed the cap on the counter. He walked back into the living room and sat down on the couch. Trent just continued to watch him intently, waiting for a response.

"Trent, I have been a cop for a long time, I know when something is wrong, especially when it comes to someone I love. Something is wrong! I am not going to sit around and wait for her to call me or wait till she happens to show up, because she isn't going to."

"What do you mean? Seriously what do you think happened?" Trent asked curiously.

Caleb took a drink of the beer, feeling the coolness of it hit his empty stomach, he had not eaten nearly anything since he was on the plane, he was too damn worried to eat.

"I don't know what happened, not yet, but what I do know is I am not sitting around here with my thumb up my fucking ass while I wait. I have to find her, and I will find her."

"So, what then? What do you suppose we do?"

Caleb took another drink of the beer, then placed it on the coffee table in front of him, and he looked up at Trent with a dead serious look in his eyes.

"It's time we go pay Isabelle Vaughn a visit and find out how much she knows about her daughter."

Caleb watched Trent's expression as he processed what Caleb had just said. He could tell Trent thought that was a horrible idea, but right now Caleb didn't care. He had to find Sophia and starting with her mother was the first step. No matter how much she may know about what truly happened that night.

NINETEEN -October 8, 2015

Zoe slammed the old refrigerator door and reeled around quickly, a bottle of water in her hand, to face Olivia who was standing closely behind her.

"What are we doing here Liv? We can't keep her here forever?"

"I know Zoe, I know. I just need some time to figure out what I am going to do here. I have to find a way to get her to tell me what happened, I just need some time." Olivia replied convincingly to Zoe. She did not like feeling pressured by her, she just needed Zoe to understand she needed time to figure out what was next.

Zoe twisted the cap off of her water bottle and took an enormous chug, Olivia watched her in silence and waited for her to reply.

Zoe brought the bottle away from her mouth, set it on the counter and walked into the living room. She stood near the fireplace, she studied the flames in front of her. Olivia followed behind her and gently slid her arms around her waist from behind. She rested her head on her back and closed her eyes.

"Baby, please just trust me," Olivia softly spoke into Zoe's back. Olivia's head softly rose then fell back down as Zoe inhaled deeply and then exhaled heavily. Zoe did not make any motion to turn around or bring her arms up in response to Olivia's embrace, she just stood there staring into the fire.

"I do trust you, I do. I just don't know what you are going to do here? I mean we cannot keep her here Liv, we can't just keep her locked in that room. I get that you want to find out the truth, but we can't force her to tell you, and we can't keep her locked away."

Olivia released her arms from around Zoe's waist and gently turned her around, their eyes locked on one another's. Olivia smiled at Zoe and rubbed her finger softly along her cheek.

"I'm going to figure it out, I promise, but I just need you to be patient okay? Nobody knows we are out here, nobody will be coming out here anytime soon, especially now that it's getting cooler out. I just need some time to think."

The look on Zoe's face told Olivia that she was desperately uncertain of Olivia's decision. Olivia didn't blame her, but she knew that she needed Zoe to remain calm and just be patient. She had to determine a way to get Sophia to tell her what happened that night. This was her only chance to put the demons to sleep about her brother's murder.

"I know, but Olivia, maybe we should just give her some more of those drugs you gave her, and I don't know, take her somewhere and just leave her in her car. We still have time, we don't have to keep her here. She won't remember anything, she won't remember where she was, right? Babe, it's not too late, I mean she has been in there sleeping the whole time, we don't have to do this," Zoe was trying her best to change Olivia's mind. Olivia knew nothing was going to change her mind, not when she had the woman who she was certain murdered her brother. Zoe was wrong…Sophia had not been asleep the whole time.

"We can't do that Zoe!"

"Sure, we can Liv… Let's just give her more…"

"Zoe! We can't do that, we can't just give her more drugs and drop her off somewhere. She has already woken up, she was screaming for help like a fuckin idiot. She was awake when I got here from grabbing some supplies. She was driving me insane, so I went in there already, I told her to shut up…I told her nobody was going to hear her, and nobody was going to help her. She already knows why she's here, so no we can't just take her and leave her…she already knows why she is here, and who brought her here."

Zoe's head dropped with defeat. Olivia felt badly that she had brought Zoe into this, she did, but Zoe did after all tell her to bring her here. So, in a way Olivia felt that she brought herself into this.

"Shit," Zoe muttered under her breath. "So now what? What the hell are you going to do now?"

"I'm going to get her to tell me the truth, I want to hear it from her mouth what she did."

"Olivia, baby, I know you want to find out the truth, and I truly hope she does tell you, so you can be at peace with it, but…," Zoe paused long enough for Olivia to respond.

"But what?"

"But what if she does tell you the truth, what if she does admit to you that she had something to do with his death, or what if she does admit that she planned it? What then?"

Olivia knew that question was going to eventually come up. She just had not figured it completely out for herself yet, let alone be able to explain it to Zoe. But she knew she needed to hear it from Sophia, she needed to know what part she had in his death. She needed to find out if she hired someone to do it, if Cat actually did murder him, and what part Sophia actually played in it. But every instinct told her that Sophia was actually the one who pulled the trigger. Sophia was the one who was responsible for ending her brother's life and destroying Olivia's.

"Then I need her to tell me, I need her to tell me everything, every motive, every action, and every step she took. I need her to look me in the eyes and tell me the look my brother had on his face knowing he was about to die. The look on his face when he realized his whore of a wife was about to end his existence. I want her to tell me what his last words were. I want to know if she made him beg for his life, did she watch him grovel, and cry for his life. I want her to tell me who helped her, who helped her do this to my family. There is no way she is smart enough to get away with something like this, there is no way she would have done any of this alone. I want her to tell me everything, and I mean everything."

Zoe asked her gently once more, "Olivia, I know what you want her to do, but what I want to know, so I am asking you again, then what? If she tells you everything, and its what you have been wanting to hear, and she confirms your worst inclinations, and you were right all along, then what?"

Zoe had tears forming in her eyes, she was clearly frustrated with Olivia's avoidance of the question. But Olivia knew that if Sophia did finally fess up and reveal the truth of what truly happened, that she did have a hand in her brother's murder or worse yet, she was the one who actually took his last breath from him. Olivia knew…she had thought about it every day since Marcus was taken from her, she knew what the answer to that was. She was just damn certain, that Zoe probably didn't want to hear it, but she answered anyways.

"Then I think it's time she knows what Marcus felt in that moment. I think then, she will know what it will feel like to have no control, to sit helplessly, knowing her life is about to end. Knowing why her life was about to end but knowing there was not a fucking thing she was going to be able to do about it. That's what, Baby, then that's what."

TWENTY -October 9, 2015

Caleb and Trent sat quietly in Trent's truck staring at Isabelle Donovan's house. They knew she was home as her vehicle was parked in the driveway. It was a very small and modest house, with big welcoming windows, light blue siding and a small porch big enough to fit two rocking chairs. Caleb remembered Sophia telling him that her mother had decided to leave her home in Imperial Beach, to be closer to Sophia when she came home…I guess a mother always knows her child better than anyone. It was midday, the sun was shining brightly and there was barely a cloud in the sky. It seemed like inappropriate weather for the conversation they were about to go and have with Sophia Donovan's mother.

"Have you figured out what you are going to say to her?" Trent interrupted the silence of the truck. Caleb turned to him and answered with not much confidence.

"The truth, I guess. I have to tell her that I think something has happened to Sophia, and I am hoping she opens up to me, and tells me how much she actually knows."

"This is risky Caleb, what if she knows too much? We don't know if we can trust her to keep quiet."

"If she knows the truth, it's because Sophia felt assured enough to tell her, and if Sophia felt she could tell her mother there is a reason for that, because she can trust her. If Sophia trusts her then I have to trust her." Caleb replied with a hint of worry behind his voice.

Trent returned to his silence and studied the house again. Caleb glanced at him and could see the concern etched in every line of his face. Caleb was worried too, the more people that were privy to the truth could only mean the more of a chance someone would say something. But right now, Isabelle was the only person that could tell them anything about Sophia.

"She is the one person who will know where Sophia is, and if she doesn't, then we know there is a problem. Trent, my gut is telling me there is a problem and it's usually right. The longer we wait, the worse it is going to get. Christ, I am praying that when she opens the door she can tell me exactly where Sophia is. Right now, I have no choice but to go to her and if she needs answers, I have to give them to her. I will do whatever it takes to find her."

Trent turned to Caleb once more. "I know you will, but Caleb, maybe she is fine, maybe she went to stay with friends, who knows. We don't know that anything has happened to her," Trent paused a second, seemingly deciding if he should continue. "Maybe, she just changed her mind, maybe she just isn't ready to see you..."

"That's bullshit," Caleb interjected, not letting Trent finish what he was about to say. "That is bullshit, Trent, and you know that. Why the hell would she call me and change her mind the next day, that does not make sense at all. She wouldn't do that."

"I'm sorry, I'm just trying to think rationally here," Trent responded apologetically.

"And I'm not? I'm thinking very rationally, my mind is crystal fucking clear, and that is why I know we have to go and talk to Isabelle. I know something has happened, I know something is not right, and I need you to understand that. Quit fucking questioning me. You do not know her like I do, so don't tell me that I am not thinking rationally, don't insult me," Caleb stared at his friend with resentment and anger, but the moment he had said the words, he felt the frustration of letting his emotions get the better of him creep in.

"I'm sorry, I didn't mean…"

Again, Caleb did not let Trent complete his sentence. "It's fine, just forget it, come on, lets just go get this done, the faster we talk to her, the faster we can figure out where Sophia might be."

Both men got out of the truck and closed the doors gently behind them. The street that Isabelle Vaughn resided on was quiet, tucked away out of the hectic LA traffic and noise. They quickly glanced for any oncoming cars and crossed the street, they both stopped before they continued onto her property.

"It's going to be fine," Trent tried his best to sound encouraging, as he gave Caleb a pat on the shoulder.

"I hope you're right."

After what felt like an eternity of standing at the edge of her property, Caleb finally made the move towards the front door and Trent followed cautiously behind him.

Both men came up to the front door, Caleb paused momentarily before he reached for the doorbell and pressed the button. He could hear the chime followed by light footsteps making their way to the door. Caleb could feel his heart rate pick up, he knew there was no turning back, it was time to find out exactly how much Isabelle Vaughn knew about him. The door swung open and both men were face to face with Sophia's mother, anxiety was evident in her face. It was unclear at first to Caleb if it was relief or anger that washed over her, but the moment Isabelle recognized Caleb standing on her doorstep she began to cry.

"Mrs. Vaughn," were the only words he could manage to utter.

Isabelle stepped aside inviting the two men into her home, she closed the door behind them and turned to back to them.

"Detective Stone, where is my baby?"

TWENTY-ONE -October 9, 2015

Olivia stood over top of Sophia and watched her intently, watching as her chest rose and fell lightly with every breath she took. She looked so peaceful, so content, so innocent, but Olivia knew that was a highly deceitful representation of the woman who lay sleeping below her watchful eye. Sophia had been asleep most of the time since Olivia's last confrontation with her, and she honestly wanted nothing more than to reach down and shake her venomously awake so she could start talking. The faster she started telling her what happened to Marcus, the faster Olivia could figure out what she was going to do next. She knew that Zoe was panicked, she was concerned that Olivia had made a horrible decision, but Olivia knew that she could still trust her. She just needed Sophia to talk so they could quit wasting anymore time. Eventually somebody was going to notice that she was gone, although Olivia still wasn't sure who even knew she was back.

A soft groan escaped Sophia, she started to squirm lightly, rousing herself awake. Olivia continued to watch her. She was waiting for her eyes to open and soon enough they did. Sophia's eyes locked directly onto Olivia's and Olivia had to admit, she loved the look of fear when Sophia realized she was still here and it wasn't just a shitty, horrible dream.

Olivia stood silently, watching her, waiting for her to say something, or do something. For several moments Sophia just lay there, staring up at her, her facial expression did not change. She did not cry, she did not utter a sound, she just lay there, and they glared deeply into each other's eyes. Finally, Sophia broke the eerie silence.

"Why are you doing this Olivia? What do you want from me?"

Olivia felt that familiar sense of rage creep up on her, but she forced it away, determined to stay as calm as she could right now.

"You know why you're here, don't act like you don't know."

Sophia slowly and cautiously sat up, holding her head as she did. Olivia knew her head must have been pounding from the lack of water, and the after effects of the drugs she had given her, but it only gave her more gratification that she was holding that much power over her. Sophia settled herself, leaning her back against the wall.

"Olivia, I don't know. I have no idea why you have me tied to a bed, being held prisoner, God knows where, and I certainly don't know why," her words were feeble, and Sophia swallowed hard, trying to moisten the desert in her mouth.

"Enough!" Olivia cried out. "Enough of your fucking lies, Sophia. You know damn well why you are here. It's about time you tell me what you did to Marcus, I want the truth, and you are going to give it to me."

Sophia closed her eyes, and gently placed her head back, she licked her lips and asked.

"Can I please have some water?"

Olivia did not want to give this woman anything, but thought perhaps if she gave her something it would encourage her to give her what she needed. She turned and left the room, went to the fridge and retrieved a bottle of water. She returned seconds later and tossed the closed bottle on the bed. Sophia reached for the bottle and barely managed to twist off the cap. She brought the bottle to her mouth and drank eagerly. Olivia impatiently waited for her to finish. Finally, Sophia brought the water away from her mouth, after finishing nearly the whole bottle. She put the cap back on and turned her attention back to Olivia.

"Thank you," Sophia muttered.

"You have had your damn water, now tell me what the hell happened to my brother, Sophia."

"Olivia, what do you want me to tell you? You know exactly as much as I do. Marcus was having an affair with my best friend, and it went sideways."

"Bullshit! That is total bullshit, and you fucking know it!" The anger was starting to get the best of Olivia again.

"Cat murdered your brother and then she killed herself, Olivia, that is exactly what happened, and why else other than the fact that they had an affair would she do that? Why would Cat murder Marcus if they were not having an affair? She obviously wanted more from him than he was going to be able to give."

Olivia did not want to hear anymore, this was all information the detectives concluded, and she was positive it was all garbage, it was all lies.

"You know what Sophia, maybe he was having an affair with her? Why wouldn't he? Do you think he was satisfied with you, do you think you could give him what he deserved? I would not blame him if he was fucking someone else, in fact I would applaud him on it. But I am not buying for one second that you didn't know, you didn't find out, and when you did, you did something about it."

Sophia shook her head slowly back and forth keeping her gaze locked on Olivia's.

"You have no idea what you are talking about, Olivia, you have no idea at all what you are talking about. I don't know what strange vendetta you have towards me, I honestly don't, but you have me tied up here waiting for me to tell you something I cannot tell you."

Olivia turned towards the door in shear frustration, and dug her hand through her long hair, she took a few deep breaths and turned back to her ex sister-in-law.

"You are a fucking liar, I know that and you know that, I lived with you guys, I know how you guys argued and fought. You tried to pretend like you were this perfect little wife, always standing by her husband, but that was a lie. You were a controlling and manipulating bitch who obviously drove Marcus directly into your best friend's arms. And you are going to sit here and tell me that you did not know about it, you did not know that your best friend was screwing your husband? That is such bullshit, Sophia. You know what I think?" Olivia asked Sophia not caring what her response would be.

"I would love to hear what you think Olivia, tell me what you think happened to my husband."

"You found out, you found out that you were about to lose your free ride, and you panicked. God forbid you have to support yourself and give up the life that Marcus gave to you, so you panicked. You did this, you hired someone didn't you? You hired someone to murder my brother."

Sophia chuckled softly under her breath and that struck a nerve deep in Olivia's soul, the fact that this woman had the audacity to laugh at her.

"Olivia, you know what I think? I think you are fucking crazy!"

The word "crazy" coming out of Sophia's mouth and being directed towards Olivia summoned the fury she was trying so desperately to keep at bay.

"You lying bitch!" and with one quick, furious motion, Olivia sprung towards Sophia, and backhanded her with vengeance, viciously across the face. Sophia's head was snapped to the side, she held it there, bringing her hand up to her cheek. The back of Olivia's hand burned and throbbed from the brunt force of the hit, but it was a pain that brought her pleasure. Finally, Sophia turned back to Olivia, blood was trailing out of the corner of her mouth. Sophia's eyes were dark as she wiped the blood from her mouth and studied it on her fingers, before looking back up at Olivia. Olivia steadied her nerves again, and in the calmest voice she could muster, Olivia probed one more time.

"Now, are you ready to tell me the fucking truth?"

TWENTY- TWO - October 9, 2015

Caleb and Trent both took a seat on the overstuffed sofa, both of them adjusting the throw pillows behind them that decorated the couch. Isabelle stood watching them and waited until they were both comfortable before she asked.

"Can I get you guys some coffee?"

"Sure," they replied in unison.

Isabelle turned and headed out of the room into the kitchen, and Caleb could hear her clattering about gathering their drinks. He turned to look at Trent, who had concern across his face.

"I still don't know what we are doing here?" Trent whispered loud enough for only Caleb to hear him. Caleb whispered back.

"This has to be done, I have to talk to her, we have to figure out what the hell is going on and this is our best option right now."

Trent reached his hand up and ran his fingers through his jet-black hair. He was just about to say something when Isabelle's return stopped him in his tracks.

"Detective Stone," was all she said before she came in and placed the steaming mugs in front of both men and took a seat across from them. Caleb waited for her to continue, but she just stared at him with worry in her puffy eyes.

"Mrs. Vaughn," he began but was cut off.

"Call me Isabelle."

Caleb nodded and replied. "Of course, and please, call me Caleb, as you know I am retired now."

"Where is she?" She continued, getting straight to her point.

"I was hoping you could tell me that."

The look of defeat, and concern was etched in every line in her face. Tears welled up in her eyes.

Trent reached for his cup of coffee and blew in it softly before he asked his question, even though it was evident he already knew the answer.

"When was the last time you saw Sophia?"

Isabelle brought her attention to Trent and looked at him blankly for a moment before she replied.

"Who are you?"

"I'm sorry Isabelle, this is Trent Ford, he is a close friend and colleague of mine, don't worry we are both here to help," Caleb answered quickly, as he could tell her bluntness unnerved Trent.

"Colleague? But you just said you are retired now, is this a case? Did something happen to my baby?" Isabelle was clearly becoming overly agitated.

"No, no, Isabelle please calm down. This is not a case, not officially, we are both just here to help," Caleb's voice was soothing and calming. He knew he had to keep her calm, but he could see anger creeping up on her.

"Help? You're here to help? I think you have already done enough damage, don't you?"

"Excuse me?"

Isabelle sighed deeply and leaned back in her chair and rested her forehead in her hand.

"I know what you did." her voice was barley audible, but Caleb heard the words loud and clear. He looked over at Trent, who also rested his head in his hands. But before Caleb could formulate the words to answer her she brought her head back up, tears now streaming down her cheeks, as she continued.

"I knew there was something happening between you two. I saw it. The way you both looked at each other whenever you were in the same room. I knew something was happening, but I did not fully understand exactly what it was."

Caleb felt his mouth quickly lose all moisture and he reached for his coffee, and took a hearty sip, nearly burning his tongue. All the while holding his attention on Sophia's mother.

"I'm a Mother, I have a certain…I guess you could call it intuition when it comes to my daughter. I know if something isn't right, even if she refuses to tell me. I knew something wasn't right in her marriage to Marcus. I voiced my concerns, but only very passively, as I did not want to offend or upset her. I knew that he wasn't treating her well, and I hate myself that I didn't know just how horribly he was actually treating her. Everyone thought they had this magical, perfect life, but that was definitely not the case. Nobody has that, and I knew that all along, but I didn't know how bad it really was, and I certainly didn't know that her life was in danger. I hate myself for not seeing how much she was suffering, I am her Mother, I am supposed to protect her…" she paused for a moment to catch her breath, and grab a tissue on the table beside her, and then she went on. "I am supposed to protect my child, and I failed."

Caleb's heart was in his chest, and he felt utterly horrible of the pain that Isabelle Vaughn was in.

"Isabelle, you did not fail her."

"She murdered her husband. She murdered her husband trying to protect herself. It should have never gotten to that point."

Trent was sitting quietly listening to the exchange that was taking place, Caleb knew that he did not want to interfere, and at this moment, he appreciated that. Although Caleb had had a gut feeling that Isabelle Vaughn knew the truth, her last statement confirmed it. He still was unaware as to what level she knew the truth.

"Sophia is strong, she fought back for her life, Isabelle, she fought back."

Silence hung in the air between the three of them, but Caleb did not know what else to say.

"Why?" Isabelle asked softly.

Caleb, uncertain how to answer, as he was confused on the question.

"Why what?"

"Why did you let her do it?"

And now it was clear, it was clear at how much Isabelle knew, so there was no sense being anything other than completely transparent with her.

"I didn't want to."

"You could have done something, anything, anything other than that."

"I tried, Isabelle, believe me I tried, but she was to determined that she needed to do it. She needed to end it, she needed to make sure for herself that Marcus would never hurt her again. She needed to watch the life drain out of his face to be sure her nightmare was over, that was the only way for her. As much as I hate the fact that she decided to do it, I would do it over again in a heart beat if it meant she was safe. If it meant that son of a bitch was never going to lay another hand on her again."

"Do you love her?" Isabelle asked matter of fact.

"Yes."

"Caleb? Do you love her?" She asked again, staring him straight in the eye.

"Isabelle, I love her, I love her more than anything in this world and I would do anything for her. I will do anything to protect her, anything."

Isabelle licked her dry lips and nodded her head slowly. Caleb was entirely unsure where her head was at in this moment, but he had to admit, it felt like a weight had been lifted off his shoulders being able to talk to her.

"Then where is she? Where is my baby? Why didn't she come home last night?"

"That's why we're here," Trent finally broke his own silence to answer her. Caleb glanced at him and then nodded his head in agreeance before he also replied.

"That's exactly why we are here Isabelle, something has happened and we are here hoping you can tell us exactly what it is."

TWENTY- THREE -October 9, 2015

Jill stared at her reflection in the mirror, she was not overly pleased with the image looking back at her. She noticed how tired she looked, swollen and hollow pockets had formed under her eyes, and deep lines were settling very noticeably in her once perfectly smooth skin. The last few years had definitely taken their toll on her emotional as well as her physical state. She began to second guess her decision to go out for dinner with this guy. She reached for her brush and ran it through her long, poker straight hair, fiddling with a random fly away strand for a moment before tossing the brush back onto her vanity and let out a sigh of nervous frustration.

"God, what am I doing?" she mumbled to herself as she grabbed a tube of mascara twisting off the lid.

She applied a thin layer to her already dark lashes as she continued to talk to the image in the mirror.

"What am I doing? Like I really need to go out for dinner with some guy, why the hell did I let her convince me to do this? Apparently, I am crazy, that is why, I am crazy, and no guy wants to sit and have dinner with a crazy person," she muttered tossing her mascara back on the table. She rarely wore a lot of make up, but she thought she could at least make the attempt to try and be womanly tonight. She opened her drawer and rifled through her sparse choices of lip glosses, settling on a soft brown. She put a light layer on, pressed her lips firmly together and inhaled a deep breath, as she studied the finished product in her mirror.

"I should cancel... no...I told her I would at least have dinner with him...but I really should just cancel... ya, I think I should just cancel." Jill reached for her cell phone, finally convincing herself that she should not be going out on any dinner dates. As she grabbed her cell it began to ring in her hand, she flipped it over and

Rae's smiling face was staring back at her, as if she could read her mind in that very moment. Jill smiled to herself before hitting the accept button.

"Are you always in my head?" Jill asked upon answering the call.

"Of course, how could you live your life if I was not there making all of your decisions for you," Rae joked on the other end. "I just wanted to give you a call to make sure you have not chickened out."

"See you are always in my head. Rae. I don't know, I think I am going to call him and tell him I cannot make it."

"No, no you are not. Listen Jilly Bean, you are going to go out with Eric tonight, you are going to have a nice dinner, some wine, some good conversation, and it wouldn't hurt to let him get in your pants you know."

"Rachell Bishop!" Jill scolded her friend, trying to sound serious.

"What? I am sorry hun, but you need to get laid, like bad," Rae replied with a playful chuckle, all the while being completely serious.

Jill huffed, denying her friends statement. "I do not. I do not need to get laid. I am just fine not being laid thank you very much. Besides I don't know this Eric guy. I am only agreeing to this for you, to satisfy your annoying insistence that I need to go out on a date with some strange man I have never met. I agreed to go out for dinner with him, what makes you think I am going to just drop my pants and let him have his way with me?"

There were a few seconds of silence on the line and Rae answered, her voice heavy with urgency.

"Because, Jill, I have to be honest with you, I have been worried sick about you lately and I know you will be okay...if...."

Again, there was silence and for a brief moment Jill's playful nature turned to a serious note, thinking there was something her friend was trying to express to her.

"If what?" Jill inquired.

"If, if you would just drop your damn pants and let him have his way with you, because girl... you need to get L-A-I-D, laid, like tonight laid."

Both women erupted in laughter, Jill feeling foolish for even thinking Rae was trying to have a serious moment with her. Rae was a lot of things, but being serious and morose was typically not one of them. She lived her life on a high, she was exploding with positivity and upbeat energy, so Jill's ears definitely perked when she sensed a seriousness behind her voice, but she should have known better.

"So, no, you are not cancelling, don't even think about calling him to cancel. He is a super nice guy, with a great job, no baggage, and yes, the boy is fine. So please, Jilly Bean, my friend, my soul sister, my partner in crime, just do me this solid and go out, enjoy yourself and please, please get laid."

Jill was still seated on her vanity bench and she continued to study her features as she spoke to her friend. A smile spread across her face as she listened to Rae. Jill thought to herself, she was an impossible brat, she meddled in her life, but she was her best friend and she loved her dearly. So, she was not going to cancel, she would go out on this dinner date, just for Rae, because that is how much she meant to her.

"Okay, I won't cancel. But that does not mean I am going to hop into bed with him, you understand? I don't need to go getting messed up with some guy I don't know, I don't need that in my life right now. I am going to go, have a nice dinner, that he will pay for. I am going to have some wine to unwind, also which he is going to pay for. And I am going to have the largest slice of chocolatey, chocolate goodness cake that I can find, and yes, he will pay for it. Then I am going to come home, and if I have the need to get laid, I will be more than happy to pull out Vern. Sound good?"

Again, laughter filled both lines of the phone call, Rae knowing full well who Vern was, the vibrating plastic toy, that was tucked conspicuously in the back of Jill's underwear drawer.

"Okay, it's a deal. Just promise me you will have fun, and call me when you get home please?" Rae answered between lighthearted giggles.

"I will, I promise I will have fun, Vern will make sure of that."

TWENTY – FOUR - October 9, 2015

Sophia reached up to touch her swollen cheek, it was still stinging and burning. The vengeance and hatred behind Olivia's hand was left there on her face, reminding her why she was here. She could not believe that this was happening to her and she desperately wished she could just go back to that beautiful serene place with Caleb. If she had not run away from him when he told her the truth, then none of this would be happening. The stranglehold of panic surfaced once again wondering how anyone was going to know where she was. Was anybody going to be able to find her here, wherever here was. She did not even know where the hell she was. It was chilly, and dim, and she was chained to a fucking bed, that is all she knew. Sophia may not have known where she was, but she knew why she was here, Olivia had made certain of that. Olivia had been tormented by finding out the truth. Sophia knew that Olivia did not trust her from the beginning. Granted Sophia's feelings towards her ex sister-in-law were very mutual. She had known she was emotionally unstable at times, very dramatic and even narcissistic, but she never ever thought she would be capable of something like this. The scariest feeling in this moment, as she laid there by herself, was wondering what she was going to be able to do to get herself out of this. Olivia knew something, she admitted she was not certain of exactly what transpired that night, but she knew Sophia was involved. What she wanted from her was the truth. No matter what Olivia said or did to her, that truth was only known by a small handful of people and Sophia had every intention on keeping it that way.

Sophia reached onto the floor and grabbed her water bottle and downed the last remnants of liquid, it barely managed to quench even an ounce of her thirst, but she did not want to have to ask for anything else from her. The last thing she wanted was to give that crazy bitch the satisfaction of knowing she had her in her grips. Although Sophia would have given her right arm for water, and lots of it, she had to remain calm, as calm as she could anyways. If she were going to get herself out of this she had to keep a clear head, and unfortunately that meant she was going to have to do what she could to stay strong. Whatever Olivia had used to get her here was rough. It made her head pound with the pressure of 1000 hammers, it made her mouth dry and difficult to swallow, and her eyes were burning with dehydration.

Now that she was fully aware of why she was here, Sophia needed to keep her shit together, to figure out what she was going to do. This was the time to plan because she knew one thing, she wasn't going to tell Olivia what she wanted to hear. Who knew what she would do to her if she discovered the whole truth. After this, she would not put anything past that woman. Just when Sophia thought she would be alone with her thoughts for awhile to be able to think of a plan of escape, the door swung open. Olivia joined her once again in the room. Olivia felt an insatiable feeling of rage spring from her gut, and she wanted nothing more than to grab Sophia by her scrawny throat and squeeze the life out of her, but she didn't, she couldn't, not yet.

"You're gonna need this," Olivia exclaimed as she threw and empty bucket on the bed beside Sophia. Sophia looked at it, briefly puzzled, then comprehending what it was for. She looked up at Olivia with a credulous glare.

"You're kidding me, right?"

"Do I look like I am fucking kidding?"

"You want me to go to the bathroom in a bucket, on the floor?" Sophia's voice broke slightly, the vision running through her head.

Olivia just stood there staring at her, her upper lip curled in hatred for the woman lying before her. Sophia remembered her thoughts before Olivia came barging in, she had to try and stay calm, she had to try to keep her wits about her.

"I can't go in a bucket, Olivia."

"And why's that Sophia? Are you just too good for that? You're just too good to take a piss in a bucket? What makes you think I would give you the benefit of going to the bathroom like a normal person? Why shouldn't you piss in a bucket on the floor, you tell me that?"

Sophia inhaled deeply and closed her eyes, defeat and weakness taking over all of her senses. She honestly did not have the strength to fight, but this, this was inhumane.

"Because I'm not some kind of animal Olivia, I am a human being."

"My brother was a human being, he was an amazing human being, so no you don't get to compare yourself to that, not after what you did. You are an animal, a disgraceful, disgusting vulture, so there," Olivia pointed at the bucket, "there is your bucket, it's that or you can go in your $500-dollar jeans for all I give a shit."

Sophia was astounded, she could not fathom what Olivia was saying to her, and Olivia still did not know the truth. It made it very clear of how far she would go and what she could do if she did find out. No, Sophia had to just give in to her right now, she could not fight her on this, besides she literally did not have the strength, not yet.

"Fine, I will do what you want Olivia."

A look of accomplishment rested on Olivia's face, triumph that she was still in control. Sophia realized that perhaps that is what she was thriving on, being in control of the situation. When Sophia was confrontational in any way, it only enraged Olivia. But if she demonstrated fragility and succumb to the power she had over her, it fortified her. It satisfied the demons that were controlling her thoughts and actions. So, for now, that is what she had to do, she would have to be feeble, weak, and inferior.

"I can't fight you on this Olivia, I just want to go home."

Olivia laughed a devious, callous, laugh.

"You're not going home Sophia, not until you tell me what happened to my brother. Not until you tell me everything that you did or were a part of."

"Olivia, I know you are hurting, I know how you loved your brother, I under…"

"No, you do not, you do not know how I feel. You don't have the capacity to understand how I feel. You are void of emotion, you have to be, in order to hurt him. You hurt my brother who did nothing but cater to your every whim and give you this life you have. There is no way you have any sense of emotions except hate. You took him from me, from my parents, I know you did. He didn't deserve to die, he was a good man, too good for you."

"Olivia, listen to me," Sophia started to reply with a calming voice, but Olivia did not allow her to continue.

"Stop saying my name, you don't get to say my name," Olivia's voice was now shrieking with frustration and anger once again. Sophia shrunk back not expecting her reaction.

"I'm sorry," Sophia replied tears stinging her eyes, as she shook her head. "I'm sorry but he wasn't…"

Olivia's outburst seemed to diminish at Sophia's words, and she came towards her, stopping just short of the bed.

"What? He wasn't what?"

Sophia knew she should not answer her, but the one thing she could not do was sit here and agree, pretending that man was a good man. He was not a good man, not at all. She was here because of him. Her life was flipped upside down because him. There was no way she was going to defend him or agree in any way, shape or form that was anything other than the maniac who planned to kill her. She knew it was going to infuriate Olivia, but she would never back down on this.

"He wasn't a good man, he was a monster, to me he was a monster."

For the first time since she had been here, Sophia saw a look like none she recognized before on Olivia's face. Desperately she tried to determine what the look meant. Tears swelled heavy on the rims of Olivia's eye's, but she did not blink, she just stared at Sophia. Almost seeming to be in disbelief that she could say such a thing. Finally, she slowly blinked, releasing the tears to slowly roll down her cheek. Sophia just held her gaze and thought perhaps she got through to her somehow.

"Olivia," She whispered softly. And her voice, her voice saying her name broke her out of her momentary trance.

Olivia quickly grabbed the bucket off the bed by the handle, and turned on Sophia, bringing it down across Sophia's head as hard as she could. Sophia's hands instinctively went up to protect her head from the attack.

"NO!" Olivia screamed while swinging the bucket. "NO, I TOLD YOU, YOU DON'T GET TO SAY MY NAME, STOP SAYING MY NAME, YOU BITCH, YOU MURDERING BITCH!"

Sophia somehow found a stitch of strength from somewhere, and she manage to grab Olivia by the wrist. She tried to wrestle the bucket from her grasp but finding it very difficult to defend herself against the rage and strength that was taking over Olivia.

"I HATE YOU, DO YOU HEAR ME?" Olivia continued to scream as she fell forward on the bed, grabbing Sophia's arms as tight as she could to force her to let go. They continued to wrestle, Sophia feeling the last of her energy draining when a high-pitched whistle filled the air.

"OLIVIA, STOP IT, PLEASE STOP!" The weight of Olivia's body was suddenly pulled off of her, and Sophia gasped for breath. Scrambling away from Olivia, she curled herself into the wall, pulling the blankets up to her chin in one motion. She watched the woman with the red hair pull Olivia off the bed. Olivia was now on the floor, looking up at the other woman. The woman stood there looking at Olivia, and the sobs escaped her.

"I'm sorry Zoe, I'm sorry baby. I don't know what happened." The woman named Zoe slowly bent down, and softly grabbed Olivia by the shoulders and pulled her up. She held her at arms length for a moment and wiped a dark hair out of her wet eyes. Sophia sat and watched the two women, a flash of memory of a red headed woman came to her. She was the bartender, she was the woman behind the bar. Zoe glanced over at Sophia, and Sophia could see it in her eyes, she knew this was wrong, she had regret, and guilt deep in those eyes. She quickly diverted her attention back to Olivia and began leading her out of the room.

"I know Liv, I know you didn't mean to, come, let's go get some air."

TWENTY – FIVE -October 10, 2015

Another day gone, and Caleb still had no idea where Sophia was. The idea that she was out there, alone, without him was tearing him apart. With every second that ticked by he knew that there was something desperately wrong, and he felt like it was his fault. If he had just tried harder to stop her from running away when he told her the truth about being hired to kill her, if we were just up front with her from the very beginning instead of waiting to tell her, then maybe none of this would be happening. It was his job to keep her safe, and now she was out there, who knows where, and it was all because of him. That realization slapped him hard in the face the moment he knew she was gone. As he stood at Isabelle Vaughn's sink, letting the water run, his mind was lost in the reality of the situation. He stared blankly out of the window overlooking the small backyard. The high-pitched whistle of the tea kettle startled him back to the moment, he reached for the faucet, stopping the water from flowing into the sink. He pulled two mugs from the cupboard, tossed a tea bag into each and reached for the boiling water on the stove. After filling both cups, he carefully walked back into the living room where Isabelle was still on the phone. He set down a cup in front of her and she smiled softly up at him with a nod of appreciation. Caleb then took his own seat next to her on the couch and listened to the last of her conversation.

"I know Samuel," she said softly into her cell phone. "of course, I will, and please if either you or Devon hear anything please be sure to do the same and let me know." There was a brief pause as Isabelle listened intently to Sophia's good friend on the other end, then continued. "We will find her, we have to," a sob clutched her throat, but she managed to continue. "We have to find her Samuel, wherever she is we will find her. I will be sure to let you know as soon as I hear anything, and please remember to keep this between us. I cannot have anybody else knowing about this, it could put her in more danger." Another pause, as Isabelle gently wiped her eye. "Thank you, you too," she spoke one last time before she ended the call. Caleb sat silently watching her, waiting for her to speak first. Isabelle put her phone gently on the glass coffee table in front of her and turned to Caleb, with desperation etched in the corners of her eyes.

"Thank you for the tea."

"Of course," he said tenderly.

"Neither of them has heard from her, Sam said he has not spoken with her since she left at the end of September, he had no idea she was even back."

Caleb nodded his head and took a cautious sip of his tea.

"I figured as much. I don't think anyone knew Sophia was back here. Which makes this so much more infuriating. If nobody knew she was back, then where is she?" Caleb asked the question more out loud to himself than to Isabelle.

"Caleb, I'm scared," Isabelle's face was pale and he felt horrible that because of him she was going through this hell. He reached over to her and gently placed his hand on top of hers.

"I know you are Isabelle, but I promise you, I am going to find her. I won't stop until I find her, I swear that to you and to her."

"But what if you don't, what if you cannot keep that promise?" The fear of never seeing her daughter again surfaced quickly and Isabelle did not even try to keep her sobs at bay. "I can't lose her Caleb, she is all that I have left in this world, I cannot lose her." She put her face into her hands and allowed herself to cry openly. Caleb as uneasy as he felt, moved to her and put his arm around her, Isabelle leaned into him and wept for her daughter. Caleb held her, softly rubbing her back, wracked with guilt. After a few moments Isabelle's breathing slowed and she pulled away from him, her dark eyes, red and swollen, looking up at him.

"I will find her," he repeated adamantly.

"What do we do now?"

"Trent is heading to the bar as soon as it opens today, it's the last place he knew she was for sure. He is going to talk to everyone there. He will find out who spoke to her last, and who remembers seeing her there. We start there!" Caleb held her gaze, and hoped she felt somewhat reassured.

"What else can we do? There has got to be something?"

Caleb could only begin to understand the determination Isabelle had to find her. That was her daughter, her baby, and he knew she would do anything and everything to help. He knew there was only so much she could do, but the least he could do was make sure she was in the loop the whole time.

"We are doing everything we can. I have someone working on a couple things, okay? We are pulling the street cams, any working ones around that bar that we can. And her cell phone, I am hoping I can find some information on where her cell phone last pinged."

"You can do that?" Hopefulness presenting itself. "I mean I know they can do that, I just mean can you do that, without having anyone find out what is going on?"

"Yes, if there is something to find, a trace that she left, then I will find it. I don't want to involve any more people in this than we absolutely have to. I know you trust Samuel immensely, and it was important to check with him, but wherever Sophia is, I know she is not there voluntarily. I don't want to draw attention to the fact that anyone is aware of it. If someone has her I want to be able to catch them off guard." Caleb continued to hold Isabelle's hand. She nodded her head slowly.

"Do you really think someone has her?"

"Isabelle, she left me that message then disappeared. There have been no accidents, nothing that has been reported. We have checked all the hospitals, so yes, as much I hate to say it, I think someone has her. Someone knew she was home, I just have to figure out who, and I will."

Isabelle shook her head in utter disbelief at what she was hearing.

"I don't understand, I just don't understand who would want to hurt her. If someone took her, or if someone is going to try and hurt her, I just cannot understand why. I don't get it Caleb, why is this happening?" I mean you don't think anybody knows do you?"

Caleb did not need her to clarify further on that last part of the question. With her questions hanging between them, Isabelle's phone rang interrupting the answers. Isabelle jumped, grabbing it off the coffee table.

"I don't recognize this number," she exclaimed, unsure if she should answer it.

"It's okay, just go ahead and answer it, it could be her." Caleb's heart was pounding not wanting to allow himself to be let down by who may be on that phone.

Isabelle took in a quick calming breath and she hit the accept button.

"Hello?" she said wearily into the phone.

Caleb watched every single line in her face wrinkle as her forehead raised and relaxed, looking for some sign of who was on the other end. It felt like an eternity before she spoke into the phone.

"Yes, of course, I will see you soon, and thank you for calling." She ended the call and stared blankly at her phone for a few seconds.

"Isabelle?" Caleb said. "What it is?"

She turned to face him, and Caleb could swear he could see a very small shimmer of optimism on Isabelle's face and she replied.

"Well, we may not know who in the hell would want to hurt Sophia, but I think we may have just found someone who possibly does?"

TWENTY – SIX - October 10, 2015

Her heart was pounding, and she was having a hard time catching her breath. The intense sensation was making its way through every part of her body, sensations she had not felt in a very long time. Jill could feel it all, a warmth of pleasure traveling through every vein, filling her body with desire. She clung to the wrinkled sheet, bunching the fabric tight in her fists as she tried to contain her senses and not move around too much. Her toes curled so tight, they almost began to cramp, and she felt like she was going to crawl out of her own skin. She did not want this feeling to stop, not yet. His hand slowly moved up her stomach and started slowly caressing one of her breasts, tracing his finger over her nipple until it hardened under his touch. Intensifying her arousal even further, if possible.

"You like that? A voice mumbled from between her thighs. Jill could feel the stubble of his newly grown in beard rubbing on her delicate skin, it should have been uncomfortable, but it only made it better.

"Just don't stop," she ordered in between ragged breaths. She could feel his tongue continue dancing wildly, between her legs, the heat of his breath driving her closer to climax. "Keep going."

He obeyed, he brought his hand away from her breast, and placed both of his hands under her buttocks, squeezing and pulling her further into his mouth. Jill let out a cry of insane gratification and steadied herself for the explosion of arousal that was taking over her entire body. She released the death grip on the sheets and grabbed a hold of the headboard as her body squirmed wildly. Within a few moments, there it was, her body ignited in a furious climax, every worry, and every stress, being demolished all at once. She let the feelings wash over her again and again, keeping the outside world at bay for just a few more minutes.

"Oh my God," she cried, panting with shallow breaths as the man responsible for it all moved slowly up her body, meeting her lips with his. She quickly returned the kiss. He collapsed beside her. Jill turned to him and studied the beads of sweat that had formed on his forehead.

Rae had been right, Eric was, as she had put it, very fine. Jill noticed that particular detail the moment he had stood to greet her at the restaurant the night before. He was tall, about 6'1, and his dark features were sexy and masculine. He was in incredible shape, his muscles toned and tight underneath his tanned skin, and he smelled amazing. Jill recalled how the smell of him alone increased her heart rate. Rae was right that he was a great guy, he had a good job, and he had a good family life. He was definitely a catch. That was all he was right now, a good catch, that she knew she would be throwing back in the lake after this.

"That was fucking awesome," he exclaimed turning his head to look over at Jill with a sly smile. Jill grinned back.

"It was, but I really have to get going into the station."

Eric pushed himself, resting against the headboard. "Can I see you tonight?" He asked, hopeful she would say yes.

Jill sighed deeply, reaching for the sheets to pull over her exposed body, then swung her legs over the edge of her bed.

"I don't think so," she replied honestly, before she grabbed her panties off the floor and slipping them on while staying covered up. She grabbed her tank top that was hanging from her night stand and slipped it on. She released the blanket and stood up, turning to Eric who was still in the bed.

He cocked his head to one side, keeping that grin on his face.

"So that's it?"

"What?" she answered casually.

"We have a night of mind blowing sex last night and then again this morning and then that is it?"

Jill took a seat back on the bed, grabbed a pillow placing it in her lap.

"Is that all I am, just some sex toy?" His tone was playful, intending to not be offended but Jill could read in his expression that he was hoping for more from her. But more she could not give him, no matter how perfect he seemed.

"No, you're great, you know that. But like I said last night at dinner, my life is just busy, crazy, complicated and really not something you would want to get yourself tangled up in. I'm not looking for anything serious, I told you that."

Eric nodded his head slowly and ran his hand through his black, thick, slightly dampened hair. He held his hand in place, holding the hair out of his eye, studying Jill for a moment. He smiled wider at her, and an insanely sexy dimple filled his right cheek.

"I know Jill, I'm just bugging you. But it was amazing! You're pretty amazing too. Rae was right about you, you don't give yourself as much credit as you deserve. You work too hard, you gotta let yourself live a bit, and allow someone in."

"Is that so? Is that what Rae had to say about me?" Sarcasm filled Jill's voice, she knew very well what Rae thought about it. "I'm just in a bad place for anything right now, nothing serious. It's not fair to anybody to ask them to be a part of my life right now. I can't give someone what they deserve, my time or the energy, it wouldn't be fair. This is all I have to give at this time."

Jill knew she was crazy, to meet someone like Eric and not want something more with him. He was obviously open to more. He was open to an honest, real, relationship, any woman would be lucky to have someone like him. She just knew she could not be that woman, not now, not when she had just come to terms with her feelings for Caleb. As much as she knew those feelings were not reciprocated, she needed time to deal with them, to sort them out, to find a way to bury them back where they belonged.

Eric acknowledged her feelings with another quick nod, and he stood up from the bed, his perfectly sculpted butt exposed to Jill. He walked around the foot of the bed, found the pair of jeans he was wearing the night before and he pulled them on. The button open, Jill eyeing the little trail of hair leading down from his belly button. He came and stood in front of her, his dark eyes looking down at her, penetrating her.

"I get it Jill, and I am not going to pressure you into something you are not ready for, that would not be fair of me."

Responses like that definitely did not make it any easier. Not only was he amazing looking, with a tremendous personality and insatiably hot in bed, he was patient and understanding. She thought to herself again how crazy she was. As he stood above her, with those dark, probing eyes, she felt the desire begin to creep over her again. She knew she would never get to work if she allowed him to look at her like that.

"Thank you, Eric," Jill replied, she stood up, making an attempt to walk him out. But the moment she stood up, Eric grabbed her, and lifted her, her legs wrapping around his waist. She threw her arms around his neck, and their eyes were locked.

"If that is all that you are able to give right now, then I sure as hell am not going to be done with you quite yet."

He cupped the back of her head and pulled her hungrily towards his waiting mouth. She responded instantly, knowing she should have just ended it at that. But the moment she felt his body next to hers, and his lips on hers, she knew she was not going anywhere yet. He walked to the edge of the bed, her body still clinging to his and he carefully laid her back onto the bed. He gently lowered himself on top of her. He yanked her tank top off, tossing it back exactly where she had just retrieved it from on the nightstand. Again, his dark eyes sunk into her soul, again making her think she was in fact crazy. And the moment she felt his warm tongue wrap around her erect nipple, she almost managed to push her feelings for Caleb Stone out of her mind, almost.

TWENTY – SEVEN - October 10, 2015

"I'll wait for you out here okay? It will be fine I promise."

"Are you sure you don't want to just come in with me?" Isabelle had her hand on the door handle of her Camry, she asked Caleb before getting out.

"No, I think it's best if you just go in and talk to him, he knows you. I don't want to intimidate him right now. If he has some info I want him to feel comfortable talking to you. The only reason he knows me is from the investigation of his best friend's murder, so I don't want to give him any reason to second guess coming to talk to you. Just remember to turn on the recording app on your phone, I want to be sure we don't miss anything he might have to say."

"Alright, well I will try not to take too long," she opened the car door, and gave Caleb an uneasy smile, before she closed it gently behind her. She adjusted her purse on her shoulder and made her way to the front doors of the small diner. Before going in she grabbed her phone out of her purse, making sure the voice memo recording was activated.

She walked inside the diner to discover it was only slightly bigger than it looked from the outside. She could see only two waitresses working the floor, the morning rush had cleared, one of the waitresses walked up to Isabelle and said, "Morning Hun, you can take a seat anywhere that's open."

"Thank you," Isabelle replied with a nod. She quickly scanned the diner and saw the back of his head, sitting in a booth in the far corner of the restaurant. She nervously made her way over to him tapping him on the shoulder as she approached. Alex jumped slightly, he turned, his face lighting up at the sight of her. He quickly stood up to greet her with a hug.

"Isabelle, it's so good to see you,"

Isabelle held him tight in an embrace and answered.

"You too Alex, it's been awhile," she pulled away and studied his face. He looked like he had lost some weight. His face was thinner, and now covered with the beginnings of a full beard. She held him at arms length, so very grateful that he called her, but not wanting to jump right into why. "How have you been?"

They slid into the booth, staring across from each other.

"I've been okay, as good as I can be I guess."

Isabelle's heart hurt for the man sitting across from her. He was in pain over the loss of his friend, not only Marcus, but Cat as well and even Sophia. Since this all has happened she is sure he has not had any communications with her, at least that she was aware of.

"What about you? How are you holding up?"

"The same as you, one day at a time." Isabelle gave him a soft smile, acknowledging they were in the same boat.

They sat at the table, silence hanging in the air. Isabelle could tell that Alex was uncomfortable or nervous, but she did not want to press him. She was hoping he would just talk to her about whatever it was he had to share with her.

"Isabelle? How's Sophia?"

This is where it got tricky, she wasn't sure how honest she should be with him. Caleb had told her to just go with her gut, but she did not want to negatively affect this conversation in any way. Then Alex continued.

"I mean I know she left LA after all this and I don't blame her, but have you talked to her lately?"

Isabelle decided to be slightly honest.

"Yes, I have actually."

"Oh, good!" Relief washed over his face and Isabelle was curious as to why.

"She came home."

"She did?" His relief turned to concern. "When?"

"Earlier this last week?" Isabelle's answers remained short wanting Alex to lead the conversation.

"Oh, how is she?"

"She is still upset Alex, terribly upset."

Alex entwined his fingers together in front of him, he stared down at them and fidgeted. He asked her the next question while keeping his gaze focused on his hands.

"Have you spoken to anyone else at all? I mean, does anyone else know she is home?"

Uneasiness began to form in Isabelle's chest, she knew his questions were leading to something. He was not wanting to scare her in anyway, so trying to pass it off as small talk.

"What's going on Alex? Why did you call to meet me here?" She decided to cut the bull and get straight to the point. No sense torturing him or herself any further. Alex drew his gaze from his hands and focused back on Isabelle's waiting eyes. He inhaled deeply then he answered her.

"Listen, I don't know if this is even a big deal, I mean it is probably nothing, it's dumb actually. It's just Olivia Donovan called me a couple weeks ago, and she was super upset and emotional about Marcus's death, I mean that is understandable, but…"

Tears began to well heavily in Isabelle's eyes, and Alex noticed immediately. She saw his concern, and he reached across the table to touch her hand.

"Isabelle, what is it? What's wrong?"

"Alex, Sophia's missing!" she answered him bluntly. She watched Alex's expression turn from being concerned about making her cry, to being shocked, and even possibly scared.

"What? What do you mean missing? When?"

The tears flowed down her cheeks now, and her hands shook softly under Alex's strong hand.

"I have not seen her or heard from her since Tuesday."

Alex shook his head, as if trying to rattle sense into the conversation at hand.

"Christ!"

"Alex!"

Alex locked his eyes onto Isabelle's pleading stare.

"I wasn't sure Isabelle, I was not sure if I should make anything out of the conversation between Olivia and myself. I've known her a long time. She has always been dramatic and craved attention, but for her to just call me up out the blue and have me meet her at some dive bar to talk to me about the case, especially after it is supposed to be done and buried. This fucking case…" Alex paused embarrassed he used vulgarity in front of Isabelle, "I mean this case is done, we were all supposed to be moving on with our lives. So, when she comes to me saying all this stuff about Sophia, I just wasn't sure if…"

"What stuff?" Isabelle interjected.

"Crazy stuff Isabelle, it was crazy ramblings. Demanding to know what was going on in their marriage. Wanting to know every detail I had about Marcus' life, and everything I knew about Sophia. When she started going on about her hatred for Sophia, I thought she was just angry and looking for someone to vent to. But when she started going on about Sophia being the one who murdered Marcus and wanting justice, I knew it was more than venting. She was losing her mind, and the scary thing was she was dead serious. She was convinced that Sophia murdered her brother, and she was even more convinced she was going to get her to admit it, one way or another."

Isabelle felt a lump form in her throat, nearly making it impossible for her to breathe, but she needed to stay calm. This was a break, this was the best clue they had gotten in days. Isabelle had to keep her wits and just stay focused, so she could find her damn daughter.

"I need you tell me everything, every single word. I need you to tell me everything she told you Alex, do not leave any detail out, no matter how small, do you understand me? Because I think you just helped me figure out exactly what happened to my daughter."

TWENTY – EIGHT -October 10, 2015

Jill Keller grabbed her favorite mug from the shelf and poured herself a cup of hot steaming coffee. It smelled delicious, but it was a running joke through out the station that it always tasted like hot tar. After her night last night, she did not care what it tasted like, she needed coffee and lots of it. She was still kicking herself for letting things progress so far with Eric last night, and this morning, but she felt she was pretty straightforward about what her intentions were and are. She walked over to the fridge in the stations break room and pulled out a carton of milk, she opened it, sniffed it, and grimaced.

"Jesus, that's disgusting," she muttered to herself as she walked over to the sink and dumped the remaining coagulated liquid into the sink. She had no choice but to forego the milk this morning, so she dumped a spoonful of sugar into the coffee gave it a quick stir. She turned around at the sound of Detective Sterling's voice.

"Morning Keller."

"Morning Detective," she replied with a sluggish tone.

"Rough night," He asked with a curious smirk?

"Something like that, let's just say coffee is going to be my best friend today."

"Where's Landon this morning?" Sterling asked as he glanced quickly around the room.

"Ah, he had to drop his daughter off at her mom's then had an appointment, he should be in later this morning," Jill answered in between a reluctant sip of her drink.

Detective Sterling walked to the fridge, and opened the door staring aimlessly inside for a moment.

"If you're looking for the milk, you're out of luck."

"Black it is," he answered as he grabbed his own mug and filled it up. He blew in it gently before he spoke further. "So, how are you guys making out on that Cassidy Ryan case? Any new leads?"

Jill shook her head slowly; a look of frustration crossed her face.

"Nothing so far, trying to get the ex in here for some questioning, so hopefully that will give us something. Hopefully!"

Detective Sterling walked up to her and his five-foot seven frame came eye to eye with hers. He placed his hand on her shoulder and gave her a reassuring squeeze.

"If anyone can catch the sick bastard that did this, it's you Keller."

Jill smiled warmly at her colleague and replied appreciatively.

"Thanks Sterling, that means a lot," with that he turned and headed back to his desk to start his day. Jill watched him as he took a seat and shuffled some papers around, then she turned and headed back to her own office.

She settled herself at her desk and she looked at the stack of cases that was piled on her desk. She really had to delegate some of these smaller cases to some other detectives. She knew she was just not going to have the time to give them the attention they deserved. Her focus had to be on Cassidy Ryan and finding out who did this to her. Whoever it was needed to be put away for good, or even better, get the death penalty. Jill had a sneaking suspicion that whoever did this heinous crime had done it before. It seemed too skillfully planned and prepared, but so far, no other cases have come about with any of the same characteristics.

Jill pivoted towards her computer and pressed a few quick buttons that lead her into her email. Every time she opened it there was a part of her that was desperately hoping for a response from Caleb, and every day she was disappointed. She wanted nothing more than to hear from him and find out where he settled at. To hear his voice, to know that he was doing okay, that is all she wanted, just to know that he was doing okay. Her thoughts were startled by her cell phone ringing beside her. She smiled to herself at her friends face on the screen and she answered it knowing exactly why Rae was calling her.

"Morning Sunshine," Jill sang into the phone.

"Well, good morning to you," Rae replied on the other end.

"What's going on?"

"Not much, just heading in to the salon right away, wanted to see if you had time to meet up for a quick coffee at the diner?"

Jill brought her wrist up, checking the time on her watch.

"Uh, sure I should be able to sneak out for a few, it's 9:00 now, and Landon isn't going to be back till later this morning. I guess I could come grab a coffee with you. You want to meet me there say in about 20?"

"Absolutely!" Rae answered her eagerly. "I have been dying to find out what happened with you and Eric last night."

Jill chuckled quietly, dropping her head back, her eyes studied the ceiling tiles of her office for a moment before she answered her friend's curiosity.

"Well I don't want to bring you down, but I don't think I have much to say that is going to be very interesting."

Jill could hear Rae smirk on the other end of the line.

"I call bull! I tried calling you 3 times last night and you did not answer so I knew you must have been either dead or getting laid, and well you're talking to me right now, so I guess you aren't dead."

"You're such a shit Raechell, you know that right?"

"Of course, I do!"

"Just meet me at the diner in 20 okay?"

Rae laughed, and replied, "Okay Jilly Bean, I would rather hear the deets in person anyways, see you soon.

TWENTY-NINE - October 10, 2015

Olivia's eyes slowly began to open, they felt like rocks were anchored to her lids and weighing them down. She felt utterly exhausted, then she remembered last night. The memory of the rage that took over her when Sophia had the nerve to utter out loud that her brother was a monster. She had tried her best to remain calm while talking to her, but when she had uttered those words she could not stop it, there was usually no stopping it. Then Zoe was there, out of nowhere pulling her off of Sophia, she could not convince herself that had Zoe not come home, she would have stopped attacking Sophia with that bucket. Maybe before she would have been able to control herself enough to stop, but she knew she was different now. Then she recalled Zoe bringing her to the other bedroom and doing her best to calm her down. She was thankful Zoe was here for this, she was the one person who could keep Olivia level, she was her voice of reason. Olivia was thankful she had someone that was finally on her side. Olivia's mind drifted briefly to the night before.

"Here baby, take this," Zoe walked into the bedroom and stood over Olivia with a bottle of water and 2 small pills in her hand. Olivia held out her hand, and Zoe handed them to her.

"What are these?" Olivia asked through the haze of her utterly exhausted state.

Zoe sat down beside her, and Olivia had sensed a small wall between them.

"They will just help you sleep, I think you're overtired Olivia. I think you just need to get some rest that's all, and these will help you."

Trusting Zoe, Olivia popped both pills in her mouth and washed them down with a drink of the water. Zoe only wanted what was best for her, and if she thought she needed some rest then she would take them. She did need to get some sleep, she needed to have a clear head to think, and to make sure she knew what she was doing.

Zoe smiled caringly at her and stood up from the bed.

"Just lie down, and rest, you're stressed, I think you will feel better in the morning."

Olivia inched over, allowing Zoe to pull the covers down, she slid underneath the covers without taking off any of her clothes. When she was settled underneath the warm bedding, Zoe knelt down, coming eye level with Olivia. The last thing Olivia remembered was Zoe softly rubbing her forehead, as she whispered lovingly.

"It's all going to be okay tomorrow baby, it's all going to be okay."

That is why she felt like a semi had hit her, she had taken those sleeping pills. She should not have taken them, she had really wanted to keep her mind crystal clear and drugs hindered that. She wanted to remain sharp and focused. Zoe had been right though, she had been exhausted and her body was stressed, and it was all because of that crazy whore in the next room. If she would just tell Olivia what she had done to her brother, then they could move on from this. She knew she needed to hear it, and she would do whatever she needed or wait as long as she needed for her to say it. Olivia knew she was not going to be able to move on from this part of her life until she got the answers that she was so desperately searching for. She was just thankful that she was not in this alone anymore and she had someone who could understand her and help her get what it was she needed. With that thought, Olivia slowly rolled over to reach for Zoe, but her hand fell on emptiness. In fact, it did not even look like Zoe had come to bed at all, her side of the bed was untouched. She sat slowly up in her bed, and rubbed the heavy sleep from her eyes, the bedroom door was closed but she could hear movement on the other side of it. Zoe must have fallen asleep on the couch, or perhaps she just did not want to disturb Olivia knowing how gravely she needed the uninterrupted sleep. She tossed the covers back and she sat on the edge of the bed for a moment, gathering herself before she stood up.

She opened the door and walked into the main area of the cabin, she did not see Zoe, but she saw a pan on the stove, a carton of eggs and some milk on the counter. Olivia smiled, knowing she was making her breakfast while she slept. Then she heard faint talking and she saw the door to the room Sophia was in was opened slightly, Olivia walked to it and pushed it all the way open. Zoe was standing above Sophia's bed, handing her a plate of eggs. Both women turned at the sound of Olivia opening the door, and Olivia could see almost panic on their faces.

"She needed to eat," was all Zoe managed to say.

"Of course," Olivia calmly answered while holding a vengeful glare on Sophia.

She watched Sophia take the plate from Zoe, and the she backed herself up against the wall with the plate in her hand obviously hesitant to eat with Olivia watching her. Zoe too could see the look in her eyes and turned around to face Olivia.

"She has to eat Liv."

Olivia's dark glare went from Sophia onto Zoe's, the woman who has been her rock since the day she met her in the bar. The anger she was feeling eased slightly, but she was still furious she gave her food without telling her.

"I said I know Zoe, she needs to eat, so eat," her glare returning to Sophia. Their eyes were locked, Olivia abruptly turned and left the room, Zoe at her heels, shutting the door behind her. Olivia walked straight to the kitchen, scooping a fingerful of eggs from the frying pan and dropping it in her mouth.

"Liv, she needed some food, she has not eaten since she has been here, and I know your not trying to starve someone, right?"

Olivia popped a few more of the fluffy eggs into her mouth and ignored Zoe's question. She brushed past her and grabbed the carton of milk off the counter, took off the cap and took a giant chug from the container, Zoe stood watching her every move. Olivia put the milk down but did not bother to replace the lid.

"Liv?" Zoe sounded concerned.

"Whose side are you on?" Finally, Olivia spoke, and the question apparently stunned Zoe, as she just stood there staring at her, unexpectant of the question.

"Well?" Olivia pressed for an answer.

"Olivia, what kind of question is that? Of course, you know I am here for you, I am trying to help you work through this, but she had to eat. I know you were not going to starve her."

Olivia stood, her hand placed on her hip, she nodded her head, seemingly in agreement with her.

"Right, yah you're right. I mean why don't we just go out and grab some delicious steaks and a nice expensive bottle of red, and let's cook her up a meal tonight," Sarcasm was flooding her response.

"Liv... Come on."

"No, no and while we do that, lets go get her some Egyptian cotton sheets, and some really fancy bubble bath, so we can treat her to a real night of relaxation and pampering. I am sure if we do that, that stupid bitch will tell me what I need to hear," Olivia's hand pointing at Sophia's door.

"I know you don't want to hurt anyone Olivia, I know you are trying to get to the bottom of Marcus's death. I get that, but I know you don't want to hurt her…"

"You don't know what I want!" Olivia's harsh words cut off Zoe.

"If you truly knew what I wanted or what I needed, then you would not be out here, feeding her, you should not be giving her anything. If you knew me at all you would just stay away from her and let me do what I need to do right now. I trusted you Zoe, I trusted that you were on my side, that you are here for me, not her. Not that crazy fucking lunatic in there that murdered my brother. You are supposed to be here for me!"

"I am here for you Olivia, I am. She is in my cabin, I told you to bring her here. I have no idea what your intentions were, and I still don't but I am trying to be here for you. But I also don't want to see you hurt anyone, I don't want to see you get hurt." Zoe stopped speaking and waited for Olivia to look her in the eyes. "Olivia, you are really scaring me, and I don't know what to do." Olivia was shaken, maybe the person she thought was her person did not get her after all. Olivia could not understand why she would be so scared. Zoe understood this was a situation neither of them had been in before. She did not want Zoe to be scared, she wanted Zoe to trust her, and trust she would make the best decision. She knew that Zoe was the only person that was still here for her. Olivia did owe her at least as much as making her feel more at ease with the situation and try to make her understand that it was all going to be okay. Olivia dropped her head forward, sighing heavily and then brought her head back up and responded.

"I'm just hurt. I lost him Zoe, and I will never be able to get him back. He was my big brother, he was always there for me when I needed him. I'm sorry if I seem crazy right now, and I'm sorry that you have to be involved with this, but I promise I am going to fix this. I will fix it, I have to, if we are going to move on with our lives, I have to fix this."

"What are you going to do?" Zoe asked her not sure if she wanted an answer.

"I'm going to fix it, that's all."

"Okay, we will fix it," Zoe pulled Olivia to her, a palpable distance was between them even though their bodies were tightly embraced. Zoe pulled away first and reached for her purse.

"Listen, I will be back okay, I just have to go into the city and get a few things, and I am going to pick up my paycheck from the bar, then I will be back okay?"

Olivia nodded her head then replied, "Okay, I will wait here. When you get back though, I need to go see my parents. If I don't go drop in on them, they are going to think something is wrong with me and I don't need anyone thinking anything is wrong with me."

"Okay, sure," Zoe came closer to Olivia again, and planted a soft kiss beside her eye.

"This is all going to be okay, we will figure this out."

Again, Olivia nodded her head, and touched Zoe's smooth cheek. Zoe turned and headed towards the front door, turning back to Olivia with pleading eyes,

"Baby, do me a favour and just leave her alone today, okay? Please, just wait for me to get back and we can talk. We will get this worked out, but just leave it alone for a while, okay?"

Olivia felt slightly offended at Zoe's request, she got a sense that she did not trust her to be alone with Sophia, that angered her immediately. How could she not trust her? But as Zoe stood there looking at her, she pushed her anger deep within her belly where it had come from. She told herself Zoe was probably just concerned, that was all, Zoe was just concerned. So, she replied calmly and sincerely.

"Zoe, I'm going to fix this, I promise, I'm going to do whatever I need to do to fix this."

THIRTY - October 10, 2015

"I so knew it, I totally fricken knew it!" Rae leaned back in her chair, a smug grin on her face.

"Shut up, God Rae," Jill laughed at her response then continued, "It's no big deal, it's really not."

Jill slouched forward in her chair, both arms resting on the table and her fresh cup of coffee cradled in between both hands. Jill had agreed to meet Rae at their regular meet up spot, a quaint diner that was conveniently located in the middle of the station and Rae's hair salon. It was a spot they met up for lunch often, and since Jill had some time before Landon arrived at the station she figured she could go give her all the details of her date with Eric.

"I told you he was a great guy!" Rae boasted.

"Well then why the hell do you set him up with me when you could have snagged him?" Jill's head cocked to one side, awaiting her response.

Her shoulders shrugged casually, and she blew a curly strand of hair out of her eye before responding. "Nah, just not my type."

"Well I'm not gonna sit here and lie to you, he is great. He is gorgeous, he is settled. Never been married which is a huge plus, and from what I gathered so far, he is incredibly patient, seems to be sincere in what he wants in life. But what he might be looking for right now is just not where I am, but we had fun, that's all that matters."

"Listen I'm not gonna push you. You went out with him like you said you would. You guys had a good time from what I hear, I just hope you change your mind and go out with him again. I think you guys could be great together. He understands your job, and the commitment you have to it. His dad was a cop, so he knows what it is like to be with someone in law enforcement. I don't know Jilly Bean, I think you should just give it a chance, it may turn into something great whether you were wanting it to or not," Rae gave her a beaming smile, a line of perfectly straight white teeth exposed.

"Not gonna be pushy huh? That sounded pushy to me?"

"No, no, it's up to you, I'm glad you met him."

"And like I said he is great, and yeah, he has Vern beat that's for damn sure!"

Both women laughed at their ongoing inside joke. Rae stuffed a piece of chocolate chip muffin in her mouth. sliding it across the table and offered some to Jill. Jill grabbed a chunk, tore it in two and popped one half in her mouth. She quickly chewed and chased it down with a sip of coffee.

"Maybe soon, but in the meantime, I'm just going to focus on my work. I have this case going on right now and I have a feeling it's going to take a toll on me. I can't say I am really looking forward to it. Shit like this, that makes me really question if I should have taken a different career path."

"Are you kidding me Jill? You were born for this shit. You love it, I mean ya I cannot even imagine having to deal with some of the stuff you have to see, especially crap like this, but you're crazy to think you should be doing anything else. You're the one that has got to keep sick pricks like that off the street. You're exactly where you belong doing exactly what you were meant to be doing. But..." She paused momentarily.

"But what?"

"I just wish you wouldn't let your career be the most important thing, I know it's important, I get that, but I just want to see you leave more time for yourself. I want to see you have a full life all around, I don't like watching you engulf yourself in cop stuff, there is more to life you know."

A few stray muffin crumbs lay on the table, and Jill swept them away onto the floor with her hand, she pulled a napkin out of the holder and cleaned her fingers off and nodded her head.

"I know." Jill replied.

"Do you?"

"Yes, I do. I just want to focus on this case right now." Jill knew she was trying to justify herself, but Rae nodded in agreeance anyhow.

Jill continued trying to explain herself, "I just need to put my focus on this case, it's going to be brutal, long hours, and I really don't want to be sidetracked by anything. I can't afford the distractions, just not right now anyways."

"I get it Jill," Rae replied, just as Jill's phone dinged loudly. Jill glanced at the text and then threw her phone in her jacket pocket.

"I've got to get to the station, Landon's waiting on me, got to start attacking this one from all angles." Both women stood up from the small table and walked towards the door. Jill opened it and held it open as Rae walked through and Jill followed her outside into the warm sunshine. Rae made her way to the driver's side of her car exclaiming, "I bet you miss the crap out of Caleb right now hey?"

"More than you could possibly know, Rae." They waved a hand goodbye to each other, each hopping in their own cars. Jill sat behind her steering wheel, pulling her seatbelt over her shoulder.

The mention of his name was still burning in her ears. She glanced at herself in the rear-view mirror and spoke quietly to her reflection.

"Well, so much for not getting distracted, thanks a lot Rae, thanks a fucking lot."

THIRTY-ONE -October 10, 2015

Olivia paced back and forth on the wooden floor of the cabin. She did not know what to feel at this moment. Zoe surprised her by just giving Sophia food like that. She could not understand why she would do that, that was Olivia's choice not Zoe's. It was really eating at her and making Olivia question where Zoe's loyalties were. After this incident she was not certain they were with her, where they should be. Even though Zoe was continuously telling her that she was on her side and she wanted to help her seek the truth, parts of Olivia just felt like perhaps that was not true. Perhaps Zoe, like everyone else, were going to turn on her. The only person that never did was Marcus and he was gone forever. There was nothing she could do to bring him back. Olivia stopped dead in her tracks and turned to face the closed door of Sophia's room. There was nothing she could do to bring him back, but there was something she could do to obtain retribution for what happened to him. Oliva began to make her way to the door, but she stopped remembering what Zoe asked her before she left.

"Baby, do me a favour and just leave her alone today okay? Please just wait for me to get back and we can talk, we will get this worked out, but maybe leave it alone for awhile, okay?"

And again, the idea that Zoe did not trust her surfaced, and again she could feel herself fighting the anger that was rising from her belly. This was Olivia's idea, this was her plan, so why would Zoe tell her to stay away from Sophia? She was hoping it was just concern, and not wanting Olivia to get hurt, but something was gnawing at her. She stood still, just staring at the door, having an internal fight as to whether she should listen to Zoe. Trusting that she was just trying to protect her, or should she go in there and continue on with why they were there in the first place? How was she ever going to get to the truth if she just left Sophia sitting in there alone? How was Sophia ever going to know the severity of the situation if she just sat in there alone, wallowing in her self pity, while Olivia was out here being tormented by the fact that her brother's murderer was in the next room. The battle continued, and she was straining her mind for the right thing to do, she was being torn in two directions. Olivia was also feeling resentful now. Resentment of the fact that Zoe gave her those fucking sleeping pills, because now her mind was unclear. She should not have taken those damn drugs, now she could not focus. That was the very reason Olivia had decided to stop taking those useless Lithium pills, all they were doing were clouding her judgment and senses. They were not doing any good, except maybe appeasing her damn parents, making them think if Olivia just kept taking them, she could be normal. Well, she was normal, and she did not need fucking Lithium to prove it. So, she stopped, she knew she had to, she needed clarity, not drugs.

"God dammit," Olivia muttered under her breath. She knew what she wanted to do, what she needed to do. Zoe would understand, she would understand that Olivia just needed to get to the truth. The faster they got to the truth, the faster they could move on with their lives and the faster everyone would know Olivia was not crazy. Everyone would know the truth, and it would all be because of her. With that final thought, she made up her mind, she grabbed the door knob and walked into the room.

Sophia was sleeping, of course, because what else was she good for Olivia thought. The sight of her was making Olivia's blood boil in her veins. Why was she just sleeping? Why was she allowing her body to rest? She was supposed to be begging and pleading. She was supposed to be begging Olivia not to hurt her again. She was supposed to be telling her the truth, so why the fuck was she sleeping? The questions were swimming frantically in Olivia's head. No drugs, why did she take those damn drugs?

Olivia walked to an empty chair and she loudly scraped it across the floor setting it in front of the bed, Sophia's eyes opened, grogginess settled deep within them.

P a g e | 151

"Wake the fuck up!" Olivia barked as she watched Sophia. Sophia's eyes adjusted to the dim room and focused on Olivia's hateful glare. Olivia did not notice any emotion that she could recognize on Sophia's face, and again that angered her. To Olivia that only meant she was getting comfortable in her surroundings and Olivia's presence was not threatening to her anymore.

"I said wake the hell up!"

"I'm awake," Sophia responded sluggishly.

"I hope you enjoyed your breakfast," Olivia asked maliciously, pointing to the empty plate on the floor.

"Thank you." Sophia replied.

"No, don't thank me!" Olivia sprung from her chair and pulled Sophia roughly by her frail arm, "and sit up while I am fucking talking to you!"

Sophia seemed to try and shrink away from Olivia's grasp, and the familiar sense of gratification mixed with the fury she was currently feeling. Her grip tightened around her arm and when Sophia was sitting up as much as her shackled ankle would allow, Olivia roughly released her arm from her grips. Olivia's eyes bore into Sophia, not taking her gaze off of her as she returned to her seat. She studied Sophia's face, she was thrilled to see that she looked like hell. Her long dark hair was a tangled mess, and the paleness in her skin would deceive any strength that Sophia was trying to portray. Her lips were dry, no doubt dehydrated, from the limited amount of water she had been given, her eyes were hollow and emotionless. No longer was she the beautiful, fresh face woman that so easily convinced others of her innocence.

Sophia remained silent, averting her eyes from Olivia's. Olivia glanced at the bucket on the floor near the edge of the bed, she noticed a small amount of urine at the bottom. A devious grin spread across her face.

"I see you decided you were not too good to piss in a bucket."

Sophia's dry tongue was doing its best to moisten her equally dry lips before she answered Olivia.

"I really had no choice, did I?"

Olivia did not bother to answer an apparent rhetorical question.

"It's time we have a talk Sophia, enough of this bullshit, I am getting very tired of your games," Olivia did not want to waste anymore time on the idle chit chat she felt like they were having.

"I can't," the reply was barely audible to Olivia's ears. She cocked her head to the side, indicating she did not hear what Sophia just said.

"You need to speak up when I talk to you."

"I can't," Sophia's tone was decibels higher now.

"Can't what?" Olivia asked annoyed.

"Olivia, I can't tell you what you want me to tell you."

"Oh, sure you can, it's actually really simple Sophia. See I just need you to share with me what happened that night at your house. I just need you to tell me what you did to my brother, that's all. It's really very simple."

Sophia's head fell gently backwards, resting on the wall behind her. She brought her hand to her head and scratched her scalp with her fingers. She closed her eyes for a brief second then opened them again.

"It's not that simple, I cannot tell you what isn't true. Dammit Olivia, he died, just like Cat died…"

Olivia cut Sophia off with frustration.

"I don't give a shit about Cat, I could care less about Cat, for all I fucking know she deserved to die, I honestly do not care. She was just a worthless whore, just like you. I care about Marcus, I care why Marcus died, and I certainly care who killed him."

"It wasn't me!" Sophia said sternly.

Olivia stood up frantically from the chair, and kicked it out from under her, sending it flying across the wooden floor.

"WHY WON'T YOU JUST STOP LYING TO ME?" Olivia shouted, throwing her hands up in the air. "JUST STOP FUCKING LYING TO ME!"

Sophia was trying to adjust herself on the bed, the ankle cuff clinking against the footboard, she reached down and rubbed her ankle, her face grimaced in pain before she calmly responded to Olivia's outburst.

"Look Olivia, I can tell you anything you want to know about what happened between us in our marriage. You want me to tell you that we did not have a great marriage even though everyone thought we did? Yes, I can tell you that. You want me to tell you that Marcus was cheating on me with my best friend? Yes, I can tell you that. You want me to tell you that Marcus was abusive, that he hit me, he choked me, and he manipulated and controlled me? Well then yes, I can tell you that. But if you want me to tell you that I killed your brother, I can't Olivia. I can't, because I didn't."

Raw hatred coursed through her body for the woman sitting in front of her, spewing these atrocious lies about her brother. How dare she? How dare she sit here and try and tell her that Marcus was abusive, and controlling, as if somehow trying to justify what she had done. Olivia bounded towards Sophia and grabbed a fistful of her tangled hair, yanking her head back as forcefully as she could, hearing a gasp of pain escape from Sophia's throat. She was in control of Sophia once again.

"That is fucking it," Olivia seethed, spit filling the corners of her mouth. "That is it Sophia. I gave you a chance, I gave you several fucking chances to tell me the goddman truth. But you just don't get it do you? You think this is some sort of fucking game? You think I am messing with you? Well you're wrong you little bitch. I gave you a chance to tell me. You could have just told me the truth, and everything would have been fine, but no, you think this is a game. If you had just told me the truth instead of sitting here and spewing lies from that dirty fucking mouth of yours then none of this would be fucking happening. If you think you're going to tell me lies about my brother to try and make me feel sorry for you it isn't going to work!" Olivia pulled even harder on the chunk of hair she had in her strong, vengeful grasp, and revelled at the sound of Sophia's rapid breath, telling her to let go. "I will never feel sorry for you, you bitch. That's it, do you understand me? It's fucking over." Olivia gave one final yank, then she spit directly in Sophia's shocked, fear covered face. She swiftly released her hair causing Sophia to fall back on to the bed. Sophia began to cry and sob heavily as Olivia smirked with pleasure. She turned on her heels, reeling, absorbing every emotion she was feeling in that moment. She stormed through the door, slamming it behind her, she came to the centre of the room and stood statuesquely still. She allowed herself to feel every sensation, every emotion, her power was back, she was in control. Her tension began to subside as she unclenched her fists, completely unaware of the huge chunk of dark hair that fell to the floor, landing softly at her feet. She smiled to herself, feeling a level of clarity she had not felt in a long time.

"Yes, I am going to fix this, I now know how exactly I need to fix this."

THIRTY-TWO -October 10, 2015

"Shit do you think that Marcus's sister could be involved?" Trent asked Caleb.

"Ya, I do. I mean shit Trent, you heard the same conversation I did. Alex Preston was worried enough about it to call Isabelle, you heard what he said. Olivia Donovan has had it out for Sophia for a long time."

"Did Sophia ever say anything about her? I mean the chick sounds pretty fucking nuts, Sophia must have said something," Trent hit the signal light indicator then turned right at the set of lights. He glanced at Caleb quickly then brought his attention back to the road in front of him.

"No, during the investigation she did not really talk too much about her. She told me they were not close at all. She said that Olivia had lived with them for awhile but that was the extent of it. I mean shit, I think Sophia had a lot going on, Olivia Donovan was probably the furthest thing from her mind." Caleb answered Trent.

"Well, whatever their relationship, somehow she fuckin knows Caleb, she knows what happened, so we need to find her and fast," Trent was not even trying to hide the worry in his voice.

Caleb snapped back, "she thinks she knows something. She is pissed off, and by the sounds of it she has a hatred for Sophia that goes back a while. But we don't know what she knows, all he said was that she was convinced Sophia was involved."

Trent pulled into the parking lot of Last Call the shitty dive bar, that he had last seen Sophia. Caleb had originally asked Trent to go snoop around, but after hearing Alex's confession, Caleb knew he needed to be there with him.

"Jesus, what was she doing here in the first place, this place is a shit hole, so out of the way? Why would she come here goddammit?" Caleb unbuckled his seatbelt letting it slide roughly through his fingers, the metal buckle banging behind his head.

"This is my fault," guilt riddled Trent's voice. Caleb turned to him, while trying to fight with his own feelings of guilt.

"This isn't your bloody fault."

"I fucking fell asleep while I was supposed to be watching her, you trusted me to keep my eye on her, and I fell asleep, now she is gone. We don't know where the hell she is, we don't know who the hell has her, we don't know anything right now and ya, that is my fault."

Caleb was not going to lie to himself, he did have his moments of anger and resentment, wanting to cast all the blame on Trent. But he also knew in the years he and Trent had been friends and partners, he had yet to let him down. He knew he would never, ever intentionally do something that would jeopardize any aspect of his life. He knew he had asked a lot of Trent to watch her like he did. He also knew that Trent was horribly concerned about how things went down because he believed his actions in this whole fucking scenario were careless, knowing Caleb's feelings for Sophia. Trent was worried about losing his friendship with Caleb over this.

"We are going to find her, we are going to figure out what happened to her. This is not your fault and I need you to stop beating yourself up over this. We are going to get her back, and we are going to deal with this crazy bitch, Olivia."

"We don't know for sure she is involved yet, this could be just a coincidence that she talked to Alex at the same time. We don't know Olivia Donovan has anything to do with this yet." Trent did not believe his own words, but he was doing his best to play devils advocate.

"No, it all makes sense now, it's her. It was her, it was Olivia. Now, all we need to do is find her, because once we find her we find Sophia. And once Sophia is safe we will deal with her. She is obviously crazy, but she is too close to this, so we just have to find her and take care of Olivia." Caleb got out of the passenger side of Trent's truck, slamming the door behind him, leaving Trent sitting behind the wheel for a moment. As Caleb began to make his way across the cracked pavement Trent got out and followed after him.

The two men walked through the doors of the empty bar. It had just opened, and the bartender was putting down the last of the bar stools. He glanced at Caleb and Trent, the glare of the sunlight falling away with the door closing behind them. The bartender made his way behind the bar and began wiping it down. Caleb and Trent both took a seat on the stools in front of him.

"Morning, fellas, you're here early. What can I get ya?" He finished wiping the bar and tossed the damp rag in the small sink behind him.

"We are hoping you can help us out?" Caleb started the conversation. The bartender shrugged his scrawny shoulders.

"That depends I guess,"

Caleb pulled out his cell phone, a smiling Sophia filled the screen.

'Have you seen this woman?"

Caleb could feel his heart miss a beat. The familiar feeling of longing and guilt filled his chest. The bartender took a quick glance at his phone and shook his head, raising his eyebrows as he did.

"Nah, have not seen her, I wouldn't mind if I did though, she is a smoke show."

An urge to reach over the bar overwhelmed Caleb. Trent obvious to this, gave him a quick reassuring tap on the shoulder.

"You guys cops or something like that?" the bartender inquired with interest.

"Ya, something like that?" Trent answered him.

Caleb swiped his phone, bringing a picture he found of Olivia, it was an old picture he had taken directly from her Facebook page, a page which did not hold a lot of useful information. It was a deceiving picture, because without knowing it, one would think she was just a young beautiful woman enjoying a glass of red wine.

"What about her?" Caleb turned the phone to him again. The bartender grabbed the phone and studied her face, again a quick shake of his head. His greasy brown hair, falling into his eyes.

"Nope not ringing a bell, but again, damn. Why you looking for these two? Someone get killed or something?"

Caleb took a deep breath, again trying to intercept the urge to knock this guy out. He knew none of this was his fault, but the edge that Caleb was teetering on was making his patience nearly non-existent.

"Look, buddy, this is very important, are you sure you have not seen either of these women, I just need you to be sure."

He held his hands up in the air, backing away from the bar.

"I'm sure, trust me I would remember either one of those chicks. But I also have not been in this last week, I was out in Jacksonville, visiting my brother."

Trent and Caleb turned to each other, evidence of frustration settled between them.

"So, who else works here then?"

"It's usually just me and Zoe, but while I was gone, I had someone filling in for me, so Zoe did not have to work every day and night."

Caleb took out a pen and a small pad of paper from his back pocket, he flipped it open, wishing this guy had just told him this in the fucking first place.

He focused his attention back to the bartender, who was staring at him with quizzical eyes.

"What's your name man?"

Bartender frowned, "Why do you need to know my name? I don't have anything to do with whatever the fuck is going on here."

Caleb pressed his lips tightly together, this was just not the time, he thought. Trent jumped in quickly.

"Just tell us your name, you're not in any sort of trouble,"

"Fine, okay, it's Carl."

"Okay Carl, so this other bartender the one that you had filling in, I'm going to need his name. We are going to have to ask him a few questions as well," Caleb took over the questions again, jotting as he spoke.

"His name is Tommy, Tommy Dixon. Like I said he only was filling in while I was gone, A few shifts here and there, so I don't know if he will be any more help than I am." Carl's hands found their way into the pockets of his jeans.

"That's fine, but we will need a number for him if you have it," Trent asked.

Carl turned and grabbed his cell phone from behind him, and as he was scrolling for Tommy's number Caleb continued.

 "You can get Tommy at 310-555-3589."

Caleb jotted the number down quickly before it escaped his overloaded mind, then continued.

"And Zoe, you said the other bartender's name was?"

Carl nodded his head and gave a quick "Yup, Zoe Cardell."

"You say she is your other regular bartender, she worked most of the shifts while you were gone?"

"Ya, she would have been here most of the time, it's pretty much just us two, the owners don't come around much. They own a few other bars around LA, much nicer bars than this. So, if you ask me I don't blame them for not wanting to come in here, as you can see, it's a shit box, but it pays my bills and I ain't got to answer to anyone."

Caleb let Carl finish his useless ramble, then reverted his attention back to the topic at hand.

"When's Zoe gonna be on next?" Caleb adjusted himself on the hard bar stool.

"Uh, she took the weekend off, but I can grab her number for you if you can't wait till Monday."

Finally, Carl managed to volunteer something useful. He began scrolling through his phone again, just as the doors to the bar opened. Sunlight flooded in, almost blinding all the men as they turned their attention in that direction. The door shut, and Carl looked back at Trent and Caleb.

"Speak of the devil and she shall appear?" A clever smirk crossed his face. He then turned back towards the door and gave an abrupt wave.

"Hey, Zoe, come on over. You're the lucky girl these guys really need to talk to."

THIRTY – THREE - October 10, 2015

An emotional battle was happening in Zoe's mind, a battle of right and wrong, and she was desperately struggling. She felt like Olivia was slipping away from her, and it was happening very quickly. They had not known each other all that long, but she seemed so different now than the woman she met a few weeks ago. That woman she met was confident, and strong. She was tormented by her brother's death, yes, but she seemed very much put together. This Olivia that has started to surface in the last five days is not someone Zoe recognized, at all. But she was falling in love with her, had been since they day they met. Zoe knew she was falling hard for this girl, they seemed to understand one another. They were made from the same cloth, and they had spent every possible moment they could together. It all started to change the moment Sophia Donovan walked into that bar.

Zoe pulled up to a red light, her radio playing softly in the background, and her mind was somewhere adrift thinking about the situation that they were currently in. Zoe knew without a doubt they needed to figure something out, she had to convince Olivia that they needed to just do something. She was not sure what at this point, but they had to do something, because Zoe knew if this continued, it was going to lead down a very dangerous path that they could not come back from. Zoe wanted nothing more than for Olivia to get answers, she deserved those answers. But watching her over the last several days with Sophia, Zoe knew this was not the way. Sophia was adamant that she had nothing to do with it, but Olivia was not going to take that for an answer. Olivia wanted to hear what she wanted to hear, and it was starting to terrify Zoe that she was willing to do just about anything to get what she wanted.

Zoe was suddenly startled by a car horn honking behind her, she looked up and realized that she was so deeply lost in her thoughts she had not notice the light change to green. She pressed on the gas and continued down the road. She just wanted to go to the bar and grab her paycheck and get back to the cabin, so she could try talking to Olivia again. Olivia had said she knows what she needs to do to fix this before she left. Zoe was praying that meant she was going to do the right thing. She did say she was going to go and stop in at her parents. Maybe she was going to confide in them, maybe they could help her make the right decision. She hoped that was what she meant, but a nagging feeling in Zoe's chest made her come to an undeniable conclusion that was not at all what she meant.

Zoe's grip tightened on the steering wheel, feelings of shear confusion and torment overwhelmed her. She just wished there was something she could do to make this right, but the fact was she was involved way over her head without a way of steering the situation. It was her cabin that Olivia had taken Sophia to. It had been five days and she was fully aware of what was going on, so she would be an accomplice to all this, and that thought scared the shit out of her. Panic rose in her throat the more she allowed herself to think about it, to actually think about how deep she was involved in this. It was like her morality was being torn in two different directions. Olivia trusted in her, she knew that. She was the only person in Olivia's life that understood her. The look in her eyes this morning when she had woken up to find Zoe giving Sophia food would stick with Zoe for a long time. It was a look of defeat and betrayal, but the thing that worried Zoe so much more than that was the look of pure hatred.

Zoe pulled into the parking lot of the bar, and she put her car into park. She glanced at the clock on her dashboard and it read 11:04 back to her in bright green digits. She knew Carl would have just gotten everything opened up. She was dreading having to go in there because Zoe knew he was going to want to chat her ear off, and right now that is the last thing she wanted or needed. She did a quick scan of the parking lot and there was only one truck, besides hers, Zoe hoped that there was someone inside that could distract

Carl's attention, so she did not feel trapped to have to sit and have a conversation with him. She was not even certain if she was going to be able to maintain a calmness. She needed to act normal and normal was the furthest thing from her mind right now. Zoe took a few more moments and tried to steady her nerves, she tried her best to put herself in a midframe of innocence. She tried to summon her normal, confident, everyday Zoe vibe, but it was hard, because the old Zoe was lost now, lost in the chaos of Olivia Donovan. Finally, she opened her car door and she made her way to the front entrance of the bar. She stopped briefly, needing one more second, then walked inside. The bar was quiet, of course it had just opened, but there were two men sitting at the bar, Carl looked to be deep in conversation with them. It did not surprise her though, most days there was usually one or two who were ready to start their day of drowning themselves in whiskey and beer as soon as the bar opened. Zoe noticed immediately that these two men did not strike her as that type though, both were very handsome and nicely dressed. The door closed behind her and all three of them turned to face her, and Carl gave her a quick wave and said something Zoe was not expecting.

"Speak of the devil and she shall appear." Zoe was unsure what he was referring to, but she gave a quick wave in response. Carl then continued.

"Hey, Zoe, come on over. You're the lucky girl these guys really need to talk to."

Zoe's heart skipped a beat, and a lump formed in her throat, she had no idea who these men were, but she knew that if someone was looking to talk to her it could not be good. She braced herself and allowed a smile to spread across her face as she cautiously approached all three men at the bar. The blonde haired one stood up and came to meet her with his hand extended, Zoe reached for his hand, certain he was going to feel the dampness of her palm.

"Hey Zoe, how's it going?"

"Good." A simple reply.

"Good, good. Listen we were just chatting with Carl here, and we just had some questions about a couple people that were possibly here in the last week or so. Carl said you were on shift most of the time last week, so we are hoping you can recognize some pictures," the man, whom she did not get his name handed her his phone, so she could take a look at the first picture. She took it from him, and it was like her lungs were in a vice. She could feel her chest tighten at the image in front of her. It was Sophia, the woman that was shackled to a bed at her family's cabin.

Stay calm Zoe, just stay calm was the only thing that Zoe could hear in her mind at the moment. She continued to study the picture hoping her expression was not betraying her. She slowly shook her head back and forth as she handed the man back his phone trying to steady a shaking hand.

"Sorry, she does not look familiar."

"Okay no problem, but what about her?" the man swiped his screen quickly and handed it back to her again. She took it and this time the face looking back at her was Olivia's. To say panic was gripping her would be an understatement. Bile rose in her throat, a hot burning sensation that was sure to suffocate her at any moment. She swallowed hard and was trying desperately to defy the intense urge to turn and run, just run away. But she did her best to push it all away, to ignore it all. Again, she shook her head and nervously blew a stray hair out of her eye as she handed him his phone back. Uneasiness surrounded her, all three men were just standing there staring at her, like they all knew her secret, like they knew she was lying to them.

"I'm sorry I don't recognize either of them, is there some sort of problem?" Zoe inquired casually, trying to undertake the role of a concerned citizen.

The man put his phone in his pocket and Zoe could see a look of displeasure and frustration spread across his features. She wanted to ask him who he was, but she also wanted to say and know as little as possible.

"No, there is no problem, not for you to worry about. We are just looking for these two women, but we will follow up with the other bartender and see if he has seen them. If you don't recognize them you don't need to worry about anything."

Zoe's legs were shaking wildly, it felt like they would betray her at any moment. She wanted to turn and run so much.

"I'm sorry I could not be of more help, I see a few faces in a week here but to be honest neither of those women look like the type that would even come into a place like this," she half joked.

"That's what I said," Carl jumped in. "If those two were in here, why did it have to be when I am not here, just my flippen luck."

Now the attention turned to Carl, standing behind the bar. She watched as the other man, with the dark salt and pepper hair shake his head at Carl. That also did not surprise Zoe, because Carl was a real piece of work, and she wanted him to just shut up, so these men would leave. So, she could leave and get back to Olivia.

The blonde man pulled out his small notepad and he jotted something down, he ripped the piece of paper out of the book and he handed it to Zoe. She took it from him and all it said was Caleb and a phone number. So now she knew his name.

"Listen, I want to thank you for your time, but if you can think of anything or if you happen to recall seeing these women in your bar at all in the last little while, I want you to just give me a call okay? That goes for you too," He turned to Carl.

"No problem man," Carl replied unphased at the gravity of the situation.

"Of course! Again, I'm sorry I could not help," Zoe was fidgeting, the paper crumpling between her fingers. She noticed the man named Caleb observe that, she immediately steadied them. He smiled at her, and the other man stood up and they both headed towards the door. Zoe and Carl both stood watching after them. Caleb turned around one more time before they went through the doors and repeated.

"Anything, if you can think of anything, please don't hesitate to call." And with that they were gone, the doors closing them back into the dark, musty bar.

Zoe let a breath release from her constricted lungs, she shrugged at Carl, he looked at her with no indicators of suspicion.

"Well, that was fucking weird," he exclaimed.

"Ya, tell me about it, hey I'm actually just here to grab my check, I've got a crazy day and gotta get running," A hurried tone was behind her request, a crazy day, again another understatement.

"Yup got it right in here," he replied as he walked into the tiny office right off the back of the bar. Zoe waited drumming her fingers on the bar, impatience enveloping her. He came back with an envelope and handed it to her.

"Here you go."

Zoe snatched it from his hands in one quick hurried motion, and he pulled his hand back in reaction.

"Holy, a little grabby, are we?"

Zoe laughed nervously, trying to control her nerves. "Ya, sorry just in a rush, I got a bunch of stuff to do today."

Carl returned her laugh with his own chuckle.

"I'm just messing with ya, you know that."

Zoe gave me him a quick smack in the arm, a playful action that was not uncommon with them, but Carl's smile turned straight face.

"You okay Zo, you seem a little, I don't know, stressed or something?"

"Stressed? No, I'm totally fine. Just got to get going, busy day like I said," she did her best to sound reassuring, and normal. She gave him a quick wave, "Have a good day today, I'm gonna run."

"You too, take it easy, I will see you back on Monday?"

"Yup, see you on Monday," Zoe headed towards the door and Carl yelled after her before she left. She turned her attention back to him.

"By the way, when you gonna bring that new girlfriend of yours around here, so I can spill all your juicy little secrets to her?"

Carl did not realize how loaded that comment was, in fact, he had no idea how many secrets Zoe actually now had, only thing was there was nothing to spill because Olivia knew it all. She was the secret now. Zoe passed off his question to her with a wave of the hand as she turned and headed through the doors, yelling behind her.

"Ya, ya, I'll see you Monday Carl."

THIRTY – FOUR - October 10, 2015

"Hey! Good to see ya!" Luke Nolan opened the door to his apartment and greeted Caleb with a hug.

"You too, wish it was under better circumstances though," Caleb replied as he pulled away from Luke and walked into the front entrance of his apartment, Trent following behind.

Luke closed the door and the three men walked into his large living room.

"I take it nothing yet?" Luke asked.

Caleb walked over to the floor to ceiling windows and looked down on the city below. He turned back to Luke and replied.

"Well, no I wouldn't say that exactly. We got some interesting information from Alex Preston this morning. Well, I should say Isabelle has some interesting information." Caleb corrected his response.

"Yup, I think we know who we are looking for but now we just need to figure out where the hell we start looking?" Trent finished.

"So? Who are we looking for?" Luke anxiously asked.

"Olivia Donovan!" Caleb exclaimed.

Luke had to take a moment to think, and then it came to him.

"Marcus's sister?"

"Yup, got some info. Turns out she might be a little off her rocker to say the least. According to Alex, Olivia has had a hate on for her sister-in-law since the beginning. But now she is convinced that

Sophia had something to do with her brother's death, she is on a mission to prove it." Caleb walked to the leather couch and plopped himself down.

"Ah shit!" Luke sighed, "That is not fucking good!"

"No, it's not, we need to find her and fast." Trent said as he took off his jacket and tossed it on the chair in the corner of the room.

Luke got up and walked to his computers and pressed some buttons. Caleb watched him, having no idea what he was doing, that was Luke's area of expertise. He needed any information Luke may have gotten to help them out.

"Well, I got her last ping here," Luke pointed to his screen and both Caleb and Trent walked over to see where he was pointing at.

"Crest Park?" Caleb asked confused.

"Ya, Crest Park, that is the last location it has pinged and that was on Tuesday, nothing since."

"Shit, that's a big area out there, I mean what the hell was she doing out there?" Caleb ran his hand roughly through his hair.

"I don't think she was out there alone!" Trent offered.

"The only thing I can think of is Lake Arrowhead, Crest Park is on the way there, I don't know where else. I mean my dad had a place up there when we were kids, and we would always stop at Crest Park for piss breaks, but who knows? That is all the info I have!" Luke explained.

"Okay," Caleb said calmly. "It's okay, you did good, we got something, we got a direction at least."

"We gotta head out there then, that's our best clue right now." Trent said hurriedly, grabbing his coat from the chair.

"Ya, we do, but I need to stop and talk to Isabelle before we go. I told her I would keep her in the loop about everything."

"Can't you just call her?" Trent asked as he put his arms into his sleeves.

"No, I need to stop on the way. She is scared senseless right now and this is our best lead. I need to just stop and see her and do what I can to make her feel at ease that we have this under control."

Both Trent and Luke nodded in unison, understanding Caleb's thinking.

"Let me know what else I can do to help, it would be so much easier if that place had cameras or something."

"That bar is a dive, they don't have cameras, we checked." Trent replied annoyed, knowing that would have helped tremendously.

"I do need you to do something else for me Luke," Caleb turned back to him.

"Anything."

"There is something off for us about that girl at the bar, Zoe, she seemed to nervous, like she knew something. I have no idea what, but Trent and I were discussing on the way here that something just seems off. She was there picking up her check and won't be back in until Monday. I'm gonna need you to do some digging for me okay? Maybe it's nothing, but just do a quick check. Caleb walked over to his desk, grabbed a post it notes and jotted down her full name.

"Zoe Cardell, that's her full name. Just dig up what you can." Caleb patted Luke on the shoulder and smiled at him. Then he and Trent made their way to the front door.

"You guys will find her, I know you will," Luke's voice sounded more reassuring then he felt.

Trent opened the door and Caleb followed him through, he turned back to Luke one more time.

"Your damn right we will Luke, you're damn right."

THIRTY – FIVE - October 10, 2015

She was going to die here! She was going to die at the hands of Olivia Donovan. Sophia was not even sure exactly how long she had been chained to this bed, but she had an urgent realization that this was going to be it. She could not tell Olivia anything, there was no way in hell she was going to tell her what actually happened to Marcus, she had just proved how unpredictable and crazy she actually was. As she was lying there her mind found its way to a dark corner of Sophia's memories, to the day that Marcus had told Olivia she was going to have to move out of Marcus and Sophia's place.

"Olivia I really hate to do this, but I think it's time you found somewhere else to stay." Sophia stood at the island of her large kitchen as she watched Marcus calmly speak to his sister.

"You think it's time?" Olivia hissed, staring at Sophia as she said it.

Marcus sighed heavily and continued, "Olivia come on, you know that is not how it is, Sophia has nothing to do with this."

"Ya, like I will fucking buy that Marcus. You know she hates me being here."

"That is not true Olivia," Sophia interjected, and Olivia glared at her with burning daggers.

"Shut the fuck up Sophia, I wasn't speaking to you."

"Hey!" Marcus's voice raised several decibels and echoed throughout the room. "Olivia you will not speak to my wife like that in my home, do you understand?"

Olivia huffed with annoyance oblivious to the fact that her brother was not taking her side this time. Sophia knew that Olivia had heard their many arguments about Olivia being there, and typically up until now, Marcus did take her side, but finally he was putting his foot down and asking her to leave.

"Fine! I will leave but only because you are asking me to." Olivia stuck a finger in her brother's chest as she walked past him towards the front entrance. "But don't sit here and pretend this was your decision Marcus, I know damn well who's doing this is."

Marcus turned and watched her head out of the kitchen, Sophia knew he was feeling horrible and she also knew that he was probably going to resent her forever if there was a rift between him and his sister after this. But she also knew she could not live another day with her under their roof, she was moody, emotional and insanely disrespectful.

"Olivia, please hold on!" Marcus followed after her. Olivia stopped with a hopeful look on her face. "I don't want you to leave angry okay, this does not have to be a bad thing."

Disbelief washed across Olivia's face.

"Marcus, you are kicking me out of your house, you know I have no where to go. I don't have a job right now, you know that I really need you right now and you're still asking me to go. You would have never done this before, not before her." A disgusted look was shot back to Sophia standing in the kitchen. Sophia could not believe what she was hearing come out of Olivia's mouth.

"Come on Olivia, you're perfectly capable of getting out there and getting a job, you know that's just an excuse."

Marcus gave Sophia a stern look, advising her to just stay out of it, as she was going to make it worse, but for Olivia she already did.

"See! Marcus, you're letting this manipulating bitch control your fucking life, and the sad thing is I have no choice but to sit back and watch it happen."

"Enough! Olivia, that is enough from you. Now go, get out, go to Mom and Dad's. I don't know but right now you are not welcome here, I told you, you will not speak to my wife like that, so go, take a breather." Marcus had both his hands planted on his hips now, his stance he often took before the anger would take completely over.

Olivia had tears forming in her eyes at her brother's outburst, and she stood staring at him perhaps waiting for an apology, but Sophia knew better than anyone, there were no apologies from him until the anger passed. But she was surprised as she watched them, she could see that Marcus's stance was beginning to soften at the realization that he hurt her feelings. He dropped his head and his arms fell to his side, he glanced back up seriously at his sister.

"I'm sorry Liv."

"No you're not, don't lie to me."

"Olivia, maybe it's a good idea to go back to Dr. Forsythe." The softness returned to his voice, and as soon as the words were out, Olivia recoiled with disbelief that her brother would bring that up.

"Unbelievable Marcus, you too? When are you guys going to fucking leave it alone, I am fine goddammit. I don't need to keep seeing that fucking quack, I am just fucking fine." She swung heavy on her heels, reached for an expensive vase, which held a bouquet of lilies and smashed it on the floor before she grabbed her purse and swung the front door open. She turned with vengeance over her shoulder and shouted loudly, *"I'll come back for my fucking things when she isn't fucking here."* And with that the door slammed behind her so hard, the walls vibrated.

Sophia was shocked. She had definitely seen Olivia have her outbursts but never at her brother. But she had never heard of this Dr. Forsythe, that was something Marcus had never mentioned before. She watched him closely and remained quiet, not wanting to interrupt this thought. She felt very nervous what his reaction was going to be now, and she braced herself at the possibility that he was going to be angry at her. He slowly turned around and walked back to the island, and he walked slowly up to her and pulled her towards him, embracing her in a hug. Her head was nuzzled into his strong chest, and he kissed the top of her head.

"I'm sorry about that Sophia, you should not have had to see that."

"It's okay, I'm the one that wanted her to leave," She brought her head back and tilted her head up so that she was looking directly at her husband. She could see the strain behind his eyes over what he just had to do.

"There's just a little more to Olivia that most people don't know, that's all." Marcus confessed.

Sophia nodded her head, understanding what he may have meant, but not pushing for further clarification.

"Dr. Forsythe is her therapist. She has been seeing him off and on since she was a teenager. At times she does really well, but when she is not seeing him, and things don't go exactly as she plans them, then it can really throw off her balance, it can be rough. It's been a very complicated time with her, with her disorder, so it worries me when I see her like this." Marcus closed his eyes for a moment, then he pulled away from Sophia and walked to the fridge and pulled out a bottle of water. Sophia stood where he left her and decided to ask.

"What's wrong with her Marcus?"

Marcus opened his bottle of water and took a sip before he answered.

"She was diagnosed Bipolar when she was 17 and trust me, it has been a struggle since. But she is good, she is really good when she is seeing her therapist, and when she stays focused on her family. I have seen her be brilliant and confident and almost forget the demons that she is battling."

Sophia looked at her husband as he explained his sister's issues, and guilt instantly flooded her conscience. She admitted to herself that she felt bad for Olivia, she did not know she had been battling this for so long. She was not sure why Marcus never told her about it, it could have definitely helped her in understanding where Olivia was coming from. Although Bipolar or not, Sophia could not understand why Olivia did not like her. The only thing she could seem to think was that in her eyes, Sophia was taking her brother from her. Sophia also had another question dawn on her, but it was a thought she knew she could not voice out loud, and that was if Olivia was suffering from this, was Marcus too? Was that why he could so easily be taken over by anger with her, and how in the blink of an eye she would be face to face with a man she did not recognize. She questioned it, but then she pushed it out of her mind and turned her attention back to Olivia.

"I'm sorry Marcus, I did not know."

"Well why would you? It's not something my family likes to talk about, but her behaviour lately just has me worried about her. I'm worried she has stopped taking her meds again," Marcus planted both hands on the island, and Sophia could see the worry in his eyes.

"Again? Does she stop a lot?"

Marcus shook his head slowly back and forth and replied.

"No, not a lot but she has. She takes them, and she feels good, she feels normal and back to life, and her mind tries convincing her that she is better, she does not need the drugs, so she stops and…" there was a pause in the air.

"And what happens? What happens if she stops taking her meds?" Sophia asked in between the silence.

"It's just not good, that is all I can really say is, it's just not good at all."

Sophia was jolted back to the hell she was currently in. It made a little bit more sense now, recalling that conversation she had with Marcus. Olivia was going crazy, and Sophia was certain she now knew why. She knew Olivia had it out for her from the beginning and she knew Olivia was always looking for someone to blame for her brother's death. But Sophia honestly thought she moved past the hate and the blame. She remembered the day at the courthouse, standing outside when Caleb was giving the press conference, revealing the findings of the case. Sophia remembered how she felt when Bruce, Adele and Olivia arrived. Sophia remembered feeling on such edge that Olivia was going to make a scene again, but she hadn't. She had walked up to her and hugged her and apologized for her actions. Why? Sophia wondered to herself, why would she do that? Just to turn around and do this to her?

Sophia sat up slowly in her bed, careful not to move her head to quickly. Her head was throbbing, and her scalp was so terribly sore from where Olivia had pulled her hair. Everyday she was here she felt weaker, and weaker. The fact that Olivia was this enraged over the fact that she was given food, only clarified Olivia's madness and desire to harm Sophia. She sat her back against the wall, with her elbow propped up on her knee, allowing her head to rest in her hand. She wanted to cry but she had no strength or energy, she did not even think she had any tears left to cry.

"What am I going to do?" She whispered to herself in the empty room. She felt alone in the house, but she knew Olivia was still out there. She could hear her moving across the wooden floor every so often, she wanted nothing more than for her to just leave. Just leave her alone, that is all Sophia wanted right now.

Sophia was then startled by the sound of a car door slamming outside, her heart skipped a beat in hope, but then she realized it was the other girl, the one named Zoe. It was Olivia's girlfriend. That in itself had shocked Sophia, because in the years that she knew Olivia, she never knew her to be interested in women. But if she was off of her meds right now that could be part of it. That could explain so much of this. Sophia cocked her head to one side and listened. She heard the door creek open and she could here Olivia first.

"Finally! Zoe what took you so long?"

Faintly but still audibly Sophia heard Zoe answer.

"I'm sorry Liv, I went as fast as I could, but baby listen to me…"

Then her voice mumbled, and Sophia strained to hear the rest but she had lowered her voice. Sophia shifted and moved forward off the bed to get as close to the door as she could without actually getting off of the bed. But still only quiet mumbles. Then again, she heard Olivia.

"Are you sure? Zoe are you sure? Who are they?" Olivia's voice sounded panicked now.

"I don't know Liv, but we have to do something," Sophia heard Zoe's voice louder this time.

The voices muffled again for a moment and then very clearly, she heard Olivia.

"I have to go." Followed by a high-pitched Zoe.

"Olivia! Olivia! Goddammit Olivia!" Then the door closed.

Sophia sat quietly and waited for the next sound, and that was the car door outside. She heard it slam and that was followed by the engine coming to life. She heard the engine rev highly and the sound of the tires, as they spun out on the gravel, trying to grab traction as Olivia sped away from the house. Sophia could hear her own heartbeat in the silence, she placed her hand on her chest hoping to quiet it. She scooted back on the bed and sat with her legs stretched out in front of her, the shackle still rubbing on her ankle. She listened for Zoe on the other side of the door, she could hear her walking and she could see a soft shadow emit from under the door. She knew she was standing there, but she did not know what she was doing. It felt like an eternity, but finally, the door to her room slowly creaked open, and Zoe was there. Their eyes met, and Sophia could see faintly the tears that were forming in Zoe's tired, and worn eyes. Zoe stood frozen in the doorway, looking defeated and scared. Sophia's gaze was torn away from Zoe's as she looked down and saw in her hand, a large clump of hair that not long-ago Olivia fiercely ripped from her head. Sophia studied it in her hand for a few seconds, not sure what to say, if anything at all. Her eyes found their way back to Zoe's, the two-woman looked at each other, and in that moment, Sophia knew this was her only chance, this red headed lady was her only chance of making this out alive.

THIRTY – SIX - October 10, 2015

Olivia's delicate hands tightened on the steering wheel, her knuckles white and strained, her anxiety peaked to its maximum and her nerves were shaken to the core. She had been watching the news daily and waiting for some news that Sophia Donovan was missing, but there had been nothing. She had not heard a single word back from that detective Keller since she went to her asking for her help. She was pretty sure she was not aware of what was happening because Olivia would have been one of the people Jill Keller contacted. So, who the hell were these two men that Zoe was talking about? Who the hell was snooping around the bar looking for her and for Sophia? If it was news that Sophia was missing, Olivia knew it would be all over the damn tv and newsfeeds, especially being quite close to what happened to Marcus. It unnerved Olivia knowing that someone was now out looking for her, but also at the same time it also excited her. She knew that she was running out of time to get the truth out of Sophia, but that was okay because she knew if she did not get what she wanted she was ready to do what she had been wanting to do for a very long time. And she knew soon people were going to know the truth and maybe stop thinking Olivia was just being crazy.

Olivia turned at the last stop sign onto her parent's street, she approached the house and pulled into the driveway. Bruce and Adele's home were a small ranch style on the corner, with white gate fencing surrounding the backyard. This was her childhood home since they had moved here from Seattle when she was 10. This is where all her memories were formed, good and bad, and this was where her parents still lived. This was the last place she wanted to be right now, but she knew if she did not stop in and see them they were going to bug her relentlessly, asking her if everything was okay, asking her if she was okay. She did not need that distraction right now, especially knowing now that there were two men out looking for her. She had to finish this and soon. She also needed her parents help. Well her dad's help even though they were unaware, they would have a part in bringing justice to Marcus once and for all. Oliva's emotions were all over the map right now, she was scared, nervous, excited and filled with an adrenaline she had never experienced before. She knew she had to remain calm, her parents had already been on her case lately about making sure she was remaining on her medications and making sure she was going to start seeing a therapist again. She was getting fucking tired of it, but after tonight that was all going to end. After tonight they would all know the truth about Sophia Donovan. She adjusted the rear-view mirror down to her eye level and examined herself in the mirror. She had to admit she looked exhausted, she hoped her parents did not pick up on that. She gave her cheeks a few quick pinches to blushen them softly, and she fingered her hair, taming the wild pieces. Good enough she thought to herself and she reached for her purse on the passenger seat and opened the door.

She approached the front door and inhaled a deep breath before she reached for the handle, she braced herself, and tried to summon all of her inner strength to remain calm and not let her parents incessant concern and worry over her get to her too much. She reached for the door but even before her hand could make contact the door swung open and her mother stood on the other side, a look of relief washed across her features.

"Olivia! I have been trying to call you!" Adele's big brown eyes were looking softly at her daughter.

"Mom! I'm fine, I don't have to talk to you every single day," Olivia walked into the house and right past her mother. She threw her purse down on the floor by the front closet and turned back to her mother who was closing the door.

"I know Liv, but you know how I worry about you."

Olivia's eyes nearly rolled into the back of her head as she walked away from her mother and into the living room. Her father, Bruce, was reclined in his favorite chair, a newspaper sprawled out in his hands.

"Livy! Your mom has been quite worried about you, you know. It does not take much to give her a quick call." His glasses were perched on the bridge of his nose, his eyes gazing up at her over the brim of the paper.

"Jesus Dad, I have been busy."

Adele came into the living room, pulling her pink cardigan around her midsection. She walked to the couch and took a seat, taking her cup of tea off of the coffee table and taking a small sip.

"What have you been doing?" Adele tried to sound as non-prying as possible.

Olivia threw herself down on a chair, directly across from both of her parents, both of them watching her and waiting for her to answer.

"Not much, I have just been busy."

"With her?" Adele clearly not wanting to say Zoe's name.

"You mean Zoe, Mom? She has a fucking name, Jesus."

The newspaper in Bruce's hands was folded briskly and tossed onto the end table beside him.

"Olivia! You do not speak that way in this house, I have told you that! Do not disrespect your mother in that way."

Again, Olivia's eyes shifted in their sockets and she fell back into the chair further, she could feel the frustration and the anger at her parents starting to boil.

"To answer your question Mom, ya, I have been spending time with Zoe, lots of time actually."

Adele nodded her head softly.

"Will we get to meet her soon?"

Olivia scoffed, "Are you kidding me?"

Bruce pushed the foot rest of his recliner in so he was now in a full upright sitting position. He took his glasses off his face and rubbed his temples and responded to his daughter calmly.

"She is just asking you a question Olivia, you do not need to get so sarcastic. You have been seeing this Zoe woman, for a little bit now, and your Mother just wants to know when you are going to bring her home, so we can meet her?"

Olivia turned to her dad and shook her head.

"Why would I bring her here to meet you guys? You're just going to judge her like you judge me. You don't agree with me seeing another woman, so why in the hell would I put her through that?"

A look of shock enveloped Adele, "We don't judge you Liv, I would never judge you like that. I was surprised, yes, but that is only because I did not know you were interested in girls, but I would not judge you for it. I would also not judge her for it."

"Bullshit Mom!"

"Goddammit Olivia!" Bruce's calmness was obviously starting to wear short.

"Okay, okay let's just change the subject," Adele uncomfortably interjected. It was clear to everyone in the room she was doing her best not to upset her daughter. Adele smiled softly at Olivia and shifted to another topic.

"How have you been feeling lately? Good?"

Olivia knew exactly what she meant by that. She could feel her skin begin to crawl at the notion that her mother was going to have the nerve to bring this up already. She just got in the damn door.

"Yes Mom, I have been good, I have been great actually."

A smile of relief crossed Adele's face, before she replied.

"Good, I am so glad to hear that."

Bruce Donovan was not so eager to walk on the eggshells that his wife always did when it came to his daughter, he always just wanted to be upfront, so he asked.

"Have you found a new doctor you can work with?"

"Dad! I am fine, I don't need to keep seeing damn doctors. I am good, in fact I am probably the best I have been in awhile, things are looking up Dad, finally."

"So, the meds are good then, the doses?"

Olivia did not answer her father, she just closed her eyes, trying to summon the strength to remain calm.

"Livy, I just want to make sure you are okay? I just want to make sure that you're staying on the meds, because you know how much they help you. And honey, since Marcus, you have really been struggling…" Adele's tender voice was cut short by Olivia, now heavily agitated at the mention of Marcus.

"Mother!" Olivia's eyes were dark as she penetrated her mothers stare. "I don't know how many times we have to go through this. I don't know what I have to say to you two to make you understand that I am not being emotional, I am not over reacting, and I am not CRAZY!" Olivia's voiced raised loudly on the word crazy.

"We do not think you are crazy, neither one of us, you know that is not true…" This time it was Bruce who was interrupted.

"God! Just oh my God," Olivia tried her best, but pure frustration at her parent's blatant denial of how they felt about her, took over her calmness. She stood quickly from her chair and paced back and forth, her glare switching between both of her parents as she continued her rant. "You both think I am crazy. Why else would you keep harassing me to find a new doctor? Why else would you just keep making sure I am on my precious meds? Did either one of you stop to fucking think that maybe I am not as crazy as you think I am, that maybe I know things… I know things that you don't. You just didn't want to hear me when I told you both that I did not trust Sophia, she was no good, and she was going to hurt Marcus. You did not want to listen to me, and now look. Your son is fucking dead!"

Bruce stood from his chair too, anger was evident on his face now, but Olivia did not care. They needed to hear it. Bruce made a step towards his daughter and warned her.

"Enough Olivia, we have been through this. We know what happened to Marcus, you need to let this anger go. I know you did not like Sophia, but enough Olivia, it is over, you need to move on."

Olivia raised a finger in the air, indicating she was not finished and she ignored her father's statement. To Bruce and Adele it looked like perhaps Olivia was just taking a breather, trying to calm herself like she was taught to do in situations like this. They both just stood watching her. Olivia turned and ran out of the living room and she headed to the stairs, sprinting quickly up them.

Adele and Bruce turned to look at each other, neither one quite sure what too say, or not to sure what was really happening in the moment.

"She is just upset, maybe she just needed a moment."

Bruce cocked his head and the corner of his mouth perked at his wife, she was always so loving and calm. Bruce walked through the living room and stood at the bottom of the stairs and yelled up.

"Olivia! Come back down here, we are not done talking," there was silence, so he hollered again. "Olivia!" Then he could hear her coming and she bounded back down the stairs. He backed away slightly giving her space, walking back into the living room to stand near his wife, who was still seated on the couch. Olivia's hand held onto the bannister of the stairs, and her eyes were still very dark with rage. She pointed her finger now at both of her parents and she continued on with her speech.

"Your son is dead because of her, but pretty soon you will know the truth, because I am going to get it from her."

"Honey, what are you talking about? Olivia you're scaring me, are you sure you are okay?" Adele was clearly confused and more worried than when Olivia arrived.

"Mom, just you wait, you're not going to think I am so crazy anymore. I am going to prove it to you all. I am going to prove to you that Sophia Donovan murdered your son, and then soon, she will be known as the crazy one, not me. Nobody will ever think I am crazy ever fucking again." With that Olivia stormed quickly out the front door, slamming it behind her. Bruce stood unable to move, stunned how quickly his daughter escalated this time. Adele looked to her husband now for assurance, that it was going to be okay. They looked at each other for a moment, and a look of dread washed over Bruce Donovan's face, and the only words he uttered before he turned and ran up the stairs were, "Oh Christ Olivia, please tell me you didn't."

THIRTY – SEVEN - October 10, 2015

Caleb followed Isabelle into her living room, and he could tell her body was wracked with stress and an overwhelming amount of worry. He hated to see her like this, it was heartbreaking. He hoped it was all going to be over soon.

"We got a little bit of a lead."

Isabelle hugged her arms tightly and a glimmer of hope sparkled in her eyes.

"What kind of lead?" she asked.

"Her cell phone, we were able to find out the last place it was pinged."

"Oh, thank God, where was it?" she asked.

"A tower near Crest Park."

"Crest Park? I don't… where is that?" she was confused.

"It's about an hour from here, towards Lake Arrowhead," he replied bluntly.

Still confused, Isabelle asked further.

"I don't understand, why would she be there? Why Lake Arrowhead?"

"Isabelle, we don't know yet. All we know is that is the last place her cell phone was transmitted. That was last Tuesday and there has been nothing since. Do you know if maybe the Donovan's have a place there or something?" Caleb remained patient.

Isabelle shook her head slowly back and forth, Caleb could see she was searching her memory though for some indicator of what would be in Lake Arrowhead.

"No, not that I can recall. I don't remember Sophia ever saying they had a place out there. I mean Marcus's parents and Olivia once in awhile would come to Marcus and Sophia's beach house but no, I don't recall anyone ever saying anything about a place out there."

Caleb nodded his head, fully expecting that answer. Isabelle gasped and her hand found its way to cover her mouth.

"Oh God!"

"What is it Isabelle?" He wondered if she just remembered something and his heart nearly jumped out of his chest.

"Caleb," tears were forming pools in her eyes now. "What if? What if she is dead?"

Caleb quickly reached for Isabelle and pulled her towards him, "Isabelle, no, she is not dead, do you hear me."

She sobbed into his chest and Caleb rubbed her hair softly allowing her to grieve a moment for her missing daughter. Pushing her away from him, he held her at arms length and he looked directly into her red eyes.

"She is not dead."

"How do you know that, why is that the last place? All the way out there? What if she is out there, lying in the woods somewhere all alone."

Caleb shook her very gently and he refocused her attention back to him.

"You listen to me Isabelle, we are going to find her, do you hear me? She is not dead…"

"Caleb, it's been five days, I am scared out of my mind, I cannot bear the thought of losing her. I can't! But why? Why is she out there? What if somebody hurt my baby, and left her out there to rot, all alone, with nobody, with nothing…" Isabelle was allowing the hysteria to take over, and every worst-case scenario entered her mind. The thought of any of it possibly being true was too much for her to take. Her body started to tremble, and Caleb pulled her back into him, hoping to calm her.

"Caleb", she sobbed into his chest. "What if she is dead?"

"She is not dead Isabelle," He tried to sound as confident as his trembling voice would allow.

"How do you know that? How can you say that?"

Caleb sighed deeply and pulled away from Isabelle once again, this time he placed his hands gently on her shoulders. The passion of his response was written all over him.

"Because, I can feel her, Isabelle. I can feel her with every ounce of myself. I have this overwhelming strength within me and I know it's because she is out there, and she is alive. She needs me, more now than she has ever needed me. I will find her, and I will bring her home, Isabelle. I am going to bring her home."

Without hesitation Isabelle replied.

"I'm coming with you!"

Caleb released her entirely and he dropped his hands to his side, shaking his head adamantly.

"No Isabelle," he replied assertively.

"I'm coming with you to find my daughter." She said more firmly this time as she walked past him towards the front door. Caleb turned and watched her.

"Isabelle! No! It's not safe, I will not put you in any sort of danger. We have no idea how long this could take or what we are facing out there. I'm sorry Isabelle, I am not going to allow you to come and risk something happening to you. No! I will not put you in danger!"

Isabelle spun around, and Caleb could see determination in her face, an unrelenting fierceness of a Mother wanting to protect her only daughter, and in that moment, he knew he was not going to win this fight.

"Caleb, you already have put us in danger. The moment you agreed to help my daughter murder Marcus Donovan, you put us all in danger. I will not sit by and wait while you try to find her, I will not for one moment longer do nothing to find her. I did nothing when I knew deep in my gut that she was in trouble before, and I will take full responsibility for that, until my last breath. But never again will I sit back and allow someone to hurt my baby girl. I appreciate everything you are doing to find her. I know you love her, God I know you must love her, but I am coming with you. And if you do not take me with you, I swear I will get in my car and I will follow you. I will go and find her myself and I will bring her home. So, either you take me with you or I go on my own, but either way I am going to find my goddamn daughter, do you understand me Detective Stone?"

Isabelle's glare burned with a fierce determination, and Caleb knew in that moment he had no choice. He could hardly blame her, considering he was at fault for putting her in this position in the first place. There was only one thing he was going to be able to do no matter how desperately he knew he did not want to. He reached for the door opening, and held it open for Isabelle, and reluctantly replied.

"Yes, I do Isabelle, now let's go find Sophia, and bring her home."

THIRTY – EIGHT - October 10, 2015

"Where are we with Cassidy Ryan?" Jill did not waste any time as she walked into the board room and took a seat at the table.

Detective Landon was in the process of pinning the last ghastly picture they had gotten of the once beautiful Cassidy Ryan. Jill glanced up at the board and cringed to herself at the horrid pictures.

She was in a line of work that was not an easy one, in fact, most people would not be able to do it. There were times that she could get involved in a case and it would not impact her at all, however this one was not one of them. This case was not for the faint of heart, and as she studied the photos on the board, her heart broke for the woman, and for the woman's family. Nobody deserved to die like that. Her face was not even recognizable, she had been beaten so severely. The thought of being tied and bound under a pier, knowing this was it, it just wasn't right, Jill thought to herself. To have to watch the tide coming in closer and closer, and to watch as each wave grew larger, and more intimidating. She could not even begin to imagine the feeling of impending doom, not even being able to at least try and fight for your survival. Whoever had done this to this poor young girl was savage and unrelenting, and a monster, evil to the core.

Detective Landon pushed the pin in, making sure to hold the picture in place and he turned around.

"I got a hold of the ex-boyfriend, he is coming in later to have a chat with us."

"Good, what's his name again?"

"David…" Landon paused and grabbed a case file off of the table in front of him, flipped it over and quickly scanned the info inside, and finished replying. "Foxwell, David Foxwell."

"Let me see, what do know about him so far?" Jill asked as she gestured for Landon to hand over the file. He obliged and she flipped it open. She too quickly scanned the limited info they had to refresh her memory. The only information that they had on him up until this point was from Cassidy's sister, Jessica. Jill studied the info speaking out loud.

"Dated for two years, no criminal record, no signs of abuse in the relationship, doesn't seem there was much negative said about the two's relationship. I guess we will find out more when Mr. Foxwell gets here," Jill closed the file and tossed it on the table, sliding it on the smooth wooden surface.

Landon sat on the edge of the table, and grabbed his now luke warm cup of coffee, and took a long sip. He said, "Something just did not seem right to me about her stepfather. I know everyone reacts different to these types of things, but the man certainly did not show a lot of emotion, not like her mother had."

Jill gently allowed her chair to rock backwards, she placed her laced fingers across her stomach and she nodded in agreement with Detective Landon.

"I got the same feeling, trust me, but he has an alibi. Cassidy's mother puts him with her all night, but I definitely did not get a good feeling from him. To be honest the guy gave me the creeps, the way he kept looking at me, and eying me up and down. I don't know maybe he is just naturally a creepy sleaze ball."

Landon chuckled at Jill's candidness, then turned his attention back to the board. Evidence pictures of everyone and everything involved in the Cassidy Ryan case was posted over the entire board.

"Maybe we will get a lead from the boyfriend, he has got to have something for us," Landon sounded more hopeful than Jill thought he actually felt.

"I hope so too, but by the sounds of it they have not been in contact much since the break-up. I don't think their break-up was an ugly one, but who knows, you just never know who holds what information in a case."

"You have been doing this for awhile, does it ever get any easier?" Concern laced Landon's voice.

Jill sighed heavily, taking a moment to think before answering his question, but then shook her head slowly.

"No, not really, these are the ones," she began pointing to the covered board; "These are the ones that can really get to you. These damn cases that just make no sense at the time. Wondering who would do this to such a young woman. These are the cases that truly make you realize the evil that exists in our world. Some homicides honestly don't even phase me anymore. The gang bangers shooting each other up in the streets, the homeless guys beating the life out of one another fighting over who gets to be closer to the fire, those are the cases that I can just drift through without it affecting me. But cases like this," this time she nodded her head in the direction of the board. "These are the ones that make it hard to sleep at night, these are the ones that make me question what the hell I am doing in this line of work?"

Jill was certain that was not exactly the answer he was hoping for, but she was not going to sugar coat it and tell this young rookie detective that it did get easier.

"I hear ya," he began, "I mean I have been a cop for a while, but it's true when they tell you that being a homicide detective is a whole other ball game. I knew I wanted it, I worked for this. Some of it fucking sucks, but this is what I wanted."

"Well, all we have to do is catch the sick son-of-a-bitch that did this and it will make it all worth it," Jill rolled the chair closer to the table and grabbed her own cup of coffee off of the table and blew softly into it before taking a sip.

"Yes, it sounds like a good plan, I am too early into this to have a case hanging over my head, wondering if there was something more that could have been done," Landon's response immediately brought Jill's attention back to the Sophia and Marcus Donovan case, and also reminded her of her most recent conversation with Olivia Donovan.

"To prove that Sophia Donovan killed my Brother," those words rung loudly in her memory. However, the longer she ended up talking to Olivia that day, the more Jill realized that the girl was distraught, she was an emotional wreck, and she was grasping at straws. That was a case that was closed, but it was one of those cases that still dangled over her subconsciousness. But it was Caleb's case, and if anything, she trusted him. She trusted him probably more than anyone in her life with the exception of Rae. Although that conversation admittedly was transfixed into Jill's thoughts, she knew that there was nothing to look into. She did not want to reopen a closed case because some over-emotionally charged relative was trying to lay the blame on the ex of her dead brother.

"You okay?" Landon interrupted Jill's musings. Jill, not quite realizing how far away she seemed bounced back to where she was supposed to be.

"Ya, I'm good, I was just thinking about something."

"Okay so where do you think…" Landon was now the one who was interrupted as Jill's cell phone vibrated loudly on the table. She reached for it and answered it without even looking at the caller ID.

"Keller," she answered abruptly.

Landon paced back and forth organizing his own thoughts in his mind, just as Sergeant Decker popped her head into the room, motioning to Landon.

"I need you for a second," she whispered loud enough for Landon to hear her, but not loud enough to intrude on Jill's call. Landon waved at her, letting her know they would be right out. He turned to Jill, who's face was set with a tone of concern.

"Okay, okay, Mr. Donovan, I will be there as soon as I can, I'm leaving right now. Just keep trying to get a hold of her, I'm on my way." She hung up the phone and stood up from her chair.

"Is everything alright?"

"I don't think so Landon, I honestly don't think so."

THIRTY – NINE - October 10, 2015

The silence hung heavy in the air, as Caleb, Isabelle and Trent drove down the 210 on their way to Crest Park. Caleb knew that Trent was not happy that Isabelle was coming with them. But if he was there in her house with her, saw the determination in her eyes, Caleb was sure he would not have been able to say no either. Caleb was terrified, because as confident as he projected himself to Isabelle, the truth was as much as he could feel that Sophia was still alive, there was a small part of him that worried that Isabelle was right. He also knew that if he was right, and if Olivia Donovan did in fact have Sophia somewhere, he had no idea just how far she was willing to go to get her to tell her what she wanted to hear. Caleb glanced over at Trent who had all of his attention focused on the road ahead of him, over his shoulder he glanced at Isabelle, who wore an expression of utter trepidation.

She had her hands folded in her lap, her face was drained of all colour and she was staring aimlessly out the back-seat window watching the trees pass by, the sunlight flittering in between the leaves as the truck drove along beside them. Isabelle must have sensed Caleb watching her, and her eyes fell on his. Caleb softly smiled at her and Isabelle smiled weakly back.

"Isabelle, I'm so sorry that you are having to go through this right now," he said as he adjusted himself, so he was looking more directly at her.

"Caleb, I'm sorry for what I said back at my house."

Caleb shook his head at her and replied nonchalantly, "I don't know what you are talking about Isabelle."

Isabelle grinned at his obvious attempt at pretending he did not know what she was referring to.

"I mean it, I know my daughter, I know how stubborn she can be when she gets something in her head…" Caleb stopped her and put his hand up to do so.

"Isabelle, you don't have to say anything, because you're right. This is my fault."

"No, Caleb, this is not your fault. I know how stubborn my daughter can be when she gets something in her head. I never thought in a million years she would have gone to such great lengths and do something like this. But I know the moment she decided to do it, you, nor myself, or anybody else for that matter, would be able to change her mind. You did not force her to pull that trigger Caleb."

Trent glanced over at Caleb, knowing full well that Isabelle was right, and he nodded his head when Caleb looked towards him. Isabelle continued from the back seat.

"I just wish I had known how bad things were for her. I don't know why she didn't tell me, I could have helped her get out of that mess before things got this bad."

Caleb turned his body towards her again.

"Isabelle, she did not tell you because she did not want you to worry and fuss about her, she tried to make things right on her own. Trust me when I tell you that there was nothing you could have done, no matter what Sophia did. Marcus was going to make sure she suffered, he was going to make sure that she did not destroy his precious reputation, and he was going to make sure she could not interfere in his relationship with Cat. He was not a good man, not at all, and as much as I hate the situation we are now faced with, Sophia was right."

Isabelle sighed heavily and wiped away one stray tear as it fell from her eye. Caleb watched her, his heart breaking for her.

"I'm just so scared."

"I know you are, and I would be lying to you if I told you I wasn't scared either, but Isabelle I promise you, we are not going to stop until we find her. I will search every square inch of this planet until I find her. We have good people, smart people helping us, it's only going to be a matter of time, and it's going to be over, I promise."

"I hope you are right Caleb, because I don't know what I would do if I lost her, I just don't know what I would do," Isabelle's sullen gaze found it's way back out the window, and Caleb turned back around and watched the highway come towards them.

"We are about half an hour out," Trent informed Isabelle and Caleb.

"Good," Caleb replied starkly.

"Do you think Luke is going to find anything interesting on that Zoe chick?" Trent asked Caleb.

Caleb shrugged his shoulders, and answered, "I don't know. I can't put my finger on what it was about her, but she seemed nervous for some reason. Maybe she just doesn't feel comfortable with people snooping around her work place. Maybe she did recognize one of them and got nervous or something, I don't know, but if there is anything interesting to find out about her, Luke is the guy to do it."

"Well until then we just follow the bread crumbs and hope that someone out there recognizes one of them. I hope that we get another lead, because right now heading out here, we are searching for a needle in a haystack," Trent took his eyes off the road and glanced at Caleb, clearly knowing that was probably not what

Caleb or Isabelle wanted to hear, Caleb's expression only confirmed that.

"We have to find her, she has to be out here somewhere," Isabelle spoke now, her attention drawn to their conversation.

Caleb glanced quickly over his shoulder, and Isabelle now sat forward her hands bracing the seat in front of her. He turned to her again and he placed his hand gently onto hers and looked at her with sincerity streaked across his face, and he said to her, "Isabelle we are going to search until we find her, I will not stop. I won't give up until I find the needle, and trust me when I say, I don't give a damn how big the haystack is."

FOURTY -October 10, 2015

The front door flew open and Jill was standing face to face with the panicked faces of Bruce and Adele Donovan. They both stepped back as they ushered her in their house. Jill walked inside and immediately out of habit began to study and observe her surroundings.

"Come in Detective Keller, please, come in," Adele's alarm was apparent. Jill followed them both into the living room and neither of them took a seat, so she continued to stand as she spoke to them.

"Mr. Donovan," she addressed Bruce, thinking he may be the more level headed one in the moment to speak with. "I need you to tell me exactly what happened here," she pulled out a small notepad and a pen.

Bruce put his arm tightly around his wife, clearly trying to ease her panic, and keep her as calm as he could. He began to answer Jill.

"Olivia came home, like she usually does. She knows her mother worries about her if she does not hear from her every couple of days. Olivia knows it makes both of us feel better if she can stop in and see us, so she did, she came, but I noticed right away that she did not seem right."

"Seem right how?" Jill asked for further clarification.

Bruce shrugged his shoulders slightly and replied.

"I don't know, I could not really put my finger on it, she just seemed more agitated than normal, and she was so easy to anger today."

"Today? Is she normally quick to anger?"

"She was doing so well, we thought…" Adele answered this time, and Bruce squeezed her and then led her to the couch.

"Here honey, let's sit," both of them took a seat and Bruce motioned for Jill to sit in the chair across from them, the one Olivia had just recently been in.

Jill sat down and waited, and then Bruce continued for his wife.

"Olivia has had a rough go of things, mentally, I mean."

Jill began to jot something in her pad, "how do you mean?"

"She was diagnosed with Bipolar when she was much younger, and things have pretty much been an uphill battle ever since. That is why we like her to stay in touch with us and drop in and see us every couple days, so we can see for ourselves that she is okay."

"And today? You're saying that she seemed to be having a bad day?"

"Detective Keller, this wasn't just a bad day. Her behavior escalated more quickly than I have seen in a very long time, that means she has not been taking her meds."

Again, Jill wrote on her pad.

Bruce watched as Jill was writing and then he continued before she asked another question.

"I think Sophia Donovan is in danger, Detective Keller."

Jill stopped cold and looked at Bruce Donovan, his face was clearly worried, and Olivia's recent visit came immediately into her mind.

"Why do you say that, Mr. Donovan?"

"Because she left here in a rage, and Sophia Donovan seemed to be an undeniable source of her anger. She did not leave here empty handed. Olivia took one of my hand guns with her, that is why I called you here, Detective Keller, because I am certain my daughter has every intention of hurting Sophia."

"She came to see me," Jill said bluntly.

"When? She did not say anything to me, did she say anything to you Bruce?" Adele's concern was heightening.

Bruce shook his head and he asked Jill, "when did she come see you? What did she want?"

"She came to see me at the end of September, right after the investigation closed."

"And? What did she want?" Bruce pressed further.

"She asked me to help her, she wanted me to help her prove that Sophia murdered her brother."

Both Bruce and Adele looked troubled, but Jill could clearly see this was not the first time they had heard this.

"We knew she didn't like her, but dammit I did not think she really thought Sophia had anything to do with this. She was angry that her brother died, she was looking for someone to lash out at. But I thought once it was closed, she had accepted that, at least that is what she said. She even seemed to be sincere when she apologized to Sophia at the courthouse that day."

"Bruce, Adele," Jill looked from one then the other, "do you think Sophia Donovan might have had anything to do with the murder of your son, Marcus?"

Both of them looked astonished that Jill would even ask them that.

"No, of course not," Adele began. "Sophia was wonderful, she was incredible with Marcus, she was good to us. No, I do not think she had anything to do with it. I was horrified when I found out that Marcus was having an affair with her friend Cat. I was angry at my son for doing such a thing and betraying his marriage like that, I felt horrible. Detective Keller, I would be lying if I said that I felt horrible for Cat as well… but I don't. I know she murdered my son because she wanted him for herself. Marcus made a mistake, he stepped out of his marriage, and I wish he would not have done that, because now he is dead because of it. He is dead at the hands of that woman, because she wanted what he and Sophia had. When he would not give it to her, she killed him, then she killed herself. I have to live without my son every single day now, and that tears me apart. But trust me when I say, I will not for one day be sad for her, I just wish she would have just killed herself a hell of a lot sooner, and left Marcus alone."

Jill was slightly shocked that Adele spoke this openly about her feelings for the woman that murdered her son, but it had been clearly on her mind and eating away at her all this time. She watched as Bruce reached for his wife's hand and squeezed it reassuringly.

"Do you know where she would have gone? Have you tried calling her?"

"Yes, I have tried several times, she is not answering, I think her phone is turned off because it keeps going straight to her voicemail, which is full, so I cannot even leave her a message." Frustration filled Bruce's voice.

"Do you know possibly where she could have gone?"

"To be with Zoe," Adele replied almost inaudibly.

"Zoe?" Jill asked.

"Yes, her girlfriend," Bruce said matter of factly.

"Girlfriend?" Jill echoed.

"Yes, her new girlfriend. That is another thing. As far as we knew Olivia was not gay, and then all of a sudden she has a girlfriend."

"Have you met her?" Jill had a lot of questions but did not want to overwhelm them.

"No, we have not met her, Adele keeps asking her when we will, but Olivia just gets angry and thinks we are judging her. All we know is she met her a few weeks ago at some bar named Last Call. She said Zoe is a bartender there and, well, that is about the extent of what we know," Bruce adjusted his glasses on his nose.

Jill noted the name of the bar on her pad of paper, she was sure she knew whereabouts that place was, and she knew it was a pretty dodgy place.

"Okay, listen, from what you have told me today, I think maybe she is just lashing out, she is angry about her brother's death, and she is just reacting. It is clear her and Sophia have never been best friends and she wants someone to blame, and right now Sophia seems to be the easiest person," Jill began but Bruce interjected.

"But she has my gun, why would she take my gun?"

Jill nodded her head and continued.

"I think she is crying out for attention, if you are right and she is off her meds, then we do need to find her before she does something erratic. Her emotions are out of control right now, and she is not thinking in her right frame of mind. I am not sure what intentions she has, but chances are she took your gun to get your attention. I am sure she went to her girlfriend's. I am going to check into this. I am going to check into Zoe, find Olivia, and make sure everything is alright. And maybe after that, you guys might need to have a chat with her about getting some more help, it sounds like she could use a lot of support to get her through this grieving process. As far as Sophia Donovan goes, I don't think we have too much to worry about. When Olivia came to see me she had mentioned that she had left LA for a bit, is that true?" Jill asked Bruce.

Bruce nodded his head, "yes, she did, she did touch base with us before she left, she said she needed to get away to clear her head and spend some time alone. I don't blame her, I cannot imagine the toll this took on her. That's why I was so concerned though, the way Olivia was carrying on, it was like maybe she knew where Sophia was, like maybe she knew exactly where she was."

Jill flipped her pad closed and she stood from her chair, Bruce and Adele both did the same. All three of them walked towards the front door, Bruce's arm still placed protectively around his wife's shoulders. In the front hallway, Jill turned to them with a reassuring smile.

"Thank you so much for coming so quickly Detective Keller," Adele gently reached and touched Jill's arm. Jill slightly pulled away, not comfortable with people in her personal space. Jill did her best to sound confident and replied, "I don't want you to worry too much about this, I am going to head out right now and I am going to go find Olivia for you. Like I said, I am sure she is just reacting, she is grieving and unfortunately if she is not taking care of herself right now, then it can really seem worse than it actually is. I am sure Sophia Donovan is fine, wherever she is right now, I am sure she is just fine."

With that Jill Keller walked out the front door, but her last words did not settle her as much as she hoped they did for the Donovan's. There was something eating at her, something relentless was nagging at her gut. Now that she knew a little bit more about Olivia Donovan, something told her that maybe, just maybe, Sophia Donovan was really not going to be fine at all.

FOURTY-ONE- October 10, 2015

Zoe gently closed the door to Sophia's room and stood briefly with her hand resting on the knob. She still held firmly the large chunk of hair in her other hand, the chunk of hair she found laying on the floor only moments before. She brought her hand up and studied the hair nestled in her palm, the long dark hair that she knew was Sophia's. Finally, after a moment she turned away from the door and walked towards the kitchen. Instead of throwing out the hair she took a piece of paper towel off the roll, placed it on the counter and then she delicately laid the hair on top of the paper towel. She was not sure exactly why she was hanging onto it, perhaps proof to tell Olivia that she knew that she did not stay out of that room like Zoe had asked her to.

Zoe knew Olivia was gone, she knew Olivia had actually lost her mind now. As much as she wanted to help her find the truth, this situation was getting out of control, and fast. Olivia was losing grip of the reality that perhaps she was wrong, perhaps Sophia Donovan had nothing to do with her brother's death at all. But Olivia was not going to settle for that, it was clear now to Zoe that Olivia was not going to rest until she heard what she wanted to hear, even if it was not true.

Zoe walked to the stove and reached up opening the cupboard doors above it, she retrieved a bottle of Jack Daniels, bringing it down and placing it on the counter. She grabbed a coffee mug and she opened the bottle pouring herself a very generous amount into the mug. She never drank alone, let alone during the day, but right now she knew she needed this more than ever. She brought the glass to her nose and inhaled the pungent aroma of the whiskey before bringing it to her lips to take a small sip. Her face grimaced at the harshness of the whisky as it burned the inside of her mouth leaving a warm trail down her throat.

"Christ, what am I going to do?" she muttered to herself before taking another cautious swig of the liquor.

Zoe was tormented in this very moment, the answer of what she needed to do was not clear to her, not right now. She knew one thing, and that was that she was screwed. She should have never told Olivia to bring Sophia here. But at the time she panicked, at the time she truly thought that Olivia would have talked to Sophia and got an answer and then just let it go. But over these last five days Zoe has watched Olivia slowly unravel right in front of her. It was scaring the shit out of her. What was worse, there were people looking, there were people looking for both Olivia and Sophia, so it was only going to be a matter of time.

Zoe leaned against the countertop and her gaze went out of the small window above the sink, it was so calm and peaceful outside right now. She could hear birds softly chirping and there was barely a breeze. The sun's midday rays were beaming through the trees casting a warm glow through the window. This was such a serene and tranquil place, it always had been. Zoe wondered to herself why they stopped coming here after her parents died, but she knew the answer was because the memories were just too painful. It was once a place of happiness and family, but that had changed. The only family she had left now was Chad, her older brother, but he did not approve of her lifestyle, so they had drifted apart several years ago. Zoe brought her attention back to her glass of whiskey, took one more generous sip and then set the glass down on the counter. She walked back into the living room and paced slowly back and forth across the floor, every so often glancing towards the door to Sophia's room.

Zoe wasn't sure what made her open that door and look at Sophia, she just stood there holding that clump of hair. The moment their eyes locked, Zoe was shocked at her reaction, she felt horrible for the woman that was shackled to the bed. Sophia looked defeated and crippled with the knowledge that she was trapped here, Zoe felt heartbroken for her. But as the two women looked at one another, nothing was said, Zoe had no idea what to say so she just gently closed the door. What was she supposed to say to her, the last time she went in there and gave her breakfast Olivia nearly lost her mind, so Zoe was not sure what she was supposed to say, if anything at all.

Zoe walked over to the worn sofa and took a seat, she rested her elbows on her knees and let her head fall into her hands, and before she knew it, she found herself weeping. She let herself cry, she let the stress of the last five days come out. As the tears came, so did the sinking realization that Olivia was damaged beyond repair. Zoe tried so hard to help her, and she even understood her pain of losing a family member and wanting to have someone to blame. Needing someone to cast your anger towards, but it was clear to her that Olivia was not well, she wasn't mentally well. Zoe still had no idea what she was going to do, and it was literally tearing her apart. She cried into her hands for several moments, and finally she managed to settle herself down, she brought her head up and she wiped both eyes with the back of her hands. She sniffled, and swallowed hard, the taste of whiskey still present in her mouth.

"What do I do? Jesus what do I do?" her voice was soft in the silent room.

Before she could answer her own question, she stood up and she walked back into the kitchen, retrieved the bottle of Jack, her own cup and then she pulled one more mug from that cupboard before heading back towards Sophia's door. This time she did not hesitate, she just allowed her body to guide her. She reached for the handle and she slowly opened the door. Sophia was awake, still sitting up, her back against the wall. Zoe thought she must have been hoping she would come back in. Again, both women just looked at each other and Zoe could read the desperation in Sophia's eyes, it was clear as day. Zoe watched Sophia's desperate look change to confusion, as she noticed the bottle of whiskey in

Zoe's hand. Zoe walked into the room, and she noticed that Sophia seemed to try and back away, the wall stopping her from shrinking any further. Zoe immediately hated the way she was feeling, she hated knowing she was causing someone that much fear, so quickly she said.

"It's okay."

Zoe placed the bottle of whisky and the two glasses gently on the floor and she pulled the chair to the edge of the bed and took a seat.

"It's okay, Sophia, I promise I'm not here to hurt you."

Sophia's tongue tried to moisten her dry lips, Zoe grabbed the bottle of Jack Daniels and poured a small amount into the mug. She reached the cup towards Sophia, but she did not accept it at first.

"I can get you water if you would like..." and before she could finish her sentence Sophia grabbed the glass out of her hand, clearly indicating she needed the booze as much as Zoe did.

Sophia cautiously brought the mug up and smelled the whiskey. Zoe was not sure if she was just enjoying the aroma, or if perhaps she was making sure it smelled okay to drink, so Zoe decided to ease her mind.

"It's okay Sophia, like I said I'm not here to hurt you."

Zoe watched as Sophia took a very small sip, and her eye's closed as the liquid found its way into her mouth. Zoe knew that as harsh as it must have tasted, Sophia was relishing in the taste of it, happy to have something to drink. Sophia swallowed slowly and opened her eyes back up and her gaze once again fell on to Zoe's. Zoe did not know what else to do so she smiled softly at the woman in front of her.

"Thank you," Sophia's voice was raspy. "But why are you doing this? You shouldn't be here talking to me."

Zoe nodded slowly at Sophia and she bent over and grabbed her own mug from the floor before she answered.

"I'm here to help you Sophia, I want to help you, but first I just need you to tell me everything you know. Just tell me what you know about Olivia, and about the murder of her brother Marcus, tell me what you know. I'll help you, but please just tell me everything you know."

FOURTY-TWO - October 10, 2015

"I'll be there as soon as I can Landon, but I have something to take care of first," Jill sat behind the wheel of her vehicle as she spoke to her partner on the phone.

"Is everything okay?" Landon asked concerned on the other end.

"I think so," Jill did not believe her own reply. "I think so. I just have to check something out, it has nothing to do with the Cassidy Ryan case, it's probably nothing but I just have to check it out."

"Okay, well I'm just about to head in to interview the boyfriend, if you're not back I will be sure to let you know how it goes," he answered quickly.

"Thanks, I appreciate it, I'm sure I will see ya soon," Jill did not say goodbye before she pulled the phone away from her ear and hung up. She turned the engine off in her car, and she studied the dingy building in front of her for a moment before getting out.

She had never had the privilege of being inside the bar, but she had driven by here a few times before. It was definitely your stereotypical, run of the mill, dive bar as they call it. And this is the place that Olivia Donovan came the day she met her new girlfriend Zoe. She did not know a ton about Olivia Donovan, but Jill had to admit it shocked even her that Olivia would come to a place like this. Jill reached for the door handle and she stepped outside, the sun warming her face.

Jill walked through the front door and immediately took inventory of everything she saw. There were a few customers scattered throughout the bar, sipping on beers, whiskeys and whatever else they felt necessary to brighten up their Saturday afternoons. There was an old pool table in the back, but nobody was playing it. Jill walked towards the bar and was barely even noticed, as nobody felt her presence was important enough to take their attention away from their drinks. She took a seat at the bar, a young man walked up to her. Jill noted to herself that he barely looked old enough to be working here, but did not really find that detail important enough right now.

"Afternoon Miss, what can I get ya?" the young bartender asked.

"Nothing to drink thank you, but I do have a couple questions for you."

"Okay…" his response was slightly drawn out and worrisome.

"What's your name?" she asked bluntly.

The bartender was silent for a moment, seemingly nervous to tell her, perhaps thinking he was in trouble. But finally, he answered her.

"Tommy."

"Hey Tommy, wondering if you can help me out today, I need to know if you have a bartender by the name of Zoe working here?" Jill began.

"Ya, we do but she is not here right now," his nerves seemed to settle realizing this had nothing to do with him.

"When she going to be in?" Jill continued.

Tommy shook his head and replied. "Not back till Monday, um…can I ask you what this is about?"

Jill pulled out her badge and quickly flashed it in his direction, something she should have done right from the beginning.

"Sorry, it's nothing, I am just looking into some things and I need to speak with Zoe, it is important. Do you happen to have a number for her?"

"Uh ya I guess, just hold on" Tommy turned and walked into a small back office leaving Jill alone at the bar. She swivelled on her chair to study her surroundings again. She truly felt sorry for some of these people that spent their days in places like this. Her life was a bit of a mess right now but at least it wasn't that bad. Again, the thought of Olivia coming in here had her wondering what the hell she was doing in a place like this to start off with. Jill swiveled back around to the sound of Tommy behind her.

"This is the only number I have for her," he said almost apologetically as he handed her the piece of paper. Jill pulled out her notepad, jotted the number in it, and readied herself to take some more notes. "Let me ask you something else Tommy, do you know Zoe's girlfriend, Olivia?"

Tommy smirked, Jill was uncertain as to why, probably some stupid lame lesbian fantasy he had in his head at the mention of girlfriend.

"Oh ya, have definitely heard about her."

"Have you met her yet?"

"No, I haven't, not yet anyways, if they are even still together."

Jill looked up at him, her look indicating she would like him to clarify his statement.

"Well, last week her and I were watching the place, I worked a lot more than she did that was for sure. I just figured she was going through some shit, so I covered for her a few times."

Jill jotted something down in her pad and then she asked.

"What do you mean? Shit?"

Tommy shrugged, "I don't know man, I mean, she is a chick, and no offense officer, but I don't get you guys. She just seemed distracted, and real pissy, just very unlike herself. Normally Zoe is a chill chick, one of the guys kinda chick."

"Did you ask her if she was okay?" Jill pressed further.

"Uh, well sort of, I just asked her what was up her ass the one day, when she snapped at me for something stupid."

Jill smirked and answered sarcastically, "You got a real compassionate side I see."

"Like I said, I don't understand women sometimes, I thought maybe she was just PMSing or something, the way she was acting. I did ask about Olivia, thought maybe they had a fight or something, cuz she used to talk about her non-stop and this last week, when I did see her, she barely said anything at all about her. When I brought her up, Zoe just sloughed it off so I thought maybe they broke up already or were fighting or something." Tommy folded his skinny arms across one another.

Jill thought back to Bruce Donovan explaining how erratic Olivia had been acting recently, and she knew perhaps it was beginning to cause a strain on this new relationship. Maybe Olivia's mental instability was just too much for Zoe to take, there was something more to this story. It was gnawing at Jill, and she needed to figure out what it was.

"Tommy, did she say anything to you about where she was going to be or what she was going to be doing this weekend? Anything at all?" Jill's intent gaze was on Tommy urging him to give her some indication of where to find her.

"No, she didn't," he answered honestly.

"Do you know if she has any family in the area?"

"I know her parents are dead, but she has a brother. I don't hear much about him either, but he is listed as her emergency contact."

"Okay, well I'm gonna need you to grab me that information Tommy."

"Uh, sure, just give me a minute," again Tommy disappeared to the back office while Jill sat and waited. Her mind already trying to put together what little puzzle pieces she had.

Tommy came back and handed her another piece of paper and she stood up from the bar, preparing to leave.

"This is such a weird day; too bad you weren't here a few hours earlier."

"Why do you say that?" Jill asked turning her attention back to Tommy.

"Well Carl was here earlier…" Tommy began but Jill cut him off.

"Who's Carl?"

"My boss, he will be back later if you need to talk to him, but he said Zoe was here this morning to pick up her check."

Jill felt slightly frustrated that Tommy was just telling her this now, she huffed heavily and replied.

"Yes, I will want to talk to your boss as well, but why is that weird? Does Zoe normally not pick up her checks?"

"No, not that, but just seems like we are a popular place today."

Jill's frustration continued to mount at Tommy's unclarity.

"Why do you say that?" Jill asked him as she quickly glanced around the nearly empty bar. "This is what you mean by popular place?"

Tommy chuckled at her sarcasm, "no, I mean, earlier, when Zoe stopped by, Carl said there were two men here asking a bunch of questions about a couple of women."

Jill's attention was immediately refocused, and her curiosity piqued rapidly.

"Two men?"

"Yup, looking for a couple missing women," Tommy answered unphased.

"Do you know who they were?"

"Nah, you will have to talk to Carl about that, or Zoe, but I hope you have better luck getting a hold of her than I have."

"Thanks, Tommy," knowing she had gotten as much information as she could out of Tommy, she turned to head out of the bar. She opened the doors, the glare of the sun hitting her directly in the eyes. She walked across the parking lot, unlocked her door then slid into her driver's seat. She sat silent, confused, trying to make sense of what she just heard.

"Two men? Looking for two missing women?" she uttered to herself.

It was then at that moment that she knew something was not right, something was definitely not right. She knew she needed to find Zoe and Olivia, and soon, and she knew the best place to start. She pulled her cell phone out of her pocket along with her notepad, she flipped it open, then quickly dialed the number before hitting send. Quietly, she sat in her car listening to the ringing on the other end, and finally someone answered.

"Hello."

"Hello, is this Chad Cardell?" Jill inquired.

There was a brief pause, "yes, it is, may I ask who's calling?"

"Mr. Cardell, this is Detective Jill Keller of the LAPD, I have some questions about your sister, Zoe, I am hoping you can answer for me."

Again, silence, this time more drawn out.

"Mr. Cardell? Are you still there?" More silence and Jill thought perhaps they lost the connection but then his voice filled the silence.

"Good God! Tell me what on earth did my sister do now?"

FOURTY – THREE -October 10, 2015

Trent pulled his truck into one of the empty stalls, at the Crest Park entrance, and turned the engine off. Isabelle sat silent in the back seat, a doe-eyed expression on her face.

"Here we are," Trent exclaimed.

"This is where we have to start, let's just get out there and talk to anyone we can. If she has her out here, someone is bound to have seen them," Caleb replied with a hopeful tone to his voice. He turned around to look at Isabelle. "Are you ready to find your daughter?"

"Yes, I am," her voice had a hesitancy behind it that Caleb did not like. He knew that Isabelle was dead set on finding her daughter, but he also could hear a slight dread in her voice, knowing there was the possibility that they would not be able to find her.

The three of them all got out of the vehicle, closing the doors behind them. The sun was still warm, and the little breeze that whispered around them was also warm. They all stood together, and Caleb brought his wrist up, looking at the time on his watch.

"We have a couple hours before the sun goes down, so we need to talk to as many people as we can. Get those pictures out there, I know this is going to be difficult but maybe, just maybe, someone has seen them."

"What do we do if we have no luck today, then what?" Isabelle asked, her voice drowning with worry. Trent glanced towards Caleb, and Caleb could read the, "you shouldn't have brought her look" clearly on his face.

"Isabelle, this is where we start, and we just have to follow any single lead we get. I told you, we will not stop looking until we find her." Caleb glanced around quickly at the surroundings, he had never been to this area before, so he quickly wanted to determine where to start.

"Trent you go that way, Isabelle and I will head this way," Caleb motioned his hand in the opposite direction. "It looks fairly busy here so hopefully we can get lucky."

"Sounds good." Trent replied. "I will meet you guys back here at the truck in an hour, call me in the meantime if you find anything." he turned and walked away from Caleb and Isabelle.

"Come on," Caleb gently placed his hand on the small of Isabelle's back.

The first people they approached was a young family sitting around a picnic table enjoying a later afternoon snack. Two small children sat happily, stuffing cheese and crackers into their mouths. The man and the woman both looked up to Caleb and Isabelle, giving them a welcoming smile.

"Afternoon," Caleb began, his phone already in his hand.

"Good afternoon," the man replied.

"Sorry to bother you guys, but I'm hoping you can tell me if you have seen either one of these women around here?" Caleb passed his phone to the man, and he studied it for a moment then passed it to the woman sitting across from him. She took the phone and slowly shook her head, then passed the phone back to Caleb.

"Sorry, I don't believe I have seen them, but we have only been here for about an hour," the woman kindly replied.

"No problem, and sorry for bothering you," Caleb nodded at them before he and Isabelle continued on.

A few feet away a young man, probably in his early twenties, tossed a tennis ball, his eager and excited golden retriever chasing wildly after it. He turned his attention to Caleb and Isabelle as they approached him.

"Hey," the young man said.

"Hi there, "Caleb replied as the happy dog bounded up to his owner, dropping the ball at his feet. The man picked up the ball and whipped it back out to the open park, the dog chasing after it again.

"Sorry to bother you, but I was wondering if you can tell me if you have seen either one of these women around here?" Caleb handed over his cell phone, the man took it and looked intently at the screen. He shrugged his shoulder and slowly shook his head.

"No man, sorry. I don't think I can help you."

"Are you sure?" Isabelle addressed him eagerly. The man handed Caleb back his phone and answered Isabelle.

"Sorry, I wish I could help." Again, the dog was at his feet, waiting, panting with anticipation of the next chase.

"No worries enjoy your day," Caleb said, as he and Isabelle continued on.

"Let's go ask her," Isabelle pulled Caleb by the arm, and briskly walked towards a young woman sitting alone on the ground, her back resting against the trunk of a tree, a book in her hand. This time it was Isabelle who approached her first.

"Excuse me," Isabelle began, "we don't mean to bother you, but can you take a look and tell me if you have seen either one of these women around here." Caleb bent down and handed the woman his phone. She placed her bookmark on her page, closed the book and took the phone. She studied the photos of the two women, for what felt like an eternity. Caleb's stomach was in his throat with the hopes that maybe this woman was recognizing their faces. But his heart sank as she handed the phone back to him and said.

"No sorry, I have not seen them, but have you checked at the store?"

Both Caleb and Isabelle quickly glanced around them, and the girl gestured her hands in front of her.

"It's just over there, around the corner, it's just a tiny little store, but if they have been around here, then most likely John has seen them."

Caleb had noticed a tiny little building as they were pulling up but did not realize it was a store, he smiled gratefully at the woman.

"Thank you so much, we will be sure to head over there."

"No problem," the woman returned his smile. "I hope everything is okay, and you find them."

"Thank you," Isabelle answered the woman, and she followed Caleb in the direction of the store.

They continued to walk briskly, both hoping the woman was right, and that this John might have seen both of them, or one of them. They approached the little store, Caleb opening the door, allowing Isabelle to go in first. The first thing that came to Caleb's mind was that tiny was barely a good word to describe the place. It was basically a little trailer, that contained some essentials that people might need for a day at the park, or for passerbys on the way to the lake. An older man, with a full head of grey hair and wire rim glasses perched on his nose, looked up at them as they entered.

"Afternoon folks," he chirped, putting his magazine down on the counter beside him. "Whatcha need?"

"Your name John?" Caleb asked as he walked up to the man, Isabelle at his heels.

"You got it, what can I do ya for?"

"I am really hoping you can help us, have you seen these women?"

The man named John grabbed the phone and adjusted his glasses, so he could see what he was looking at, he fiddled with the phone turning it sideways and then back again.

"Darn phones, I remember the day when we would just take normal pictures."

"Do you recognize them?" Isabelle's impatience was evident.

He looked intently, examining the photo of both Olivia and Sophia Donovan, and then he slowly started nodding his head. Caleb's heart leapt into his throat.

"You recognize them?"

"Nah, not both of them, but I have definitely seen this one here," John turned the phone around pointing at the picture of Olivia.

"Oh, my God, you have?" Isabelle exclaimed.

"Ya, seen her a couple times in the last few days, just came in grabbed some water, and couple other things, but I recognize her for sure."

"You don't recall seeing her?" Caleb pointed to Sophia's beautiful smiling face on the screen.

"Nope, not that I recall. But I'm here everyday, so anyone that comes in here I can usually remember. I may be getting old, but the one thing I still have is my mind, still sharp as knives." John spoke proudly as he gently tapped the side of his head.

"Do you know when she was last here?" Isabelle asked John. John thought to himself, searching his mind for the answer.

"Well, I believe it was Thursday, she came in here with another young woman, not that one there in the picture though, but another one."

Caleb's ears perked at this information, any information right now was extremely relevant, so he pushed for more details.

"Another woman? Do you remember what she looked like?"

John adjusted himself on his stool that he was nestled on and rested his hands on his round belly.

"Oh ya, that one is hard to forget, a real beaut."

"I'm gonna need a little more than that," Caleb tried to hide his annoyance.

"Big you know…" John started off his description by placing his hands in front of his chest.

Both Caleb and Isabelle shook their head but allowed him to continue.

"She was about, I don't know 5'7, white girl, and long beautiful hair, beautiful auburn hair."

The moment John was finished his description of the woman, an immediate image of the bartender from the bar came rushing to

Caleb's mind; Zoe. He was uncertain about how long her hair was, as she wore it piled up on top of her head, and she had a hoodie on, so he barely noticed the size of her chest, as John had so delicately described, but it was enough to make him question it. Before Caleb could ask John anything further, his burner phone started ringing in his pocket. He pulled it out and put up his finger.

"Excuse me, I need to take this," and he walked outside. He flipped it open. "Hello."

"It's me," Luke Nolan's voice was on the other end.

"Hey, what you got for me?" he replied anxiously, the thought of the girl Zoe now overtaking his mind.

"Oh, you're gonna love this," Luke began, and Caleb impatiently interjected.

"What, what did you find out?" he pushed Luke, as he turned around, realizing Isabelle was behind him, watching, listening, and waiting for answers.

They stood face to face, there eyes transfixed on one another, as Caleb listened to each and every word that Luke spoke on the other end. Isabelle did not move, she was cemented in place as she watched Caleb's expression shift. As Caleb processed each and every word uttered by Luke, he felt his first real prospect of hopefulness, and clarity. After a few agonizing moments for Isabelle, Caleb took the phone away from his ear and flipped it shut. They continued to stand there, in silence, staring at one another and finally Isabelle could wait no longer.

"Caleb? What? Tell me!"

"I knew it Isabelle…I just fucking knew it!"

FOURTY – FOUR -October 10, 2015

"Hey Raj, it's me Keller. Can I ask you to do me a big favour, under the radar?" Jill spoke into her cell phone, as she was driving towards her destination.

"Of course, I think I owe you a few of those." Raj Mandeep answered on the other end of the line. Raj was one of Jill's favorite people down at the station. A young IT tech who could always help her out.

"I need you to search a number for me, tell me if you can determine its last location."

"Sure, what's the number?" Raj asked, Jill quickly recited the phone number she had for Zoe Cardell. The number she was given at the bar but was not successful in reaching herself.

"Just remember under the radar, right?" she clarified to Raj, whom she knew she could trust, but needed to reiterate to anyways.

"Don't worry Keller, I will let you know what I find out in a couple minutes."

"Thanks Raj. Has anyone ever told you, you're the best?" Jill joked into the phone.

"Enough that I know I am," he joked back, before he hung up, disconnecting their call.

Jill continued on, thankful she had someone like Raj at the station that could help her out right now, she needed to do this for herself, she needed to keep it quiet for now. Her LT would not be impressed if he found out she was looking into this; this case was closed. But Jill knew she had to find Olivia, to put her own mind at ease as well as her parents, who were at this moment worried sick about their daughter. She only wished she would have had time to stop at the station to try and see if she could dig up Olivia Donovan's phone number, but she could do that later when she got back, if she was still unable to get a hold of this Zoe, to find out where Olivia might be.

Jill pulled into the parking lot of the Holy Spirit Lutheran Church, the massive structure looming over her, almost intimidating her. She struggled to remember the last time she was at a church, and she honestly could not recall the most recent time. She was however raised in a partially catholic household and the memory of her mother, every Sunday making Jill put on her nicest outfit, with her only pair of patent leather Mary Janes, and her hair in a perfect little bow. Her father never came, he was not a believer, and every Sunday there was a slight bone of contention between the two of them. Jill's mother knew how he felt about religion when she married him, so it had always been something they agreed to disagree on. Jill always wanted so desperately to stay home with her father, even if it meant sitting in front of the TV watching sports, but her mother never allowed it. Her mother was a wonderfully sweet woman, she was kind and caring towards others and her loyalties laid with God. As Jill got older, she was given the choice if she wanted to continue going, and she did for a bit, that was until her father died on the job. He too was a cop, that was what led Jill to where she was. She was proud to say that her father was an incredible cop but being incredible at what you do can sometimes be your demise, just as it was his.

Jill sat in her car, staring up at the grand building, the memory of her father haunting her mind. It had been a long time since she thought about him, but being here brought it up for some reason. She could still feel the lump in her throat when she looked out the window that September evening and seeing a police cruiser parked in front of her house. Jill could feel her chest tighten, just as it had that day when the doorbell rang. She had wanted to get up and lunge in front of her mother to stop her from opening the door, but she didn't. She had sat transfixed on the couch, knowing, without any valid reason, just knowing that her life was about to crumble around her. The pain crept back after 20 years. The memory of watching her own mother fall to the ground, wailing and sobbing for her husband who had just been killed by a drunk driver. Her father, the best cop she knew was only doing his job that day, pulling someone over for a routine speeding ticket, what could possibly go wrong with that? Everything that day, Jill thought to herself. Everything. Jill heard the officers, as much as she wished she hadn't she heard them explain to her mother that he had someone pulled over, and out of nowhere came barreling a sports car, taking out both her father and the car he had pulled over. She remembers the officers saying he did not suffer, but Jill knew that was lie, because how could they know that? How could they possibly know what her fathers last thoughts, or when his last breath was? How could they possibly know the anguish he felt at knowing he was leaving his family behind, knowing he was leaving his baby girl behind?

Jill was torn back to the present, as she noticed the front doors of the church open and a younger looking man came out and stood holding the door open. He gave her a quick wave, indicating he was waiting for her. Jill inhaled a deep breath and tried to force the painful memories of her father back into the deepest recesses of her mind. She got out of her car, closed the door and walked towards the front doors. As she approached she reached out her hand, "You must be Chad."

"Yes, nice to meet you Detective Keller," he answered as he took her hand in a firm handshake. He continued to hold the door open for her, and she walked into the church.

"Please follow me, we can go chat in my office." Jill followed him, the church was eerily silent, the sun's rays washed over the stained glass, emanating a beautiful colour. She was surprised at just how large it was, and she had to admit, she felt very out of place even just walking inside. They came to his office and she followed Chad in. He gestured for her to take a seat at one of the chairs in front of his desk. He continued on around and took his spot behind his desk. Jill sat down.

"Thank you for seeing me today," she began.

"It's not a problem, I hope I can help. I'm sorry, it was just easier to meet here. My wife is eight months pregnant and I really don't want to put any unnecessary stress on her." Jill glanced quickly around his office and then replied.

"How long have you been a minister?"

"It's been going on eight years," Chad answered her. Jill nodded, and just by her own nature, studied the man in front of her. She figured him to be around 40 or so, maybe a couple years younger. He was a very gentle looking, he seemed to give off a nurturing and welcoming presence. He had a full head of deep auburn hair, the colour of burning embers, and his skin was softly tanned with a spattering of freckles on his nose.

"Good for you."

"Detective Keller, can you tell me what my sister has done?" Chad obviously wanting to cut straight to the chase.

Jill smiled understandingly at his concern and replied.

"So far, nothing actually."

A look of part confusion and part uncertainty spread across his features, so Jill continued.

"I'm actually just really needing to get a hold of your sister, I have some questions for her that I think only she can help me with."

"So, she is not in trouble?" he asked seemingly relieved.

"No, not that I know of anyhow."

"Well, I can try calling her for you," he offered.

"I actually got her number from her place of work." Jill watched as Chad's eyes nearly rolled in the back of his skull.

"If you can call that place a job?"

"I take it you have been there?" Jill answered his sarcastic comment.

"Yes, I have unfortunately. I don't know why she is working there. I don't know what she is doing wasting her time and her education in a place like that."

"Oh, so Zoe has education in something else?"

"Yes, she was going to school for social work, she was working hard at it, but then she just quit during her last year in. She said it just wasn't for her, and that she did not want to be tied down to a job like that, she wanted to travel a bit."

"So, she quit school to go work at the bar?" Jill asked, leaning back in her seat.

"Well, no not really. See Zoe was in school and doing well, but we lost our parents, after that it just seemed like she gave up on everything."

Again, her mind tried to summon up the memory of her father, but she pushed it down, now was not the time.

"I am so sorry to hear that, how long ago?"

"Hard to believe but it has been a little over five years now. It was very difficult on both of us, but Zoe took it quite hard, and that is when she quit school and took off for a bit. She went to Thailand for a couple months, she explored around the country doing odd jobs to pay her way. She changed after that."

"Changed how?" Jill asked.

"Lots of ways, she just came back and decided life was too short to be tied down to anything like a serious job, life was too short to not be happy and carefree. So, after going through job after job, she ended up there, where she is now. I don't know how a place like that can be fulfilling to her but, hey it's her life. I don't agree with her decision on her career, and I certainly don't agree on her decisions on most other parts of her life either."

Jill shifted in her seat, gave him a curt nod and then asked,

"What other parts of her life are you referring to?" Jill knew she already knew the answer to this question, but she needed to get the information from him.

"Her lifestyle, her choices in partners. As far as I know Zoe is not gay, but since their death and going on the trip, she is all of a sudden gay now? I mean I just don't understand it."

"You don't accept her for that?" Jill felt a little unnerved at that fact, Zoe's own brother did not accept her because of whom she chose to sleep with, but Jill also knew everyone had their own opinion on the topic.

"I love Zoe, and God loves Zoe, regardless of her lifestyle choices, but personally I just don't accept it. I don't think that is who she truly is, I think it is an act, sort of a façade to hide her pain maybe." Chad paused a moment and realized Jill was waiting for him to continue. "Do I love my sister dearly? Yes, I do, very much.

Do I agree with her choices? No, no I don't. I would be lying if I said it has not done damage to our relationship. When Zoe got back, trust me I wanted nothing more than to have her in my life, she is a wonderful person, and she is a great aunt to our daughter, but Detective Keller…" another short pause. "I just do not agree with it, and I am not comfortable with her bringing her "girlfriends" around our daughter. I don't want to confuse her, but Zoe just could not understand that. Zoe could not understand my viewpoint on any of it, and it eventually just tore us apart."

Jill brought her hand up to her face, rubbing her cheek, determining in her own mind where she should go next with the questions. As much as she personally did not agree with what Chad was saying, it was not up to her to voice that opinion.

"Mr. Cardell, when's the last time you spoke to Zoe?"

Chad answered quickly, not having to think about it.

"It was just a couple weeks ago actually."

Jill was surprised it was so recently, she suspected it would have been a couple years.

"Oh, really? Did she by chance tell you about her new girlfriend?"

Chad nodded his head, again and rolled his eyes. Jill could clearly tell he was trying to be nonchalant about it.

"Ya, she told me about her, what was her name? Olivia. Ya, she wanted to call and talk. She wanted me to know she found someone that made her happy, and that she was sure she was it."

"You don't sound very convinced of that?"

"No, I mean I have heard that a couple times, even before our parents passed, she had said the same thing about a man. This is why I think she is just lost and confused. She is searching for a happiness that she will not find if she continues down the path that she has chosen. This Olivia person sounded great, but just not for Zoe, her and I both know that. Zoe is lost, she is just terribly lost." Chad rested his elbows on his desk, his hands folded together, almost as if in prayer.

"Have you tried calling her?" He asked Jill.

Jill nodded, "Yes, no luck, and it seems like her voicemail is full. So, when is the last time you have actually seen her then?"

This time Chad had to take a longer moment to find that answer to the question.

"Well, it would have been shortly after the last time we were at Lake Arrowhead together. Had a bit of a dispute, and then we saw each other once more after that. Gosh, that was the Labour Day weekend of 2012."

"Three years? Wow, that is a long time considering you guys do live so close. So, what's at Lake Arrowhead?"

"Our family cabin, well what used to be our family cabin. I have only been up there a couple times in the last couple years to check on it."

"That's too bad, that is a beautiful area. It's a shame a place up there would go to waste." Jill replied.

Chad shrugged his shoulders not seeming to agree with her.

"I don't know, I want to get rid of it. Actually, that was what the dispute was about. Since Mom and Dad died, it just does not seem the same there. It just seemed like more of a hassle than anything to hang on to it, but Zoe insisted that she wasn't ready to let it go. So, of course it turned into a big fight, and that was that. That was the last time we spent time at the so-called family cabin. I just wish she would see that and let us sell the darn place, but she won't. Now it is just sitting there empty, unused, costing us money, money that I know she doesn't have."

Jill and Chad sat across from each other, Jill wondering to herself if he was actually going to be of any help to her when her phone buzzed. She took it out and a text message from Raj was displayed on her screen, a pin, locating the last area Zoe's phone was pinged. Jill studied it closer for a moment, zooming the map out to get a full view of the area, and she couldn't believe what she was seeing. Maybe there was a God, she thought sarcastically to herself.

"What is it?" Chad asked concerned. Jill looked up, a stern expression staring back at Chad.

"Well good news Mr. Cardell, I don't think your cabin is sitting empty anymore, in fact, I'm pretty sure it's not empty at all."

Again, Chad seemed confused, not entirely sure what Jill meant by that, before he could ask Jill continued.

"I'm gonna need you to get me detailed directions to your cabin, Mr. Cardell, and I'm gonna have to ask you to do it now."

FOURTY – FIVE -October 10, 2015

Sophia's head was slightly fuzzy, because of the fact her body was starved and dehydrated she could feel the effects of the whiskey almost immediately. She had to admit it tasted horrible, but she enjoyed the way the first few sips were making her feel. This was the most relaxed she had truly felt since being trapped in the hell that she was in. Sophia was still hesitant of Zoe's intentions with her, but something about the woman's presence made her feel secure. Sophia believed Zoe when she had told Sophia that she wasn't there to hurt her. But after this morning, and seeing the look of anger course through Olivia, Sophia could not quite comprehend why she was back in here talking to her.

"I know you don't have any reason to trust me Sophia, and I won't blame you if you don't want to speak to me at all or tell me anything. But, I need you to believe me when I tell you I want to help you, I do, because I know this is wrong," Zoe sipped from her mug, then placed it on the floor beside her feet.

Sophia's internal battle continued in her mind, she knew this was her only hope of getting out of here alive, but she was scared that this was some sort of sick game, engineered by Olivia. But Sophia recalled the last conversation between them, when Olivia stormed out of here and Zoe was calling after her, with apparent worry and concern. Maybe Zoe was telling the truth, and maybe she knew how horribly wrong it was for her to be helping Olivia keep her here. Sophia knew she needed to connect with this woman on some level, to get her to trust her as much as she possibly could. Sophia adjusted herself trying to get as comfortable as she could.

"Your name is Zoe?" Sophia asked politely.

Zoe nodded her head slowly and answered.

"Yes, my name is Zoe."

"How do you know her?" Sophia continued, referring to Olivia.

"I have only known her for a couple weeks. We met at the bar I work at."

Sophia was surprised it had only been a couple weeks. To do something like this for someone would usually take a lot of trust and loyalty, so Sophia was slightly baffled.

"You have only known her a couple weeks? And you're just friends with her?"

Zoe pressed her lips together and shook her head.

"Not exactly, we have been more than friends since the day we met. It was fast, I have to admit that, but from the first moment there was just an immediate connection between the two of us, we clicked. We have barely spent any time apart except when I have had to go to work."

Sophia studied the woman in front of her more closely, now that she had the opportunity. She was a very attractive woman, Sophia admitted to herself. Her hair was a deep auburn that she was certain did not come out of a bottle. Her skin was like porcelain, smooth, and nearly flawless, and her eyes were a deep blue. Sophia could understand the attraction, but she had no idea that Olivia was ever interested in women that way.

"I never knew Olivia was interested in this type of relationship, I have only ever known her to date men."

"I know, I was her first, she did tell me that. Like I said though, when we met there was just something between us that neither one of us could resist."

Sophia's mouth was still dry, so she took another sip of the whiskey knowing it was probably not what she should be drinking, but it felt good. It was slowly giving her the courage to continue to build some trust with Zoe, now while she still had time to do it.

"Well, I guess it is true when they say we can't choose who we fall in love with, I know that just as much as anybody," Sophia answered as she continued to study Zoe.

"Sophia, she has been tormented by her brother's murder. I knew that, but I know this is wrong, what she is doing. I know that now."

"You know that now?" Sophia repeated Zoe's words, anger laced her words.

Zoe closed her eyes for a moment, she reopened them and leaned forward, her elbows resting on her knees, her eye's locked on Sophia's.

"I knew it was wrong, from the beginning. I'm so sorry you are here now. I am so sorry she is doing this to you..." Zoe's words were cut short, Sophia putting her hand up.

"But why? Zoe why is she doing this?"

"Sophia, you know why. Olivia thinks that you murdered her brother, or at least had something to do with it. She wants to hear you say it, she wants you to admit that it is true. I don't think she will stop until you tell her what she wants to hear."

Frustration now claimed Sophia, and she brought her hand up to her head and rubbed her forehead.

"I can't tell her that Zoe, I can't tell her that because it is not true."

"I believe you Sophia."

Sophia dropped her free hand back on to the bed, relieved at Zoe's words.

"You do?"

"Yes, I do. But Sophia, please, please just tell me what happened, so I know everything. Maybe I can convince Olivia to stop this craziness."

Sophia sighed heavily, her chest felt tight as it held on to every ounce of oxygen it could.

"I was in love with my husband, I was so desperately in love with my husband I could not see the truth that was right in front of my face. When I met Marcus, it was much like you described with Olivia, we clicked the moment our eyes locked. There was an undeniable force that drew us together, and like you and Olivia, we were inseparable. He was everything I had ever wanted in a man, and out of nowhere he was brought into my life. It was amazing Zoe, it was truly amazing." Sophia paused, she could see Zoe was captivated already, so she continued. "I had it all, I had the life most women would have killed to have. I had money, I had a beautiful house, I had a fantastic job, amazing friends and I had him. We were in the public eye a lot, and I know people were envious of us as a couple. I would be lying if I said I did not enjoy that. I knew I had a great life, and I was grateful for it, every single day of my life I was grateful for it. But…" Sophia paused thinking back to it all.

"But what?" Zoe did not want to be left hanging.

"But it was all a lie."

"Sophia, what happened?" Zoe's voice with filled with concern.

"He slowly changed right in front of me, and because of my love for him, I refused to see it. At first it was just little things, like bouts of jealousy. Then it started with a little more control, manipulation, and eventually it turned physical. I should have known the first time he laid his hands on me that my marriage was in trouble. But every single time he would apologize to me and he would make me forget it all, I believed him every single time. I could not tell anyone, there was no way I could shatter the perfect image we had. So, I continued on, and as sick as it is to hear myself say it now, I continued to fall in love with him. Every time he manipulated or controlled me or laid his hands on me, I forgave him. I always forgave him."

Silence hung thick in the air, and Sophia briefly questioned herself if she was saying too much. Some of this nobody knew, not even Olivia.

"I was blind Zoe. I think I knew deep down there were other women. I mean he had them throwing themselves at him all the time, I convinced myself that he was faithful and loyal to me, I refused to see the truth. I turned such a blind eye that I completely missed it," again a pause.

"Missed what?" Zoe asked.

"Cat was my best friend. For as long as I had known Marcus, Cat was my best friend. I knew her inside and out. I trusted her as much as I had trusted Marcus. I would have never ever thought it was even a possibility that she would betray me. I did not see it, until that day, I had no idea. Until that day she murdered my husband, I had no idea that either one of them would betray me like that. Zoe…" Sophia leaned forward now, "Zoe, I lied, I did, I never told anyone what was truly going on in my marriage, had I been stronger, none of this would have happened. But, I had nothing to do with his murder, I had no involvement in his murder.

I know it was shocking to Olivia, I know she is in pain, but I can't tell her what she wants to hear."

Zoe bent down and retrieved her mug off the ground, she downed what was left in her cup, and swallowed hard, she licked her lips and then she replied to Sophia.

"I know you can't. I am so sorry that you had to go through that alone. I have been in harmful relationships in my past, I know how hard it is. I could not even imagine though being married and in love with the person, and not wanting to face the truth. I am so sorry that Olivia refuses to hear the truth, I am so sorry that she is doing this to you. I know how wrong this is, I knew it from the beginning, Sophia. But honestly, I thought maybe she would just talk to you, hear it from you and then be able to move on. But, over these last five days she has slowly started to slip away from me. The Olivia I met and started to fall in love with is not there anymore. She is losing touch with reality."

"Zoe, she is sick, she is very sick," Sophia was not sure if Olivia had shared that part of her life with Zoe, but Sophia needed her to know.

"I know that now, I didn't want to see it, but I know that now."

"Olivia and I have never gotten along, that I can admit to you Zoe, but she has to accept the truth. The truth is her brother Marcus was having an affair with my best friend Catarina Warner, and things turned ugly. Cat murdered my husband, and then she killed herself, that is the truth. We know that is the truth because Detective Jill Keller and Detective Caleb Stone proved that. They proved that is exactly what happened. I have accepted it, and now Olivia needs to accept it as well." Sophia watched Zoe, her compassionate look quickly changed to another expression, one which Sophia could not decipher. Zoe held that expression, and remained silent, as if searching for something to say.

"Zoe? What is it? Are you okay?"

Zoe nodded her head, but to Sophia she did not look okay at all, she looked rattled to the core.

"Detective Caleb Stone?" Zoe reiterated.

Sophia nodded her head quickly, "Yes, why? Zoe what is it?"

"He is out there Sophia, Caleb Stone is out there, and he is looking for you. He is looking for you and he is looking for Olivia."

Sophia's heart woke from its relaxed resting place, it came alive in her chest with a fury she had never felt before. She had no idea how Zoe knew that information and right now she did not care because all she needed to know was that he was out there. He was searching for her, just like she prayed he would be. But she panicked almost instantly, panicked at the thought that maybe he would not find her in time, what if he did not find her in time?

"You have got to help me Zoe, please! Unlock me please, do the right thing Zoe, help me and just do the right thing."

FOURTY – SIX -October 10, 2015

Jill tossed her cell phone on the seat beside her, she had just got off the phone with her partner, Detective Landon. She had not anticipated for her day to be completely taken up by hunting down Olivia Donovan, but the more and more she dug, she was convinced that she needed to find her and tonight. A part of Jill was still resting easy knowing Olivia was probably just crying out for attention by taking that gun from her parents' home. However, finding out from that bartender, Tommy, that things did not seem to be going great with Zoe and her, that concerned Jill, she could not deny that. The other factor that had Jill reeling, was the information given to her that two other men had been into that bar earlier looking for two women. She did not have all the information yet, but she needed to find out who was looking for those women, and which women were they looking for? There was something not adding up, and Jill knew she had to figure it out. If someone was out searching for Olivia, that could mean Olivia was in danger. Maybe that was why her and Zoe were staying out at this family cabin, to hide from someone, but who? Jill was just happy that Raj had sent her the map of the last tower Zoe's phone was pinged to when she was with Chad, because he was sure that was where Zoe must be.

The sun had already made its descent into the horizon, and the day was quickly turning into night as Jill's headlights started to light the road in front of her as she continued on the highway. From Chad's directions it was a little over an hour to get to the cabin, she had been on the road for nearly 45 minutes, so she had about 25 minutes still to go. She would have preferred to take this drive in the daylight, but there was no way she was going to wait until the morning to drive up there. Who knows what could transpire in that amount of time. Someone was in danger, Jill was just not entirely sure who that was yet. She was hoping her instincts were wrong this time, and that she would find Zoe and Olivia at the cabin, just escaping the city and escaping the reality of Olivia's disorder.

Perhaps Zoe convinced Olivia that they needed to get away, alone. Maybe Zoe was fully aware what Olivia was going through and was taking her away for a few days to refocus. That is what Jill was desperately hoping, that would make this all so easy, but usually her instincts did not lie to her. And as much as she prayed this was one of those times, Jill could feel it in her bones, she could feel that something was really wrong. Right now, more than any other time since he had been gone, Jill wished he was here with her, to help her, because he would know what to do, Caleb always knew what to do.

The other apprehension that crossed Jill's mind as she drove into the impending darkness was the fact that her Lieutenant Vasquez was going to be pissed at her if anything serious were to happen. She knew he was going to be furious that she did not clear any of this with him first, especially with the Cassidy Ryan case on the go. But Jill wasn't prepared to bring this to his attention, not until she knew more. Because, as of right now, she could be wasting her time, chasing nothing more that an over emotional, dramatic, woman who is trying to grab the attention of anyone she can. If that is the case, Jill knew she did not even want this on her LT's radar, she can definitely handle this on her own, nobody needs to know a thing.

Jill's memory shifted back to the day that Olivia Donovan came to see her in her office. Olivia was determined that Jill help her prove that Sophia Donovan murdered her husband, Marcus. This was not, however, the first time a grieving relative had come to them after a case was closed, desperate for them to help them. Many times, after a homicide case is closed, the findings do not appease someone involved. Many times, those people, filled with grief and anger, do not want to accept the truth, they need someone to blame, anybody to blame. As much as Jill had to admit to herself there was always something about Sophia Donovan that did not sit well with her, she also had to trust in their investigation and more over, she trusted Caleb. That day as Olivia pleaded with her to reopen the case, Jill felt for her, she could clearly see she was tormented over the loss of her brother. Now, after learning a little bit more about Olivia Donovan, Jill realized that she was not in a clear frame of mind, and that would make it almost impossible for her to heal.

Jill's full attention was drawn to the sign coming up ahead, she was not far from Crest Park, so she knew she did not have much farther to go. She had been up here a handful of times with her family when she was younger. She remembered her father would pack their station wagon full of camping gear, and drive Jill and her mother up here for a weekend of camping. Her father loved to camp. He loved the outdoors, and Jill cherished those times with him. They would stop at Crest Park so Jill and her dog, Shadow could run around, Jill throwing a stick for the excited black lab. Her mother would stay in the car, her knitting needles at work, while she would smile at her daughter running happily in the park. Her father would get out and lean against the hood of the station wagon and light his Marlboro. Enjoying it as much as he enjoyed watching Jill laughing, Shadow barking with anticipation. Jill smiled softly to herself at the memory of him, and again for the second time that day, her heart ached. He was such a good man, and such a good cop, he was always doing his best to protect everyone he could. He taught her about people, he always taught her that not everyone was going to be good and follow the rules. He would always say there was not very nice people out there, and that was why he was a cop, because he wanted to protect the nice people from the mean people. That was always what he would say when he knew his daughter was worried about his job and would ask him why he wanted to be a police officer. As Jill got older though, she could see how much her father loved what he did, and how compassionate he was towards everyone, sometimes even to the people Jill considered the mean people. She had asked him once, if it was hard to be nice to people who did bad things, and his answer always stuck with her, it was an answer that she tried to enforce in her career today, as hard as it was. He said to her,

"Everyone has a story Jilly Bean, sometimes people do things, bad things, and yes, sometimes it's simply because they are bad people. But Jilly Bean, sometimes good people do very bad things, but for very good reasons. Read their entire book, know their entire story, and then you will truly know who deserves your compassion, and who doesn't."

His words penetrated her memory, as she drove past Crest Park, his words clung to her more than ever right now. As she continued on her path to Zoe Cardell's family cabin, Jill Keller was not fully yet aware just how significant those words of her father were, are, and would be.

FOURTY – SEVEN - October 10, 2015

Sophia was alone again in her room, and her emotions were running rapid. Caleb, he was out there looking for her, he knew she was in trouble and he was out there. Sophia knew in her heart that he would not stop until he found her, but without Zoe's help, she feared it might be too late. Sophia needed Zoe, she confided in her as much as she could without telling her the truth. Sophia needed Zoe to do what was right, and she had told her that. But then Zoe just got up and left Sophia alone in the room again. With every moment that she left her in here, Sophia knew her chances were dwindling, and even Caleb would not be able to help her. She wanted to yell for Zoe to come back in the room, but she decided to wait and hope she would come back in on her own. And after a few agonizing moments, she did. The door opened, and Zoe stood in the doorway, looking at Sophia, her eye's looked red and puffy from crying.

"I don't know what to do," Zoe muttered, almost inaudibly.

"You know what you need to do Zoe, please just do the right thing," Sophia answered calmly.

Zoe walked into the room, and Sophia could see the struggle that was over taking her, but she just had to keep her calm and thinking rationally.

"Zoe, Olivia is sick, she needs help."

Zoe nodded her head in full agreement, then replied.

"I know she is, but I'm here too Sophia, I am part of this too."

It was clear now what was stopping Zoe from doing the right thing, the fear of what would happen to her. The fear of not knowing what would happen to her in all of this. Sophia could fully empathize with her, she knew full well this was not Zoe's doing, and she needed Zoe to understand that.

"This isn't your war Zoe, this is all Olivia. Olivia is not in the right frame of mind, and she has manipulated you into thinking this is the right thing to do. You have done nothing wrong here, I know that, and if I know that, everyone will know that."

Zoe stood motionless in front of Sophia, and Sophia could see just from Zoe's outward expression that she was internally trying to fathom each and every circumstance. She was trying to find a way to rationalize the entire situation and trying to determine if she should trust what Sophia was saying to her. Zoe inhaled deeply, her nerves evidently shaken.

"I'm just so scared, I want to do what is right, I know that, but I'm terrified of what is going to happen to me. What will they do to me knowing my part in this. Knowing that I helped Olivia get you here," tears of utter fear escaped Zoe's eyes and fell down her cheek. Sophia slid her body towards the end of the bed, so both feet were now on the floor, her shackled ankle stinging in pain yet again.

"Zoe, listen to me, I know you are a good person. I know you had no idea what was going to happen when you let her bring me here. I know that, and I know you have no intentions of hurting me. I will be sure to tell them that, I will tell them everything. If you help me I promise you, I will help you. I will make sure they know what really happened here, but please Zoe, we are running out of time. She is going to come back."

Zoe absorbed every word, Sophia knew she did, and a quiet stillness permeated the room, and Sophia just felt like screaming to her, "GODDAMMIT HELP ME ZOE" but she contained her desire to do so. Zoe reached into the pocket of her jeans, and retrieved a small key, she sighed deeply, and knelt down in front of Sophia.

"I'm so sorry, please forgive me for helping her with this. Please forgive me," Zoe knelt down in front of Sophia, looking up to the ceiling, and Sophia knew it was not her she was asking the forgiveness from, it was God's forgiveness.

"He will forgive you Zoe," Sophia spoke softly to Zoe, reassuring her as best she could, and then she continued. "And so, will I."

Zoe's gaze immediately left the ceiling and her focus was now locked onto Sophia, and she hoped that Zoe could read the sincerity in her eyes. The two women looked at each other intently, and in that moment, Sophia knew Zoe trusted her, and she also knew that she could trust Zoe, she had too. Zoe fumbled with the key and reached for the lock around Sophia's ankle, and a shock of pain shot up Sophia's leg the moment Zoe's hand touched her ankle. She winced, and Zoe instinctively pulled her hand away.

"It's okay, I'm okay," Sophia reassured her. Zoe reached for the cuff around her ankle again, being careful not to hurt her any further.

"I have to get you out of here," Zoe said bluntly as she fumbled with the key, her shaking hands struggling to place the key in the lock.

"I can go, alone…" Sophia started but was cut off by Zoe.

"No, you can't go out there alone in the dark, you don't know where we are. There is a ton of wildlife out there at night. There is no way you are going alone, wandering around in the dark. I will get you out of here."

The cuff around Sophia's ankle released, and an instantaneous sensation of relief washed over her. For the first time in however many days she had been here, she was entirely certain, she felt optimistic, and confident that this was going to be okay. Sophia looked down at her ankle, it was red, swollen and raw from the shackle rubbing against her bare skin. She wanted to jump up off of the bed, but she knew she needed to be careful. Her body was weak, and her strength was very limited, not to mention a fuzziness still enveloped her from the whiskey she finished off not too long ago. Zoe stood up, she backed away and gave Sophia some room, ready to help her stand if needed.

Sophia steadied herself, her hands bracing the bed as she slowly pushed herself up into a standing position, and the moment she was upright, the blood drained from her brain down to her extremities. For a brief moment she thought she might pass out, but she stood there allowing her body to adjust to the new position. Zoe reached for her, and gently hung onto her arm. Sophia looked at her.

"Thank you, Zoe."

"I'm so sorry," was all she replied.

Sophia made her first step, and her legs were wobbly beneath her, she could not recall a time she had ever felt this weak, her body begging her to sit back down, but she knew she could not listen, she had to keep moving.

"Are you okay?" Zoe asked with sincere concerns.

"Yes," Sophia took another step.

"We have to go now, grab onto my arm," Zoe held out her arm and Sophia took hold of it, and they began to make their way out of the room. Sophia limped carefully not to put too much pressure on her ankle but moving as fast as she could.

They were in the living room, Zoe continuing to be a crutch for Sophia, she grabbed her purse off the coffee table as they walked by, Sophia holding Zoe's arm as she reached down. As quickly as they could manage they walked towards the kitchen towards the door. Sophia's chest tightening with anticipation and liberation to soon be free of this hell. She turned to Zoe, and Zoe turned to her.

"Take me to him, take me to Caleb," Sophia muttered faintly, the weakness of her body wanting to take over.

And just as Zoe was about to answer her, the room was flooded with lights, headlights. Only two words managed to escape Zoe's lips.

"Oh shit!"

Both women stood frozen, their feet planted to the floor, the headlights washing in on them coming through the kitchen window. Sophia's stomach sank with a vengeance, and she literally felt like a deer stuck in headlights. Sophia continued to cling to Zoe, staring at one another, searching each others' internal thoughts, scared to move and scared to talk. Zoe reached in her back pocket and retrieved her cell phone with a scrap piece of paper. As the lights continued to shine on them, Sophia watched Zoe's thumb race across the screen, the words displayed so both of them could read them.

"Help us! Caleb, hurry!" followed by the exact directions that would lead him directly to the women, he was so desperate to find.

FOURTY – EIGHT -October 10, 2015

The motel room was dated to say the least; however, it was comfortable and all they needed for the night. It had two double beds, both dressed with matching floral comforters. Isabelle had her own room right next to them, a single door that attached the rooms between them. Right now, all three of them sat together in the one room. Isabelle sitting on one bed, Trent on the other and Caleb stood near the dresser, an old tube TV was on in the background but on silent.

"I just can't believe this," Isabelle exclaimed, looking up at Caleb.

"This is good, Isabelle, this is going to lead us to Olivia I know it is."

Isabelle nodded her head, and Caleb could see the latest news they got had escalated her hopes of finding her daughter.

"Well you were right," Trent also looked towards Caleb, "you knew there was something up with that Zoe chick. When we showed her that picture of Olivia it spooked her, caught her off guard. Either she lied about knowing her because she was nervous, or she lied because she knows where Sophia is, I think it is the latter."

Caleb nodded his head, then walked to the bed and sat at the empty space beside Trent, directly across from Isabelle.

"Zoe and Olivia Donovan are dating, or whatever... but they are involved. And I have no doubts about it now. Zoe Cardell knows exactly why we were in that bar looking for both Olivia and Sophia. She was a part of this, we know that now, and we are going to find them," Caleb's comment was directed at Isabelle.

"I believe you Caleb, I am just so relieved your friend was able to come up with this information."

"Luke came through that is for sure. He is going to lead us right to them," Trent assured her now.

"But we only know from her phone number the area her phone last hit right? I mean this is a big area. Where do we even start?" Concern returned to Isabelle's voice.

"We have started, we are here, we are closer, and tomorrow, when the sun comes up we are going to start again. We are going to knock on every door in the area, we are going to stop at every tiny store and we are going to find someone who knows one of them. If that John guy from that little store back at Crest Park has seen them, then I can guarantee other people will too," Caleb leaned forward and allowed his arms to rest on his knees, his head was beginning to throb from the lack of sleep and food the last few days.

Isabelle sighed heavily and ran her hand through her bob, "I still cannot believe this is happening, why would that lunatic do this?"

Caleb knew all three of them knew exactly why she would do this, but only the three of them knew the whole story. Right now, Olivia Donovan was following an intuition, a need to cast the blame on someone for her brother's murder.

"She and Sophia have obviously had a very tumultuous relationship through the years, and Olivia somehow wants to prove Sophia had something to do with Marcus's murder. She is desperate and sometimes desperate people take desperate measures, I understand that part completely."

"Caleb, how does she know anything? How does Olivia know that Sophia did this?" There was anger in Isabelle's eyes thinking of what Olivia could have possibly done to her daughter.

"She doesn't know, she thinks she knows. There is a big difference Isabelle. Olivia Donovan is determined to find out the truth, she wants to find out the truth from the only person that can give it to her, and that is Sophia. But she doesn't know the truth, she never will, she never can."

Isabelle stood briskly off the bed, she walked over to the mini fridge and pulled out a bottle of water. She twisted the cap off and took a healthy chug. She placed the open bottle on the dresser and Caleb could see her expression shift.

"That crazy bitch better not hurt my daughter, I swear to God, when we find Sophia she had better be okay. If Olivia Donovan put one goddamn finger on my baby, I am going to kill her, I swear to God I will kill her."

Trent and Caleb glanced at each other, and Caleb stood up and walked over to Isabelle. He took her by her shoulders and looked her square in the eyes.

"Listen to me Isabelle, I made a promise to you that we were going to find Sophia, and I mean it, we will. I know you are angry, I know you are scared, I know you are desperate right now, but I need you to stay calm. I need you to not do anything, and I mean anything, when we find her, do you understand me? Trent and I will take care of this. When we find them, and we will find them, I do not want you to do anything stupid, anything that can jeopardize yours or your daughter's safety. I cannot make myself clearer than that Isabelle, I did not want you to come because it is not safe, but I get it, I get why you had too. But please, you need to now promise me something. You need to promise me that no matter what happens you will not do anything, and I mean that- anything. Can you promise me that?"

Caleb and Isabelle stood firmly on the ground, staring at each other with intensity, Caleb waiting for her to acknowledge his only request. He could feel Isabelle shaking under his grasp and watched as tears formed in her eyes, and finally she answered.

"That is my daughter out there. My only child. Someone has her, against her will, and she is probably terrified, and tortured at the thought that she may never be found. I cannot even fathom the idea of what she must be going through right now, but I know she is strong…" Isabelle paused, the tears now escaping and running down her cheek. Caleb released his grasp on her arms and straightened. She continued. "She is so strong, she will fight. So yes, I can promise you, I can swear to you right here and now, that I will not do anything to jeopardize my daughter's life…" Caleb exhaled a sigh of relief, but Isabelle clearly was not finished. "But, I will do whatever it takes to save my daughter. If that means putting my own self in danger or jeopardizing my own life for hers, then no, that is part of the promise I cannot keep. I will gladly give up my life for hers, if that is what it comes to, I will not hesitate, not for one second." Isabelle then turned away form Caleb and walked around the bed, taking a seat again, as Trent watched her, with both unease and complete understanding.

Caleb placed both hands on his hips, and his head dropped to the ground.

"Jesus! Isabelle."

Isabelle turned herself on the bed so she was facing Caleb's direction and she quickly replied.

"Let's just find her okay, let's just all get some rest tonight, or at least try, and tomorrow let's get out there and find my daughter."

Silence was suspended heavy in the air, nobody wanting to break it, Caleb knew Isabelle was right. They just all needed to get some rest, they needed to start fresh tomorrow, because right now they were all exhausted and frustrated and scared.

"You're right Isabelle, we are all tired, we just need to take a break, rest and in the morning, we regroup, and we get out there. We will find her, and we will bring her home," Trent interjected for Caleb, Caleb dropped his hands from his hips and nodded at both of them. Before anyone could say anything further, Caleb's phone vibrated loudly against his hip, he quickly pulled it from its holder and flipped it open. It was a text, it was text that he was not expecting. He read the words, his brain trying to process them, his guts twisted, and his heart pounded fiercely in his chest. Isabelle and Trent both sat starting at him, but Caleb just stared at his phone.

"Caleb? What is it?" Trent finally asked.

"We need to go now," he flipped his phone closed, pulled his gun from out of the side table drawer. Trent without another question followed suit. Isabelle stood up, panicked unsure what was happening. She raced after them slamming the motel door behind them, they ran out to Trent's truck and jumped in. Trent barely giving them enough time to get seat belted before he tore out of the spot.

"Caleb?" Isabelle's voice was stern now. "Caleb, what the hell is happening? Where are we going?"

As terrified as he felt in that moment, after seeing the words "Help us! Caleb hurry!" written across his screen, he knew in that very moment Sophia was still alive. He knew she was alive and knew where she was. And as much as the idea that they would not make it to her in time horrified him, he had needed to stay courageous and strong, not only for himself, but for Isabelle and for Sophia.

Caleb gestured to Trent which direction he needed him to go, the directions that were laid out for him on his phone, and he turned back to Isabelle, looked her dead in the eye and replied.

"We are going to get your daughter Isabelle, we are going to bring her home tonight. This all ends tonight."

FOURTY – NINE - October 10, 2015

Olivia pulled up to the cabin, the headlights beating brightly against the wooden structure in front of her. Zoe's car was here, that was a good sign, it meant that she was still here and that she had not abandoned her, like everyone else had. Olivia was still very angry at her for this morning, and the fact that she went into that room and offered her food while she slept. Olivia knew Zoe was a softer person than she was, she knew Zoe was weaker so maybe she should just let it slide. She had to, Zoe was the only person that understood her, Zoe was the only person that was here for her.

Olivia sat in the driver's seat, the engine still purring softly, and she continued to stare at the cabin, knowing she was in there, sitting in that room, whimpering like a scared animal, while being chained like a wild one. Even just the thought of that now made Olivia's skin crawl, it made her blood boil, knowing she continued to lie to her face. If Sophia would have just told her the fucking truth, then none of this would be happening. Olivia would not have had to waste these last five days babysitting a grown woman, keeping her locked in a room. Instead her and Zoe could have just continued on with their relationship. They could have just continued on in their happy bubble, where nobody judged her, where nobody thought she was crazy. No, instead Sophia had to make the choice to lie, every day, and force Olivia to continue this nonsense. And now there was someone else out there looking for her, someone out there that knew she was missing. Olivia tried to figure out who it was, Zoe said two men, but who? Olivia glanced at her self in the rear-view mirror, she was not surprised that she had bags under her eyes, and stress etched in the corners of each. Look what this bitch was doing to her, look at the amount of stress she was causing her. Olivia had to admit to herself, since she went off all those horrendous meds, she was much more capable of keeping a clear mind. There was no fogginess, no false mood stabilizers hindering her from making the decisions she knew she should be making. As anxious as she was feeling, she knew her mind was not altered, it was clear. Her choices and her actions were not being manipulated by some drugs that everyone claimed she needed to be on. No, she was herself again, Olivia.

It was almost time to go in, she just hoped Zoe was ready to help her, because it was time to end this. It was very clear to Olivia now that Sophia just did not want to cooperate. If she wasn't willing to cooperate and tell her the truth, then what else was Olivia supposed to do? What other option did she really have? If that lying bitch would have just done what she was told then none of this would be happening, but now Olivia was forced to take-action. Zoe would understand, Olivia knew she would. Zoe was the only person that truly got Olivia. She was the only person that could relate to what Olivia was going through. Although Zoe had expressed her concerns about the whole situation, Olivia knew she could count on her in the end. Zoe would never let her down, that couldn't happen. Zoe would recognize, just like Olivia has, that there was nothing left to do, this was it, and it had to happen tonight. Then they could move on, Olivia could be at peace with Marcus. She and Zoe could go back to LA and they could continue what they started, they could go back to their bubble and be happy again. Olivia turned off the engine, glanced over to the passenger seat, and smiled slyly to herself at the 9 mm lying there, waiting. She grabbed the gun and got out of the car. She tucked the gun into the waist of her jeans, and she walked with purpose towards the front door of the cabin.

She opened the door, and slipped inside, Zoe was not in the kitchen or the living room. Olivia came all the way in, and before she had a chance to call Zoe's name, she came out of their bedroom, a nervous smile spread across her face.

"Zoe," Olivia was relieved she was still there, even though her car was parked out front.

"Hi Olivia," she replied, as she walked up to her and gave her a soft kiss on the cheek.

"See", Olivia thought to herself, she had Zoe.

"How did it go?" Zoe asked her, and Olivia could not help noticing that Zoe seemed rattled for some reason, but she smiled at her girlfriend and answered calmly.

"Great, everything is going to be okay."

"It is, it is," Zoe gently touched Olivia's arm and she walked into the living room.

"Baby?" Olivia addressed her as she followed behind her, and reached to gently grab her arm, Zoe turned around to face her again.

"Ya?"

"Are you okay?" Olivia asked her, sincerely worried that she was upset about something.

"Hmm mmm, ya of course, I am." Zoe continued to allow her to slide her grip down her arm and take Zoe's hand in hers.

"Good, good, I just thought maybe something happened. I was scared you would not be here when I got back. Silly, I know. Of course, you're here. You've always been here for me."

Zoe's nerves were becoming more difficult to supress, Olivia could sense it, starting to worry herself.

"Right?"

Zoe nodded her head quickly, not wanting to pause in her answer.

"Yes, I'm here. I'm here for you." Zoe held Olivia's hand firmly in hers and she led her to the couch, Zoe sat first then patted the seat beside her, indicating she wanted Olivia to sit with her. Olivia obliged, she could feel the gun, pressing up against her lower back.

"This is all going to be okay Liv, it's going to be okay, I promise," Zoe smiled warmly at her.

"I know it is. Thank you for helping me," Olivia watched as the smile faded from Zoe's face, but she continued anyways. "You helped me, and I am thankful. You get me, and for that I am thankful. It's all going to be okay after tonight."

"Liv?" Zoe swallowed hard. "It's over, this is all over?"

Olivia nodded at her and replied in agreeance.

"I know baby, it's over, tonight it's all over. I am so happy you agree, I was so worried you wouldn't understand, but I know you do. It's time to end it. I can just take care of her now, I can take care of her and then we can just be together. We can forget this happened, we can forget all about her. I can move on from this, and we can forget all about Sophia Donovan. You're right, and I knew you would understand." Olivia felt a release, any doubts she had were gone, and she knew Zoe was here for her. Olivia went to stand and this time, Zoe grabbed her hand, and Olivia looked down at her. Zoe's face was frozen, her eyes laced with a paralyzing fear, which confused Olivia because she just told her it was over, so why did she seem so afraid?

"Olivia, what do you mean take care of her?" Zoe held firm her grip on Olivia's hand, as if trying to prevent her from doing anything stupid.

Olivia laughed coyly at Zoe, and she pulled the gun from the back of her pants and held it up for Zoe to see.

"You know what I mean silly, how else did you think we were going to kill her?" she turned towards Sophia's door and Zoe jumped off the couch, every shade of colour drained from her skin, and she yelled.

"Olivia! Stop! Please!"

Olivia stopped before her hand reached for the door knob and turned back to Zoe.

"What baby?" Olivia dropped both hands to her side, the gun's barrel facing to the floor. Then she sighed, her shoulders dropping, and then it was clear to her, why Zoe was acting so strange.

"You wanted to do it for me? God, you wanted to do it for me, so I would not have to live with that right?" Olivia cocked her head to one side, and she looked at Zoe with admiration. However, that same look was not directed back at her.

"Olivia…please! Just…don't. It's over!"

Olivia became fully aware of her emotions, and she could feel them shift. As she stood there staring at Zoe, the woman who she trusted, the woman who she loved, the woman who meant the world to her, she felt it all disappear. In one brief moment, she knew she had betrayed her, she knew her doubts earlier today were real. A dawning of truth came rushing at her with a force of a freight train, she was angry at herself, for being so naive. Zoe stood there, waiting, and watching her, her eyes flooding with scared tears. Olivia glared at her now, the hurt and the utter betrayal nearly suffocating her. Olivia could only bring herself to shake her head slowly and she faintly murmured.

"What the fuck did you do?"

"Olivia please!" Zoe cried out again, but not moving.

"What the fuck did you do?" Olivia shouted loudly this time, and in one quick motion she turned, and forcefully pushed the door open, as she rushed into the room.

She stared wrathfully at the empty bed in front of her. Her brain was swimming, her heart was thrashing in her chest, and she could feel the veins in her head pumping with anger. Olivia quickly turned around, and Zoe was still transfixed with fear in the spot she left her. But now instead of love, and trust and admiration when she looked at her, she could only see disgust, and utter betrayal. Olivia bolted back out the door, the gun no longer at her side, but pointed directly at the one woman she thought she could trust forever.

"Where the fuck is she?"

Zoe was now sobbing, and she was crippled with fear, unable to move her feet. All she managed to do was bring both of her hands up, trying to calm the madness in front of her.

"Please, Liv, please!"

"God dammit, Zoe! Where the fuck is she? What the fuck have you done? You stupid bitch!" Before Olivia could pull the trigger, she heard a sound behind her and she turned quickly. Sophia was there, coming at her, swinging something directly at her.

"You bitch!" Sophia yelled, as she came at her. Olivia had heard her much too soon, and she was able to quickly duck. Sophia, still weak and feeble, fell forward, just barely missing her. Olivia spun on her heels, not allowing her a second to get back up, and the object fell to the floor, Olivia glanced at it and realized it was the fire poker. She stood over Olivia, and she watched as she scrambled to get to her feet, and Zoe made a move to help her.

"Sophia!"

"Do not move!" Olivia ordered, and Zoe stopped in her tracks, as Sophia got onto her hands and knees, her head hung low, knowing she fucked up her only opportunity. Olivia kept the gun pointed at Zoe, and she calmed her voice and looked down at the floor.

"Get to the fucking couch, both of you sit on the couch." She watched as Sophia made her way to the couch, and sat beside Zoe, the two women grabbing each other's hand, clinging to one another. Olivia stood in front of them, the gun pointed in their direction. She chuckled out loud and shook her head in disbelief.

"Are you fucking kidding me right now? You thought you would be able to fool me? You thought you would be able to win? How miserably stupid are you?"

Sophia was not crying, not like Zoe, instead she looked defeated, and crushed with the overpowering realization that she failed.

"Olivia, listen to me," Zoe pleaded. "It does not have to be like this. We can fix this, we can work together, we can fix this!"

Olivia's eyes darted to Zoe, venomously shooting daggers in her direction.

"No Zoe, WE cannot fix this, there is no more we. You selfish whore, you destroyed that, didn't you? I will fix this! Only I can fix this now. I will make this all go away, like it never fucking happened."

Olivia's body was trembling, both with adrenaline and an overwhelming rage. She kept the gun pointed at both women, doing her best to steady her hand. She wanted nothing more than to just pull the trigger, to end both of their miserable lives. But as she stood there with both of them at her mercy, she knew she would not be able to do it, not until she heard the entire truth from Sophia.

Only then would she be able to pull the trigger and be at peace with her decision.

"You," Olivia aimed her weapon in Sophia's direction, Sophia's void and empty eyes looked back at her. "Tell me what you did to my brother."

Sophia's eyes shifted away from Olivia's, and Olivia literally watched the darkness in her eyes fill with light. Olivia, keeping the gun trained on Zoe and Sophia turned her head at the source of Sophia's changing expression. She was taken aback, surprised at the unwelcome company that had decided to grace them with their presence. She did not recognize one of them but the other, she immediately remembered.

"Don't do this Olivia, we can help you," Detective Caleb Stone calmly spoke as he cautiously walked inside the cabin, the other man following behind him, both of their guns drawn.

Olivia scoffed at them, unphased by them even. They were not going to stop her from getting the truth, nobody was.

"You're a fucking liar, just like her. She needs to tell me what happened to Marcus."

"Olivia there is nothing to tell, you know what happened to your brother, so please..." Caleb coolly replied, as he very easily continued towards the living room. Olivia not unaware of it, barked.

"Do not move another fucking step, do you hear me?"

Caleb stopped in his place, Trent stopping behind him. "Its okay, I'm not going move, we will stay right here, okay? Just put the gun down, we are here to help you."

Olivia's aggravation climaxed, as he kept saying they were here to help, she knew the only person he was here to help was her.

"She tells me everything or she dies!" Olivia's head swung viciously back towards Sophia.

"Olivia!" Caleb's voice was heavy with desperation to get Olivia's attention away from Sophia, but she was like a dog with his bone, she was unrelenting.

"Fine!" Sophia shouted at Olivia. "Fine, Olivia, you want to know the truth? You want to hear it all? Fine, I will tell you everything about the murder of Marcus, I will tell you everything."

Olivia felt her body relax, she felt a tremendous sense of accomplishment at those words uttered out of Sophia's mouth. Finally, she thought to herself, finally she is going to hear the whole story, right from the source. She is going to finally hear the truth, and then she can end it all, she will finally end it all tonight.

FIFTY - October 10, 2015

Darkness was all around her now, and as Jill drove her car up the short road that led to the small cabin she immediately felt a menacing sensation wash over her. Even though she had yet to know anything, she could sense that something was wrong, and this was not going to be as easy as she had hoped. Before she even pulled up in front of the cabin, she cut her lights not wanting to draw any attention from inside. She wanted a moment to determine what she might be up against. She slowly pulled her car up to the side of the cabin, and the first thing she noticed was the other vehicles that were already there. Two other cars and a truck, but from where her car was now parked that was all she could see. She could not see inside the windows of the cabin, but her uneasiness was only intensifying, with worry that perhaps whoever was looking for Olivia Donovan may have already found her. Jill just prayed she was not too late. Jill was aware of the fact at this point, she should have called for some back up, but she was not willing to do that, not yet, not until she knew the full situation that she was going to be faced with.

Jill reached for the car door handle and opened it gently, she then got out of her car and gingerly closed the door behind her. The October air was slightly crisp, and the silence of the woods was almost haunting. That mixed with the darkness swallowing everything around her, made Jill feel a very unfamiliar sense of dread. Since she was not one to show her fear, she very easily made her way towards the cabin. As she approached she noticed straightaway that the front door of the cabin was ajar, and a soft glow of light was escaping from the opening. Her heart was beating in her chest, and her adrenaline was starting to kick in just a little bit. As she slowly approached the door, the faintest of memories of that dream she had came barreling into clarity. The dream of her walking petrified down the dark hallway, the dark long hallway. The door, she could remember now fumbling with the handle urging herself to open it up and find what was on the other side. The empty room, illuminated by candles, and then she remembers the gut-wrenching feeling of turning around and seeing him, seeing him put a gun to his head. Then she recalled the ear shattering blare of the gun. It had taken her days to erase the memory of that nightmare, but as she was approaching into the unknown in front of her, every emotion, every fear, and every sensation of sheer panic emerged from a dark recessed memory of her mind. Jill tried her best to bury back where it came from, the same spot that she kept all of her emotions buried, all the emotions that were resurfacing today, she needed to keep them all buried.

She came up the door, and she could hear the voices, so she pulled her gun out of the holster, and held it up protecting herself of a potential threat. Jill inched close enough to the door, she stood as quietly as she possibly could to hear what was being said.

"Fine!" A woman's voice shouted, and then continued. "Fine, Olivia, you want to know the truth? You want to hear it all? Fine, I will tell you everything about the murder of Marcus, I will tell you everything."

Jill recognized the voice, it was the voice of Sophia Donovan. What the hell was Sophia Donovan doing here, and what did she mean, by "I will tell you everything about the murder of Marcus?" Jill crept, ever so silently to get just one inch closer, so she didn't miss a word of what was being said. As she did so she allowed herself to peak around the corner, and when she saw him, her pounding heart seemed to stop cold in her chest. Her breath caught in her throat, and her mind was swimming in every direction possible. He was there, his back to her, a gun aimed towards Olivia Donovan who was also armed. Jill could not see Sophia or Zoe sitting in the living room, but she knew that it was Sophia in there. She did not recognize the other man that was standing at his side, and she honestly barely even acknowledged his existence. The second she realized Caleb Stone was there, standing only a mere few feet from her, she was shaken to the core. Part of her wanted nothing more than to bolt through the door and grab a hold of him and never let go, not this time. The other part, however, her sensible part, her instinctual part, automatically went on defense. She knew things were going to change tonight, whatever it was that Sophia Donovan was about to say, it was going to change everything, for everyone tonight. And somehow and in some way, Caleb was involved. Caleb had always been involved. In the midst of her own ramped emotions, she did not even notice Isabelle Donovan, sitting in the darkness of the truck watching her. Instead Jill cocked her head, trying to allow for the best position to be sure she could hear everything clearly, not wanting to miss a single word.

"Yes Sophia, I want you to tell me everything, why the hell do you think you have been here for the last five fucking days? You think I was just trying to bond with you?" Sarcasm was laced over Olivia's statement.

"I had no choice Olivia, you have to believe me when I tell you I had no choice." Sophia's voice was unwavering.

Jill watched Olivia from around the corner of the door. Her gun still at its ready position. Olivia continued to point her gun in Sophia's direction, and Jill wondered where Zoe Cardell was when another female voice, one that Jill had not heard before, spoke.

"Olivia please, you don't have to do this!"

Olivia's head swung slightly to her right and she scoffed with frustration.

"Yes, I do! Jesus Zoe, I thought you understood me? I thought you understood why I was doing this? But you are just like the rest of them. So please do me a favor and shut the hell up, so she can finish telling me her little story." Olivia returned her attention back to Sophia and shouted at her. "Now go on, tell me how you had no choice, in murdering my brother."

"I was in danger Olivia, my life was in danger. There was a side of Marcus that you did not know Olivia, I know you don't want to believe that, but Marcus was a dangerous man…"

"Quit it! Quit lying" Olivia's voice filled with fury, cut Sophia off.

"I am not lying, just listen to me. I loved him very much, I did, but things turned very ugly between us, and we kept as much as we could to ourselves. But Olivia he hurt me, he put his hands on me in ways that I didn't deserve, in ways that nobody deserves."

Jill's focus shifted for a moment back to Caleb, and she watched him, as he steadied his aim, prepared to take a shot if needed.

"I don't believe you, if he was so mean then why the hell did you stay with him? Why continue to stay and allow it to happen?"

"I loved him, and I did not want to admit to myself what was going on. I was waiting for him to change, I was waiting for him to realize that what he was doing was wrong. Because every time it happened he would say he was wrong, and every time I would forgive him. And before I knew it, 11 years of our life had gone by, but by then the damage had been done. By then it was too late," Jill was admittedly surprised at how composed Sophia Donovan was acting.

"So, for that you killed him? Because he hit you a couple times and wasn't nice to you, you decided to kill him? Is that what you are telling me?" Olivia's question seemed rather calm but contempt.

"It is not like that Olivia, that is not how it happened."

"Then how did it happen Sophia?" The anger was presenting again.

"I told you I had no choice, and I meant it. Marcus was going to hurt me, he was going to really hurt me, and I had to protect myself. You wanted to know the truth Olivia, so I am telling it to you now. I had to protect myself."

Jill watched as Olivia took a small step towards the women sitting in front of her. Her arm held straight in front of her. Jill could see from where she stood that Olivia was shaking, her arm trembling with rage as she aimed her weapon at them.

"I just want to hear you say it, I want to hear you say the words, look me in the eyes and tell me." Olivia demanded menacingly.

"I just told you Olivia…" Sophia began but was immediately cut off by a fuming Olivia, her voice loud and booming.

"JUST SAY THE FUCKING WORDS!"

There was a momentary stillness, and everyone's attention was on edge, waiting for Sophia to answer her, wondering if Sophia was going to release those words into the air.

"I killed him. I killed Marcus."

Olivia's shaking only intensified at the words, Jill was about to make her presence known when Olivia pressed further.

"You did it, I knew you did it, you killed him. But how did you get away with it so easy? Who helped you? Who helped you do this?"

"Nobody Olivia, I did this, this was me. This was all me!" Sophia answered convincingly but Olivia did not believe her.

"You killed him, you bitch, I knew you did. But you didn't do this yourself, you are not smart enough to do this by yourself. So, tell me."

"I did this by myself, you wanted to hear the truth, well here it is, I killed him, I did, nobody else but me."

The tension was mounting at an increasing rate, and Olivia was becoming more and more agitated hearing the words she had so desperately been wanting to hear, but still not satisfied, still not appeased, not until she heard it all. And with one swift redirect of her arm, she aimed the gun now at Zoe.

"You tell me who helped you, now, right now or I swear to God I will shoot her. I will kill her right now, if you don't tell me the full truth. I will put a bullet straight through this deceiving whore's head, unless you tell me who helped you kill my brother."

Sophia went to answer but was interjected. It was Caleb who answered this time, and Jill's full attention went to him, waiting to hear his voice, waiting to hear what he would say.

"It was me Olivia, I helped her, I helped her kill your brother."

The words struck Jill sharply in the chest, and she struggled for breath. Why would he say that? She thought to herself, why would he possibly say that? Before she could contemplate anything further, Olivia released her heated gaze from Sophia and looked directly at Caleb. A look of utter disbelief and shock spread across her face. Her dark eyes, shifted immediately, looking directly past him and locked tightly on Jill. Jill watched Olivia, hold on to her every move, analyzing what she might do, preparing herself for what she could do. Jill released her stare from Olivia's as Caleb slowly turned his head and the two of them faced each other. Jill could read the bewilderment, the utter confusion, him wondering what she was doing here? More over she saw dread, dread of what she just heard. In the corner of Jill's eye, she saw Olivia turn away from Sophia and Zoe, and face the three others in the room. Jill reacted, and she stepped into the cabin, everyone was aware of her presence. Now she could see Sophia and Zoe sitting together, horrified, gripping each other hands. Zoe with tears streaming down her face, and Sophia looking pale and weak.

"Olivia, it's okay." Jill assured Olivia, as she held up a hand indicating she was not here to harm her. Olivia began laughing, a blood curdling sound.

"See!" Olivia exclaimed vindicated as she redirected the gun directly at Caleb, her hand shaking wildly. "See, Detective Keller, I knew it. I told you, didn't I? She did it, she killed him, and he helped her do it." Jill's instinct was to just shoot her, but she knew she couldn't do that. No matter what was going through her mind in this very moment, no matter if she was being tormented as to why Caleb would say he helped Sophia Donovan murder her husband, her instinct was to protect him no matter what. And right now, in order to protect him, she needed to protect Olivia.

"I know Olivia, I know you were right. I should have listened to you, I should have helped you when you asked me. I am so sorry for that." Jill calmly spoke to Olivia, and she glanced at Caleb, and Jill knew he was wondering what she was talking about.

"See I'm not crazy! I am not crazy. They are." Olivia now targeting Caleb with her vengeful stare. She continued staring at him, her eyes now black. "You son-of-a-bitch, you helped her kill my brother."

"Olivia!" Jill exclaimed, and when Olivia would not release the death stare she had on Caleb, Jill said It louder this time. "Olivia, look at me." This time she got her attention and Olivia looked towards Jill.

"I'm here now, I am here to help you. This is all going to be okay, I promise. You just need to put down the gun and come with me. We will make this right. Just put down that gun and come with me." Jill dropped her own weapon now down to her side, and she held out her free hand towards Olivia. Olivia stood looking at her, seemingly contemplating if she should in fact go with Jill. Just as Jill was confident she had got through to her, Olivia looked back to Caleb and uttered morosely. "You don't know what you have done, neither of you."

Caleb held his gun firmly at Zoe but kept his wits about him, he stayed as relaxed as he possibly could, and Jill stood frigid, but ready.

"You don't want to hurt anyone Olivia," Caleb began. "You are a good person and it's not too late, this doesn't have to end badly. I know you don't want this. You heard the truth, it's all over now. I know you don't want to hurt anyone, I know it's not in you."

Olivia did not answer him right away but instead a smile spread across her lips, then quickly vanished again. And she simply answered, "It is now," and made a swift motion to turn back towards the two terrified women on the couch, and before anyone could even move, a shot rang out, vibrating through the walls of the cabin.

Jill did not even have a chance to aim her gun and shoot, before Caleb pulled the trigger of his own gun. One landed directly in the side of Olivia's left arm. Jill fully expected her to drop her weapon and fall to the ground. Instead the demon that possessed her reared its' head and she glanced towards Caleb and Jill, her expression no longer bearing any resemblance of humanity. She brought the gun up and aimed at her next target, determined to finish the job, however Caleb was much too quick for her. Without missing even, a single beat, he fired one more shot, this one landing in the centre of her chest and jolting her back. Jill watched her, it was as if she could see the light go out in her eyes, and the reality dawn on her in that very instance of what had truly just transpired. She fell lifelessly to the floor of the cabin, the gun falling to the floor beside her.

The echoes of the shots still rang in Jill's ears, and before she even had a chance to think her next thought, Isabelle Vaughn rushed through the front door of the cabin, almost shoving Jill to the ground as she did so.

"Sophia!" she shouted as she rushed past Caleb directly towards her daughter who was still on the couch, shocked, even more pale if that were possible. "Sophia, oh my God are you okay?" Isabelle stopped dead in her tracks, at the sight of Zoe, the once vibrant, beautiful red head, gone. Her head slumped to the side, resting on her shoulder, a single bullet hole in her head, a gruesome and unsightly splattering of blood cascaded on the wall behind her.

"Mom," Sophia cried, in shock, but relieved at the sight of her mother rushing towards her. Jill watched them, Sophia leaping from the couch to rush to her mother, as they embraced each other. They both crumbled to the floor, sobbing and weeping as they clung to each other. Olivia's still body lying behind them.

"Baby, oh my girl, I am so sorry. I am so sorry this happened to you. You're okay now, do you hear me?" Isabelle exclaimed as she pulled away from her daughter and held her head firmly between both of her hands.

"I love you Mom, I'm so sorry." Sophia replied between tormented sobs.

Jill noticed how pale and weak Sophia appeared, and she wondered exactly what happened in this cabin. She wondered just how long Olivia had had her here and what she did to her. Unfortunately, Sophia Donovan was the only one left to tell the whole story. She knew she needed to hear it from Caleb, she needed to know if it was true, if any of this was true. Sophia embraced her mother again, tightly, and over Isabelle's shoulder Sophia stared at Caleb, and Jill watched him, she watched him look at her. She could see it, she could see how badly he wanted to run to her. She could see he felt the same way that she had felt when she saw him standing in that cabin, how badly she wanted to run to Caleb in that moment, was how he was feeling right now. She knew that was exactly what he was feeling.

Caleb walked over to the two women, and he knelt down, helping both of them to their feet. He steadied Sophia by the arm and gestured for Trent to come and help him.

"Get them out of here, take them to the truck, Jesus, they shouldn't have to see this," Caleb glanced at Zoe's lifeless body, then behind him to Olivia's. "Just get them outside please."

Trent walked over to them and he led Sophia by the arm, Isabelle clinging to her other one to make sure she did not collapse. And as they made their way to the door, Jill looked directly into Sophia's eyes, and Sophia hers. No words had to be spoken, nothing had to be said. Jill could see the pain, she could see the devastation and the nightmare she had endured, not only tonight, and not only the last few weeks, but the pain from the beginning. It was then, at that very moment that Jill knew at least part of the truth, maybe not all of it, but a very important part of it. After they left and walked out the door, Jill was alone with him, a nervous energy filling the space between them. Caleb stood there, looking at her. Waiting for her to say something, but she did not know what to say.

"Jill, what are you doing here?" he broke the silence.

Jill placed her hands on her hips and tried to convey an appearance of unshaken confidence.

"I think I need to ask you the same thing Caleb? What the hell is going on here?"

"I didn't want to drag you into this," he answered her. That really did not satisfy Jill's question, so she asked him once more.

"What is going on Caleb?"

"Isabelle got a hold of me, she was worried about Sophia when she did not come home. She also had gotten some worrisome information from Alex Preston about Olivia, so when Olivia did not come home, she got scared. She said she did not know who else to get a hold of. I came to help that is it."

"That's it? Really? Jesus Caleb."

"I know how this looks, I know how this all must have sounded. But Jill, it's not what you think. Not all of it." Caleb shifted his stance but remained where he was.

Jill released her hands from her hips and dropped her head for a moment before she looked back up at him.

"Olivia has some serious problems, she was searching for someone to blame for her brother's death and she settled on Sophia. Jill, she is sick, and she stopped taking care of herself and well, she went after her. She did not care if it was not real or true. She hated Sophia so much, that she was willing to let her take the blame for this."

Jill rubbed her hand on her forehead, her long dark hair was loose around her shoulders. She sighed heavily, she was battling with her own emotions.

"I know she is sick. That is why I am here, she had a confrontation with her parents earlier today, and they told me everything. I know she was highly unstable, I know her hatred for Sophia, and I know she took the gun. That is why I am here. I did some digging and I was led here by Zoe's brother. I know that much. But Caleb…" she did not finish she just looked across the room to him, unsure if she should continue.

"What Jill?"

"Why would you say that?"

Caleb was silent, she knew he knew what she meant, and he answered quickly.

"I was trying to diffuse the focus off of Sophia. I knew it didn't matter what anyone said, she wanted to hear what she wanted to hear. I was just trying to diffuse the situation, and get Olivia's focus off of Sophia."

The pit formed quickly in Jill's stomach. As much as she did not want to face the reality that was smacking her directly in the face, Jill knew that was not why he said it. But as she stood here looking at him, she had never seen him like this. He was desperate to save her, he was desperate to save Sophia. It was all true, the realization was stifling but seeing him, standing there, tormented by it all. Jill knew what a good man he was, she knew there was a reason for it all, and as much as it pained her to ask him, she knew she needed to hear it.

"Do you love her?"

Again, the cabin was filled with silence, and she could see his struggle of wanting to tell her the truth. But she knew as soon as he said the words out loud, that would be it. Jill would know the truth, and as much as he had always trusted her with his life, she knew he was unsure if he could trust her now. She ripped her eyes away from his, spun around on her heels, and taking a deep breath, she slowly turned back to him for an answer. She turned back to him, and he was still standing there, tormented on how to answer. But the fear of his answer was gone, it was taken over by adrenaline, and immediate reaction. Jill pulled her gun out of her holster and screamed as she did so.

"Caleb, watch out!"

Olivia Donovan, fragile, and weak, as she lay in her own pool of blood, summoned the last of her demons, and aimed the gun that had been left lying by her side at the man who helped murder her brother. Caleb swung around, standing over Olivia and already instinctively protecting himself, but it was too late. The shot rang loud, but that was not quite as piercing as the sound of Jill screaming in anguish as she watched Caleb fall to the floor. Jill did not even give Olivia Donovan enough time to take one more breath. The final shot filled the cabin with a roar, as Jill buried one last final bullet into Olivia Donovan's heart, her cold, callous heart.

Caleb was lying on the ground, and Jill rushed to him, fell onto her knees, he was conscience but barely, his eyes opening and closing as he tried to remain lucid. Jill cradled his head into her hands and the tears were already falling heavy down her cheeks as she sobbed over him.

"Caleb," she shook him frantically. "Caleb stay with me; do you hear me? Stay with me. Do you understand me?"

Caleb looked up at her, his eyes were struggling to focus on her, she could see he was trying so hard to stay with her, but she could see he was losing the fight. She shook him again desperately, slapping him firmly on the cheek.

"Caleb, no, you stay with me. Wake up."

His eyes fluttered open one more time, and he reached his hand up to his chest, and Jill grabbed it in hers and squeezed it tight. In between her flowing tears she smiled warmly down at him. He managed to return a weak smile.

"Keller, I'm so…I'm so sorry, please…forgive me."

"I will always forgive you Caleb, no matter what you have done. You don't need to worry about that right now, do you hear me? Just please don't you dare leave me again."

He gave her one more forced smile, and his eyes slowly drifted closed. She continued to hold his head in her lap, and complete and utter desperation overtook her senses. He could not die, he could not leave her. She did not care what he did, or who he helped, he just could not die on her, she couldn't let him die. He did not open his eyes this time, and she shook him forcefully again, desperate for him to look at her again.

"Open your eyes Caleb!" she shouted loudly this time, weeping uncontrollably now. "Open your damn eyes, do you hear me? You can't leave me, not again. Caleb, please, I love you, I love you. God dammit Caleb, please, you don't get to leave me."

The floor creaked and Jill turned at the sound behind her, she looked up to see Sophia standing above her, crying heavily, but compassion surrounding her. Sophia knelt down, and the two-woman looked at one another, pain and desperation, shared between them. Unexpectedly Sophia, pulled Jill close to her, holding her in a sympathetic embrace. Surprisingly Jill did not pull away, she did not fight, she only muttered.

"Please don't let him die Sophia, please don't let him die.

FIFTY-ONE - October 12, 2015

Caleb wrestled with his eyelids, they did not want to open at first, but he kept trying. He knew he could have kept on sleeping for hours, but he heard the rustling around him and he wanted to wake up. He just prayed she was there, he prayed she did not leave him. Finally, his eyes opened, and they adjusted to the lights in the room. He immediately realized he was in a different room, different than the one where he had first woken up in. The first time he woke up, he was disorientated, confused, and all he felt was pain in his chest. That was when he first found out where he was, the memory of it was very foggy at first. That night at the cabin did not take long to come back to him. He struggled to remember it all though, the last thing he could recall was being with Jill alone in the cabin, well not completely alone. He had been shot by Olivia Donovan. He hated himself for being so careless as to not grab the gun off the floor beside her. At the time with all the commotion, he honestly only cared about one thing, and that was getting to Sophia, and making sure she was okay. God... he thought to himself, from the moment he saw her in that cabin, sitting on that couch, terrified as a wild woman pointed a gun at her, he wanted nothing more than to run to her and take her in his arms, but he couldn't... not with Jill there.

"Caleb," a soft voice said his name, the moment she noticed his eyes opened. Caleb rolled his head and smiled at the woman in front of him.

"Jill, hey," he managed to get out with parched lips and throat.

Immediately she got up and walked to the tray sitting near the other side of his bed and poured him a glass of water. She put a straw in it, and held it under Caleb's chin, allowing him to take a small sip from the straw. He swallowed, the coolness of the liquid was a very welcoming sensation. Jill smiled at him, Caleb could tell from her immensely puffy and red eyes, she had been crying, and he instantly felt guilty for the fact that she had gotten pulled into this mess. He was just so thankful that it was he who got shot, not her, and God forbid not Sophia. She placed the glass back down on the side tray and she walked around the bed and took her seat again.

"You scared me Caleb, you know that?" Her smiled faded at her words, and again Caleb's chest was filled with regret.

"I'm so sorry Jill," was all he could say. Jill gently held his hand in hers, and it surprised Caleb. Jill was not a touchy person, as she held his hand in hers, and tears slid down her cheek, Caleb also realized this was the first time in all the years he had known her that he had ever seen her cry.

"You don't apologize, you don't…" she paused trying to stifle an impending sob. Caleb squeezed her hand.

"Jill, its okay, I'm okay."

This time she only nodded, allowing herself a moment to regain her composure, Caleb knew as he watched her, she did not want him to see her this way. She quickly wiped the wetness from her cheek, and her head fell to the side as she looked at him.

"I thought I lost you again."

"Again?" Caleb reiterated. "What do you mean Jill, you never lost me."

Jill's free hand came up to her face and held it over her mouth. Caleb's heart was breaking for her as he watched her try to remain strong, and not cry, but she was failing. She brought her hand away from her face, and she quickly shook her head and smiled at him.

"I'm sorry, I'm being silly," she started with a forced chuckle. "I know that, I just mean after you left, that's all. I have not heard from you, that's what I mean when I said lost you."

Caleb smiled sincerely at his partner and his friend, then he quickly glanced around the room. Jill knew exactly who he was looking for, and she answered his silent question.

"She is here."

Caleb looked back at Jill and did his best to feign confusion.

"Who?"

Jill's head fell softly to her shoulder one more time, and she just held his gaze with her own for a moment before she replied.

"You know who Caleb, don't worry she is here."

Caleb's mind went back to their last conversation in the cabin, he was desperate to convince Jill that it was not true what Olivia said. He needed Jill to believe him when he said that what he said was only to deflect the attention away from Sophia. He needed her to believe that it was all just to appease Olivia's madness, but then it ended.

"Jill, I am so sorry I didn't tell you what was happening, I did not want to bring you into it. And when Isabelle contacted me to tell me she was worried about her daughter, I honestly did not know what was happening, and I…"

Jill brought her finger and placed it gently on his lips, silencing his explanation. She replied. "Caleb, it doesn't matter. You're alive, that is all that matters right now."

"I just need to make sure you know the truth Jill."

Caleb watched her, she swallowed hard, and inhaled deeply, as if she were trying to physically hinder her emotions from exposing her.

"I said it's okay Caleb. I know the truth. You don't have to explain any more, please, don't explain it anymore." Jill released his hand now, and she reached up and pushed a stray piece of dirty blond hair out of Caleb's eye. Her eyes locked on his, and in that moment, he knew. The unspoken understanding and acceptance floated there between them, and the trust and respect they had for one another over the years was read clearly in each of their eyes. Nothing further was said about it before Jill stood from up from her chair and looked down at him.

"I've got to go," she said reluctantly.

"You don't have to go," he reached for her arm, she mustered the most playful tone she could.

"Oh yes I do, because you had to go get shot, I have a ton of paperwork to do. Not to mention I'm going to get an earful from the LT for this."

"I can help…" Caleb began, but Jill cut him short.

"It's all taken care of, they will get your statement when your feeling better, don't worry Caleb, I have it all taken care of. It's over… this is all over." Her words hung there, and Caleb felt an insurmountable amount of gratitude, respect and love for his partner, and his friend.

"I love you Jill…" He said the words, and he knew she understood what he meant, he knew she clearly understood. She forced herself to look away from him and shrug off the feelings that were clearly fighting hard to surface.

"Enough with the mushy shit, you need to get some rest, besides I think there is someone here to see you," Jill gestured to the door, and Caleb's heart pounded in his chest at the sight of her. Jill grabbed her jacket from the chair beside her and smiled one last time at Caleb and she walked towards the door. Caleb watched Jill walk past Sophia, and even from where he lay in his bed, he could understand the unspoken acknowledgment shared between the two women. A subtle smile crossed Sophia's lips as Jill walked past her and made her way into the hallway. Sophia watched her walk away, then she looked towards Caleb, and she did not try to hide her emotions like Jill had. She raced over to the bed, and leaned over him, careful not to hurt him.

"Caleb, do not do that to me again, do not scare me like that ever again." She placed her hand gently on his forehead, and her dark eyes were flooded with water.

"Sophia, I love you, I love you so much."

She bent over carefully and kissed him on the forehead, then very softly on the lips.

"I love you too, God I love you so much. I don't know what I would have done if I would have lost you. I honestly don't know what I would have done," Caleb could see her genuine fear, in her still pale face. He reached for both of her hands and enclosed them in his.

"You will never have to find out, I will never leave you, do you understand me Sophia Donovan? I will never ever leave you, and I will never let anyone hurt you again. I am so sorry you had to endure this, I am so sorry I let this happen."

"Stop it!" Sophia cried out softly. "This is not your fault, not at all. And it doesn't matter, not anymore, because it is over. This nightmare is finally over."

Caleb's breath caught as he looked up at her, this woman, this amazing, strong, and beautiful woman. He loved her with his entirety and he did not want to ever to lose her, not ever again.

"I'm going to get out of this hospital you know that?" he asked her.

Sophia nodded her head and smiled, "Of course you are, the Dr. said your lucky the bullet hit your lung though, any closer and…"

Caleb laughed interrupting Sophia, "I'm going to get out of this hospital soon, and when I do, you're going to marry me, did you know that?"

Sophia's lips pressed tightly together, and tears crept down her cheek, but this time they were not tears of pain, struggle, or fear, this time these were tears of pure happiness and love. These were the tears of admiration for the man lying in front of her, admiration and respect for just how far he was willing to go to save her and protect her.

"Oh, you better believe I know that, because I am not letting you go ever again."

She bent over and kissed him on the lips, a little more firmly this time. Caleb wanted nothing more then to be able to grab her and pull her into the bed with him, but he couldn't, not yet. He kissed her back and they were interrupted by someone at the door.

"Ahem"

Caleb and Sophia both turned towards the door. Caleb was astounded at the person standing there, smiling at him, that familiar smug smile. A smile Caleb had not seen for several years. His friend, and his partner when he started out as a patrol cop in Atlanta. He was someone who Caleb had always been able to count on, and someone he could trust.

"Jesus Christ, this is why you wanted to come out here to this fucking town? To get yourself shot? You could have just called me up man, I could have helped you out."

Vinny D'Angelo walked into the room and Sophia stepped aside so he could hug his long-time friend. Caleb embraced him, thrilled to see him, but at the same time curious.

"What the hell are you doing here Vin?" Caleb asked him, after Vinny stood back up and glanced towards Sophia with a smirk on his face.

"He called you, he had left a message on your phone, Trent checked it, and I called him back. I told him what happened, and he was here on the next flight out. He got here this morning, so we have had some time to get to know each other," Sophia explained to Caleb, Vinny giving her a quick wink.

"Where is Trent?" Caleb inquired.

"He will be back soon, he had some stuff to do, but he will be back." Sophia answered Caleb.

"I still can't believe you're here," Caleb said to Vinny.

"Well believe it, you think I would miss this? You're stuck in a hospital bed, I can give you all the grief I want, and you can't do nothing about it," Vinny joked, but his smiled faded to a more serious look, and Caleb noticed immediately.

"What is it Vin? Is everything alright?"

Vinny slowly nodded his head, Caleb looked back to Sophia, and she also wore a look of concern, Caleb felt uneasy, so he pressed further.

"Vin, what the hell is it?"

"It's time Caleb," Vinny answered bluntly. Without a moment of thought Caleb knew what he was referring too, Sophia still confused, did not.

Caleb swallowed hard before he replied.

"It's time? When?"

"October 26th."

Sophia shifted her attention between Vinny and Caleb, listening to their exchange but Caleb knew she was not entirely sure what they were talking about. Turning to her he spoke softly, "Norman Blair."

"Norman Blair? she asked, needing further clarification.

"Norman Blair is the monster who murdered Kirsten. He is the man who mutilated her and left her behind a dumpster to rot."

Without another word Caleb knew Sophia fully understood now, he had shared his history with her, he had shared his early life with her. She knew all about Kirsten and the baby. She had known all about that man who took it all away from him. But, like he told Sophia, it was that tragedy that shaped him, it was that tragedy that led him here, to her.

"Caleb," Sophia walked back to his side. "You have to go." Vinny nodded in agreeance to her statement and they both turned to look at Caleb. He also nodded and answered her.

"Yes, you're right. I do have to go, and I will go. I need to go and look him in the eyes, I need to go watch him take the last breath of his miserable, pitiful existence. I need to watch the life drain from his body and know that he is dead…" he paused and reached for Sophia's hand once more. She grabbed it and held it tight and he continued. "And then Sophia, that is when this nightmare will truly be over and that is when we can truly begin."

The Forgotten One

Thank you for reading my books. I hope you have enjoyed them. Please take the time to leave me a review on Amazon.com.

You can follow me:

Facebook.com/debbralynnredcarpet

@debbralynn21 on Twitter

You can go to my website www.debbralynn.com and go to the contact me link. Send me an email with your email address and I will add you to my email list so you can keep up to date on the release of my future novels.

Made in the USA
Columbia, SC
09 September 2020

18746768R00165